I0637471

DANCING
WITH THE
VIPER

AMY BEATTY

STICKPIN
PRESS

DANCING WITH THE VIPER

Copyright © 2018 by Amy Beatty
All rights reserved.

Edited by Julie Frederick

Published by
STICKPIN PRESS
Amy Beatty Studios, LLC
www.amybeatty.com

ISBN: 978-0-578-41274-0 (Paperback)
AISN: B07K43T4HJ (Kindle Edition)

First Edition

For the warriors who stand
between evil and the rest of us.

And for those at home
who make them feel safe.

DANCING
WITH THE
VIPER

Chapter 1

H ANNA STOPPED IN THE MIDDLE of the street, shifting the covered cake plate to her other hand so she could wipe her sweaty palm on her jeans. This was what came of three grown women playing truth or dare while watching the new neighbor move in—not that there had been much to see with that big flutter pod squatting in the way. It was gone now, but there was still nothing to see. Watching an extraterrestrial move in ought to be more entertaining.

More than eight years had passed since the first embassy ships landed, but the aliens kept to themselves, evidently preferring to observe humanity from a distance. The few Talessanins who came to Earth tended to stay in the embassy enclaves, and most people still hadn't seen one of the aliens in person—especially not in small towns like Freebridge.

Hanna glanced over her shoulder at her own little house, where Rachel and Tiffany peeked through the curtains of her living room window.

"Keep going." Rachel's voice came from the phone in Hanna's back pocket.

"I'm going." Hanna drew a determined breath. "But if you don't stop talking, I'm taking you off speakerphone and hanging up. This is bad enough without getting caught letting my friends listen in."

Her pocket was silent.

Hanna made it to the other side of the street before her phone chirped, alerting her that a new text message had been received. She stopped again, juggled the cake back to her other hand, and fished her phone out of her pocket.

The message came from Tiffany's phone and said:

IS THIS BETTER?

"What is wrong with you people?" Hanna muttered in mock irritation. She didn't want to admit how reassured she felt, knowing someone would call the police if she screamed. None of them said so, but all three of the women knew this was the real reason Hanna had invited her friends over in the first place. The dare was just her friends' way of giving Hanna the courage to face the man who had purchased the acreage on the other side of her dead-end country road. It would've been hard enough if he'd been merely human. This was so much worse.

But Hanna needed to do this, and she needed to do it alone—needed to know she *could* do it alone. After all, the guy was going to be her only neighbor; she couldn't avoid him forever. Best to get this over with.

Squaring her shoulders, she stuffed the phone back in her pocket and marched across the neighbor's newly sodded lawn and up the steps to the front porch. Not giving herself time to back out, Hanna thumbed the doorbell once, hard, and plastered a fake smile across her face.

He answered the door so quickly that he must have been watching her out the window this whole time, and Hanna abruptly found herself staring at the middle of a broad, well-muscled chest covered in snug black t-shirt. He was tall. Really tall. Hanna's breath caught in her throat, and her cheeks warmed in a blush that would perfectly complement the fake smile. Oh yes, this was going well already.

"Good afternoon." His voice was a rich baritone. And apparently he spoke English—that was something, at least, even if his slight accent was a bit unsettling. "How may I help you?"

Hanna steadied herself with another deep breath and looked up into his face. He could almost have been some kind of Latin pop star, all olive skin and high cheekbones with solemn hazel eyes rimmed in dark lashes. His black hair, pulled back into a complicated arrangement of tiny braids, fell nearly to his shoulders.

As calmly as she could manage, Hanna gave the speech Rachel had made her memorize. "My name is Hanna Bradley. I live across the street. I saw you moving in this morning, and I wanted to welcome you to the neighborhood. I brought you a chocolate bundt cake." She held out the cake plate, hoping he didn't notice her hands were shaking. What if they didn't eat cake? What if chocolate was toxic to them, like it was to dogs?

His generous mouth stretched into a smile, and as he reached for the plate, Hanna's eyes flicked to his hands. Sturdy, flexible membranes webbed the spaces between his long fingers. She'd expected that. Everyone knew what Talessanins looked like; pictures of them were all over the internet and in the media. But seeing one in real life, in broad daylight, was different.

"How very kind of you, Hanna Bradley," he said solemnly, with a slight bow. "I am Jonantathinel of House Kanestelan Ehr, and I am most pleased to make your acquaintance. Will you come in?" He took half a step back, giving her a little space to breathe and inviting her into his home.

Hanna's heart stuttered. "Oh," she said. "I just ... um ..." Her phone chirped again; Tiffany was not letting her off the hook. "Um ... sure, but only for a minute. I don't want to interrupt your day."

Her heart pounded harder as she followed the tall alien through a spacious living room and formal dining room and into the kitchen at the back. It looked like a regular house any human might live in—at least, any human with a little more money than average. The floors were all hardwood, the furniture was all new, and the kitchen had mahogany cabinets with granite countertops and high-end appliances. One side of the kitchen opened out into a large, casual family room with luxurious-looking carpet, an enormous television, a sprawling sectional sofa, and a scattering of oversized beanbag chairs. It was a disconcerting kind of ordinariness.

"You have a beautiful home," Hanna said, feeling a need to make some attempt at conversation. "I've enjoyed watching it being built and wondered what the inside would be like." It sounded stilted. She didn't care. *Just keep breathing.*

"Did I hear the doorbell?"

Hanna jumped at the sound of the new voice and felt the fading warmth of her blush deepen again as her heart climbed up into her throat. *There were* two *of them.*

The second Talessanin man emerged from a hallway behind them, which presumably led to the home's bedrooms, and offered Hanna a friendly grin. Considerably shorter than the first and with a stockier build, this alien had short brown hair and an open, freckled face.

The first man hurried to make introductions. "This is our neighbor, Hanna Bradley, from across the street. She has come to welcome us to the neighborhood."

The second man offered a small bow. "It's a pleasure to meet you, Miss Bradley."

"Please," she said, looking back and forth between the two. "Just call me Hanna. There's no need to be so formal."

The shorter man grinned. "I'm honored, Hanna. Call me Tomin. And my friend is Jon. I suppose he introduced himself so fast that you have no idea what he actually said?" Tomin's English had hardly any accent at all.

"W-well . . ." Hanna stammered.

"Jon," Tomin scolded, "I told you, you have to slow down. Maybe you should let me answer the door for a while."

The big man grinned and shrugged. "It is my house, and I need the practice." He held up the cake plate as if it were a rare prize. "Hanna has brought us a . . ."—he looked sheepish—"what did you call it, Hanna?"

Hanna felt her blush deepen even more. "A chocolate bundt cake. It's a type of dessert."

Tomin's face lit up. "I love chocolate cake! Chocolate is definitely one of the things Earth got right without us." He took the cake plate from his friend and set it on the counter. You'll have to forgive Jon. He spent a little time here in the early days, but he's been assigned off world ever since, and he's still getting used to how things work here." He took the cover off the plate and eyed the cake with pleasure. "You'll stay and have a piece with us, won't you?"

"Thanks," Hanna said, edging backward, "but I can't. I need to be getting home." Her phone chirped. "I haven't had lunch yet." It chirped again.

"How very fortunate!" Jon exclaimed. "You must allow us to reciprocate by buying you lunch. I am sure you know which restaurants here are best."

Hanna's phone chirped again. "I'm supposed to meet up with some friends for lunch today," she explained. Again, the phone chirped.

"Do you need to get that?" Tomin asked.

"Maybe I'd better at least check." Hanna fumbled the phone out of her pocket and looked at the display.

Tiffany's texts read:

> SAY YES!!!
> R U NUTS?
> TELL THEM 2 MEET US @ MACS.
> WANT 2 C THEM2.
> DARE U!

"Is everything all right?" Tomin asked, and Hanna realized she was scowling at the phone.

"Yes. Sorry about that." She stuffed the phone in her pocket and pasted the fake smile back on her face. "Um . . . listen, my friends are waiting for me, but why don't you join us for lunch? Mac's Bar and Grill is only a couple of miles up the road on the edge of town, and we can save you some seats at our table."

Chapter 2

THERE WERE NOT TWO BUT *three* Talessanins when they arrived at Mac's for lunch. Hanna gritted her teeth and waved them over to the table where she waited with Rachel and Tiffany. The addition of the slender, dark-skinned man with the striking amber eyes and quiet, reserved manner blew Rachel's careful seating arrangement all to bits. Her strategy had been Divide and Conquer: Rachel and Tiffany facing Hanna across the table, with the fourth chair and another one filched from a nearby table placed at the ends for the aliens.

As it was, Tomin and the new guy took the ends, and Jon pulled another chair up on Hanna's side of the table, making her wonder if their seating strategy was Surround and Subdue.

She certainly felt surrounded, with Jon's bulky presence dominating the space on her right and the new guy occupying the end of the table to her left, but she refused to be subdued so she took a deep breath and cheerfully introduced her friends. After the three men had made their apparently obligatory bows and declared themselves honored to meet everyone, Jon informed the women that the new guy was called Chance. Since Hanna's knees were practically wedged up against Chance's under the table, she reflexively put her hand out to shake his as she said, "It's nice to meet you."

Chance hesitated, glancing first at Jon, then at Tomin, and Hanna realized her mistake; they didn't shake hands, they bowed. She froze, hot blood rushing to her face again, but Chance nodded solemnly and reached over to grasp her hand in a firm shake. The chestnut-brown membranes between his even darker fingers wrapped around her hand, and she was pleasantly surprised to find the touch warm, and soft, and not at all disagreeable. What had she expected, cold and clammy?

A flustered waitress interrupted the moment, handing around menus, and the ensuing food recommendations and explanations gave Hanna's heart time to slow to a normal pace again—at least until she noticed the uncertain, curious stares their table was drawing from the restaurant's other patrons. Talessanins were supposed to appear on TV, not in the neighborhood bar and grill. Well, Hanna supposed they would all just have to get used to it.

After everyone ordered and the waitress went away, an uncomfortable quiet descended over the table. Rachel arranged and rearranged her knife and fork. Tiffany pretended to read the advertisements on the folded cardboard centerpiece and surreptitiously stared at Chance's hands, which rested on the table. Hanna tried desperately to think of something to say as she glanced around the group. She almost came up with something, but then she caught a glimpse out of the corner of her eye of Jon gazing at her, his head tilted quizzically to one side, and whatever she'd thought of evaporated.

It was Tomin who finally broke the silence. "Hanna," he said, "Chance was very sorry to have missed your visit."

Chance took his cue. "Yes," he said, "I was in the back yard repairing connections on Jon's hot tub, and when I came inside there was chocolate cake, like a gift from the Sower."

Tiffany's eyes lit up at the mention of the hot tub, but then confusion clouded her face. "The Sower?" she asked.

"The predominant Talessanin creation myth," Tomin explained in the tone of an experienced tour guide. "An omnipotent being who scatters the seeds of life throughout the universe. The tradition offers a very poetic explanation for the similarities between Talessanins and humans, actually—seeds from the same tree sown in different gardens, but growing into trees that yield the same fruit."

Jon interrupted him. "Tomin has been working as a media relations officer at the Talessanin embassy in North America," he said. "He can tell you a great deal about Talessanin history, culture, and tradition if you let him. But you do not have to let him."

Tomin laughed. "I do have a tendency to lecture. The point is, it was kind of you to bring us a cake, Hanna. Thank you."

Hanna blushed. She seemed to be blushing a lot today. "It was no trouble," she said, floundering in her head for a way to shift the conversation away from herself. "So . . . an embassy media relations officer; that's impressive, Tomin. What do the rest of you do for a living?"

For a moment nobody said anything, and she worried that she'd shut the conversation down again. Then Chance said quietly, "The three of us served in the same unit during our basic military service, before Jon joined one of the specialized forces, and Tomin went into the diplomatic division. Jon recently retired and decided to come experience Earth culture first hand for a while, and he invited us along for company." He shrugged. "I mostly fix things."

Tomin grinned. "You certainly fixed the hot tub." *Was he changing the subject?* "It should be filled and heated by the time we get home. I can't wait to try it out."

Tiffany was starting to relax a little and didn't let another opportunity slip past; she beamed her full, blond, Tiffany simper at him. "I love hot tubs! You should totally have a party!"

Tomin stared at her, then chuckled. "You know, maybe we should. It would be a great community relations move, Jon. People wouldn't be as nervous to have us in the neighborhood if they'd been to our home and had a good time." His eyes flicked sideways, seeming to indicate the watchful locals, and his head tilted slightly as he looked back at Jon.

"Ever the diplomat, Tomin." Jon sighed, and Hanna tried not to flinch as the big man shifted to lean forward. "But whom would we invite? We have met only one neighbor and her friends. And I am not certain even you know enough about human culture to do it properly."

"Oh!" Tiffany practically squealed. "Rachel could help you with the planning. She does great parties!"

Rachel laughed. "And Tiffany has a lot of friends she'd love to invite."

"Are you serious?" Hanna demanded. "You two just met these guys, you can't invite all your friends over to their house!"

"Of course they can!" Tomin protested. "It would be fun. Say yes, Jon."

Jon frowned.

Chance reached across Hanna and poked his big friend hard in the shoulder. Grinning, he said, "Live a little. You just retired."

Jon sighed. "Yes. When?"

Tiffany did a little flutter clap under her perky chin.

Tomin thumped his webbed hands down on the table and asked, "Rachel, how quickly can you plan?"

Rachel grinned. "How quickly do you *want* me to plan?"

"Could we do it tonight?" Tomin asked.

"Wait a minute," Hanna interrupted. "Don't you need to finish unpacking or something?"

Tomin shrugged. "The furniture store set everything up when they delivered it, and when you're in the military like Jon and Chance, you cart everything you need around in one trunk. I'm only here on extended leave, so I just had a few things to put away, myself. There's really no unpacking left to do."

That opened the floodgates, and by the time the food arrived, Rachel and Tomin were talking animatedly about budgets and caterers, and Tiffany's fingers were flying on her cell phone texting all the "right" people in Freebridge.

Jon sat silent, his face bemused.

Hanna shook her head and chewed the end of a french fry. When she caught Jon looking down at her, she swallowed hard and cleared her throat. "I apologize for my friends. They do this sometimes. You can't stop them once it goes this far." The expression on his face made her smile as she looked away.

Tiffany kicked her playfully under the table and kept on texting. "You're coming this time, right Hanna?" she asked.

Hanna took another bite of french fry to give herself a moment to think. "I'm not sure," she said. "I might have a date with Mr. Bickles tonight."

Tiffany stopped texting. "Are you serious Hanna? You'd throw over a hot tub party with the only extraterrestrials in town for a date with Mr. Bickles? You need to have your head examined."

Hanna shrugged. "A girl's got to do what a girl's got to do, Tiff."

Chapter
3

J ON DRIFTED THROUGH HIS HOUSE, hardly recognizing the place. He'd had it built in a human style both to blend in better with his new community, and to enhance his experience of Earth culture. Perhaps in time it would come to feel like a home to him, but tonight it only felt artificial and foreign. Strange humans sprawled on his new sofas and beanbag chairs, their conversations dropping to whispers as he passed. Alien music thumped at him from the back yard, where more strangers filled his soaking pool and spilled across the lawn that stretched toward the tree line and the small lake beyond. Tomin was out there dancing with a pack of human women who were clearly fascinated by his forearm fins. Chance leaned against the refrigerator with a rapt expression on his face, listening as Rachel enthusiastically explained the various items of unfamiliar food that filled the platters and bowls covering the kitchen counters. A knot of human men picked over more food in the dining room, arguing energetically about some kind of sporting event. Jon felt like an intruder in his own house.

On the front porch, the music was more muted, but Jon was glad for the acres of forest and fields that separated his house from those of his neighbors. Except for Hanna. Did Hanna resent him for erecting his new house across from her little patch of dead-end road? He had chosen the site partly for its privacy, without thinking how he would be intruding on the privacy of his new neighbor. He remembered her face as she hesitated on his porch, brown eyes wide and startled, cheeks flushed most becomingly. She was small, even for a human, with pale skin kissed only slightly golden by the sun, and ash brown hair that escaped in wisps from a braid that fell to the middle of her back. She was afraid of him, but that was only to be expected. And she had smiled at him anyway—a brave, defiant smile.

He'd liked that smile. He'd liked her smile at lunch even better.

He lowered himself to the top step and sat staring out into the night. It was full summer at this latitude but compared to the humid swelter of his last duty station, the air here felt dry and chill, and Jon was glad he'd put on a jacket.

The tiny white cottage across the street was dark except for a dim, flickering light in the front window.

He heard the door behind him open and close, and Tiffany plopped down next to him on the step. "Chance said he thought he saw you go out here," she said. "Look, Jon, I'm sorry if we went overboard. If it helps, everyone is having a great time. And Rachel hired a cleaning service to come in the morning."

Jon attempted a reassuring expression. "Not at all, Tiffany. I am grateful for your assistance. Tomin was right about this creating a friendly relationship with our new community. It is only that I find this sort of gathering somewhat . . . overwhelming. I hope I have not offended you."

Tiffany laughed merrily, "You sound just like Hanna. She's not a party person either. Look at her over there—best party of the year, and she's sitting on her couch, alone, watching sappy movies."

Jon's brows rose. "Does she not have a date?" His gaze shifted back to Hanna's house.

Tiffany was silent, and Jon watched from the corner of his eye as she studied his face intently. After a moment, she leaned closer. "I'll let you in on a secret," she said in a half-laughing stage whisper. "A date with Mr. Bickles is code for sitting at home alone watching sappy movies. It's what she says when she wants to get out of doing something without offending anyone."

Jon studied the house across the street. "An interesting strategy."

"She's an interesting person," Tiffany said, her voice more subdued. "Please don't be angry with her for avoiding your party. It really is nothing personal; she just needs to be alone sometimes." She paused, and again Jon felt her scrutiny. He turned to look more directly at her, and she met his eyes for a moment before turning away, brow furrowed slightly, lips compressed. All laughter was gone when she spoke again.

"Listen, Jon." She hesitated again, looking sideways at him. "Since it seems like we're all going to be friends, I'm going to tell you another secret about Hanna. But this one is serious, and you can't tell her I told you."

"Then perhaps it would be better not to tell me."

Tiffany chewed her lower lip and studied his face again. "I think maybe you should know. At least, someone in this house should know, and you seem like a man who can keep a confidence."

He frowned.

Tiffany swatted at a small flying insect that landed on her arm and brushed its tiny corpse off into the night. She'd managed to hit it, even without finger webbing. "Aren't these mosquitoes bothering you?" she asked.

Jon shrugged. "Perhaps they do not like Talessanin blood."

"Lucky you!" She was thoughtful again for a minute, her face solemn. "I've known Hanna since second grade," she said finally, "and she's amazing. She made that cake herself, you know, from scratch."

"Scratch?" his brow furrowed.

"Sorry," she said. "That's not really the point. The point is, she's my friend, and I don't want her to get hurt."

"Tiffany," Jon said solemnly, "No one in this house would ever hurt Hanna."

"Of course not!" Tiffany exclaimed. "At least, not on purpose. But the thing is . . . well, as I said, Hanna and I grew up together. When we were little we had the most amazing adventures, always getting into one kind of trouble or another. And Hanna always thought it up; she was fearless. But . . . something happened to her when we were in high school. She never talks about it, and I'm not really even sure what it was, except that it was bad. Really bad. She quit coming to school and stayed in the house all the time. She had terrible nightmares. She actually tried to kill herself once." She shivered, remembering. "Her parents sent her to a residential treatment place for a while, and she came back a few months later with . . . well, with Mr. Bickles. She's been a lot better ever since."

Jon frowned, confused. "A moment. I thought you said Mr. Bickles was a fabrication."

Tiffany shrugged. "Mr. Bickles is a big pink teddy bear. He's probably watching the movie with her."

Jon's frown deepened. "Tiffany," he said carefully, "I like to think my English is adequate, but occasionally a word I hear does not quite make sense to me. I have been given to understand that a teddy bear is a child's comfort toy. Is there another meaning with which I am not familiar?"

Tiffany studied the house across the street. "Nope. You heard me right. Mr. Bickles is a large, pink, plush bear, like you might give a four year-old for her birthday. Some kind of therapy thing, I guess. I don't really understand it, but he makes her feel safe." She was quiet again while Jon processed this. Then she continued. "This is actually the third Mr. Bickles. She replaces him every few years when his eyes start falling off and he has too many holes. The first one was purple and named Fred."

"I see," Jon said, musing.

"Anyway," Tiffany went on, "Hanna's a little strange sometimes, but there's a reason for it, and she's really coping very well under the circumstances. But Jon," she turned to look at him, her face deeply earnest, "whatever happened to Hanna, it left her terrified of men." She let that sink in for a moment. "And what we have here, Jon, is a house full of men—intimidating *alien* men—moving in across the street from her home at the end of a dead-end road outside of town, where she lives all by herself except for Mr. Bickles."

She looked sideways at him and shrugged one apologetic shoulder. Then she sighed heavily. "I'm only telling you this so you and your friends will give her some space. She hid it well at lunch today, but you make her very nervous. Please don't tell anyone else what I've told you. It's really none of my business, but she's my friend, and I don't want to see her hurt. Just, if you could maybe keep an eye out for her, and don't let your friends get too . . ." She paused, searching for the right word.

"Enthusiastic?" Jon suggested.

"Exactly." Tiffany sounded relieved.

Jon frowned, looking over at the cottage again. "I believe I understand. I am glad you told me. I will respect your confidence."

"Thanks, Jon." Tiffany smiled at him. "I thought you seemed like the kind of guy who'd get it. Why don't you come back inside and eat some of that food you're paying for?"

Jon groaned softly. "I mean no offense, Tiffany, and I am sure your friends are all very nice people. But I think I would prefer to watch a sappy movie with Mr. Bickles."

Tiffany laughed. "No offense taken. Some of my favorite people would rather hang out with Mr. Bickles than go to my parties." She studied his face again soberly, hesitating before she added, "She might let you, you know, if you're serious about that."

"What do you mean?"

"She might let you watch the movie with her, if you asked nicely and behaved yourself."

His brow furrowed. "Would it not frighten her for me to arrive at night, unannounced?"

"You do understand!" She beamed at him. "Yes, it probably would frighten her a bit. But sometimes she does this thing where she intentionally walks right into things that scare her, just to prove to herself that she can handle it. She already brought you a cake and went to lunch with you today. She might be willing to let you sit on her couch and watch movies for a bit." She held up a dainty, warning finger. "Just don't make any trouble."

"I never make trouble," Jon said, with mock indignation.

Tiffany giggled. "That's not what Tomin says." She stood to go.

"Thank you, Tiffany," he murmured. "You are a good friend."

Tiffany hesitated, looking down at him, her pretty mouth pressed into a slight frown. "Don't hurt her, Jon." Then her mouth shifted into its habitual coquettish grin. "And if you do go over there, watch out for Mr. Bickles. Hanna is the nicest person you'll ever meet, but there's more to that bear than meets the eye." She winked at him and went back inside.

Across the street, a light came on in the front room.

Chapter 4

HANNA HAD JUST SHAKEN THE popcorn kernels into an even layer in the hot oil at the bottom of the pot when she heard the knock at her door. She clapped the lid on and ran to get rid of whoever it was so she could get back to the popcorn before it burned. A quick look out the window showed Jon standing on her front porch, shoulders hunched, hands stuffed in the pockets of his jeans. Freed from its complicated braids, his hair hung loose to his shoulders and fell into his face, making him look oddly vulnerable.

Hanna leaned her forehead against the back of the door. He was her only neighbor; she'd have to get used to talking to him.

She flicked the deadbolt back and opened the door a hand's breadth. "Hi, Jon. Need something for the party?"

He shifted his weight uneasily, and Hanna's grip on the doorknob tightened. He was so *tall*. "Hello, Hanna," he said. "Tiffany said you might be at home."

"I . . . well, yes, I am." She remembered suddenly that she'd given her date-with-Mr.-Bickles excuse earlier to get out of the party. Maybe she shouldn't have answered the door. Oh well, too late now. "How's the party?" she asked with forced brightness. "It sounds like somebody is having fun over there."

"Rachel and Tiffany did a very good job. It is a wonderful party." His face didn't show much enthusiasm.

Hanna heard a loud pop from the kitchen and wished he'd skip past the niceties and make his point, so she could get back to the popcorn. "That's great," she said. "Was there something you needed?"

"It is only . . ." He hesitated, and she heard three more distinct pops. "To be honest . . ." he started again and then stalled out.

In the kitchen, the popcorn started clattering in earnest. She couldn't stand here all night waiting for him to figure out what he wanted to say. And he seemed harmless enough, despite his size. "Please," she said opening the door wider, "come into the kitchen and tell me. I don't want my popcorn to burn." She motioned him in with her hand and dashed for the kitchen.

The front door thumped shut as she grabbed the pot and shook it, and she wondered whether he'd come in or decided she was crazy and left. The popcorn continued to rattle in the pot as she placed it back on the burner and turned the flame down a little. When she looked around, Jon was leaning against the kitchen door frame, which cleared his head by only an inch or two, watching her with an amused expression. She was suddenly, painfully conscious of her faded tie-dyed T-shirt, baggy gray sweatpants, and sloppy ponytail. Not to mention the oversized oven mitts decorated to look like rainbow trout. She summoned up what she desperately hoped was a nonchalant smile and asked, "You were saying?"

He cleared his throat and shifted against the doorframe. "The truth is, Hanna, I do not enjoy parties. Tomin and Chance are having a wonderful time, and it makes me happy to see them smile. But for me, the music is too loud, and there are too many people, and they all want to stare at me and talk about me, but not to talk *to* me."

Hanna half stifled a nervous giggle. "Party people." She rolled her eyes.

"Yes." He smiled hesitantly. "Tiffany found me hiding on the porch and said that you might take pity on me and allow me to hide here with you instead, if I am very quiet and mind my manners."

Hanna stared at him. "Do you mean to tell me that my friends have run you out of your own house on your first night there?"

He shrugged and looked at the floor. The pot gave a couple of loud bangs, and she realized the popping had nearly stopped. She whirled around to pull the pot off the heat and turn off the flame, giving herself a little time to think. He was going to be her neighbor. He hadn't done anything too alarming, at lunch he'd even been quite pleasant. Tiffany knew he was here.

Jon shifted again behind her. "I am sorry. I should not have come. It was rude of me to intrude on you without an invitation. I will go."

"No," Hanna said without turning. She drew a deep breath to steady herself. "It's all right, you can stay." Another loud pop punctuated the silence that followed. She gave the pot one more shake, then turned to face him.

"But there are conditions," she said, hoping her smile looked playful instead of forced.

"Conditions?" he repeated gravely.

"Yes," she said, "conditions. First, the movie I'm planning to watch is considered by humans to be created strictly for a female audience. It features lots and lots of silly romance, overblown dialog, and ludicrously inventive situations in which no rational human being would ever actually find himself in real life. Human males avoid movies of this kind like the plague, and when they're forced by their girlfriends or wives to watch the things, they inevitably feel a need afterward to lift heavy objects or bang around with tools in order to reassure themselves of their masculinity. I'm not willing to alter my movie selection just because a man showed up unexpectedly on my doorstep, so if you stay, that's what you'll be subjected to. The party might be less painful for you than the movie."

He grinned. "I understand. What else?"

"Secondly," she continued, "I will be eating popcorn and drinking strawberry slushies. I'll feel horrifically self-conscious if I'm sitting there eating in front of you, and you're not eating too. Therefore, if you stay, you must eat large quantities of popcorn, and you must drink at least one strawberry slushy, even if you don't like it, and even though it might also threaten your masculinity because it's pink." The popcorn pot fired off one last loud pop. "Unless, of course, you're allergic to strawberries, or they're toxic to Talessanins, or something. In that case, I also have lemonade and bottled water."

His grin grew wider. "I understand. Is there anything else?" He straightened in the doorway and took a step closer.

Hanna fought back a flinch and reminded herself to breathe. "Yes," she said as firmly as she could manage. "Mr. Bickles is my date, not you. So no funny business."

Jon tilted his head quizzically to one side. "Funny business?"

Hanna's cheeks warmed, and she looked away. "Um . . . it's an expression," she explained. "It means . . ." She trailed off, trying to think what to say.

"Do you mean . . ." His voice was soft. Hesitant. "Do you mean . . . romantic advances?"

"Exactly," Hanna said emphatically. "None of that."

Jon laughed. "And that is all?"

"Those are my conditions." She swallowed hard and kept her smile firmly in place.

"Miss Bradley, I find your conditions acceptable." One of Jon's hands made an odd, flicking gesture at his forehead, again at his mouth, and came to rest over his heart, webbed fingers splayed. He bowed formally. "I humbly beg asylum on the terms stated and solemnly promise that there will be no . . . funny business."

Hanna bowed back. "In that case, welcome to my humble refuge. Are you any good in a kitchen?"

Jon looked mournful. "I regret that I have not spent much time in kitchens during my military career. However, I am very good at following orders, if you can explain what I must do."

"Good enough. First, you'd better wash your hands. That's always the first rule in a kitchen—wash your hands. And you might want to take your jacket off. I'd hate to get something unfortunate on that nice leather. After that, you can start by getting me the big ceramic bowl on top of that cabinet." She pointed. "That'll save me from having to get out the stepstool."

"Ah," he said. "If you cannot be useful, at least be tall. I understand."

Hanna laughed. Jon draped his black leather jacket over the back of one of the two chairs at the tiny kitchen table and went to the sink to wash his hands, careful not to wet the long sleeves of his snug black t-shirt. Hanna watched him from the corner of her eye as she drizzled melted butter over the popped corn. He moved with a lithe, efficient grace, slowing his movements when he came near her and giving her a slightly uncertain half-smile whenever he caught her looking.

Hanna found her wariness beginning to unwind a bit as he carefully followed her instructions. The vaguely breathless sensation that began to seep into the empty space it left was . . . unsettling.

Chapter
5

JON SET THE CERAMIC BOWL filled with popcorn on the battered coffee table in Hanna's tiny living room as instructed and regarded the large plush animal that occupied the sagging couch. He had seen a bear once, and this did not look much like a bear.

"Have a seat," Hanna said brightly, coming in from the kitchen with two large plastic cups filled with the pink slush she had made by pulverizing strawberries, ice cubes, and some kind of white powder. She handed Jon one of the cups and plopped down on the end of the couch nearest the door, dumping the teddy bear, if that was what it was, on the worn carpet and motioning Jon to the other end of the couch.

Jon sat where he was told. "Mr. Bickles, I presume?" He gestured at the plush thing on the floor.

Hanna sighed. "I guess Tiffany told you what a date with Mr. Bickles means."

"She said he keeps you company."

"Yes. And he keeps me from lying to my friends. This is, as you can see, most definitely a date. With Mr. Bickles."

He grinned. "Do you always toss your date on the floor?"

"Of course not," Hanna replied, miming outrage. "Sometimes I use him for a pillow. Or a footrest. He's very accommodating that way. Now, you're supposed to be minding your manners, so eat your popcorn like a good boy and be quiet; the movie is about to start." She picked up a remote control and pointed it at a small television that nested amid a collection of paperback books, old bottles, and pressed plants sandwiched between sheets of glass that cluttered some shelves against the far wall. She pushed a button. Nothing happened. She pushed more buttons. Still nothing.

She heaved a big sigh and said, "Never mind. The management regrets to inform you that we are experiencing minor technical difficulties. You two feel free to talk amongst yourselves while I consult with the facilities manager." She got up and went back into the kitchen.

Jon settled deeper into the decrepit sofa and looked around. Hanna's living room was small, and welcoming, and felt like a real home. Like her kitchen. Like Hanna. The sofa took up most of one side of the room, and there was just enough space between it and the shelves across from it to be able to move comfortably around the coffee table. A tired-looking upholstered chair rested in one corner with its back turned half against the shelves and a fluffy throw draped invitingly over one arm. A book lay open on the seat of the chair, its upturned pages bearing a careful drawing of a stand of trees. A sketchbook.

He sucked some strawberry slushy up through the drinking straw in his cup. It tasted somehow both sweet and tart, and he wondered how it would taste with the chocolate cake. "This slushy is very good, Hanna!" he called after her.

"I'm glad you like it." She bustled back in and dropped onto her end of the couch, laying a small box of tools and a package of batteries on the coffee table. "We can make more if you run out. I have another quart of strawberries in the fridge." She examined the back of the remote control and selected a tool from the set. Next, she propped her feet on the edge of the coffee table, resting the remote on her raised knees, where she could presumably see better to work on it. Her feet looked small and pale against the scarred dark wood of the table. There was no webbing between her delicate toes. And her toenails had been painted.

She caught him staring at her toes and shifted uneasily. "I'm afraid your new neighbor is a bit uncivilized, Jon. But I promise I only put my big, ugly feet on the furniture in my own house. I can be quite charming when I choose to be." She smiled at him, and something in that smile, unguarded as it was, made Jon's pulse quicken just a little.

He cocked his head to one side. "Your feet are neither big nor ugly, Hanna. They are tiny and pink, like little mouse feet."

Her eyebrows shot up. "Mouse feet?" She sounded displeased.

He cleared his throat and looked down, then back to her face. "Please forgive me, I did not mean to offend. On my home world, mice are admired for their cleverness and resiliency and their ability to create a home nearly anywhere."

Hanna's face relaxed into a smile again. "I'm not offended, you just caught me off guard. You have mice on your home world?"

Jon shrugged. "There are mice of some kind on nearly every planet we have ever visited. The ones at home are marsupial, though, not placental like the ones here." He waved a hand at her feet. "But I was admiring your toenails."

"My toenails?" She frowned at them. "Don't Talessanin women paint their toenails?"

"Occasionally," he said. "However, I do not remember ever seeing toenails painted to look like tiny slices of watermelon before."

Hanna laughed. "I was in a whimsical mood. Could you hand me a couple of batteries out of that package?"

Jon carefully pried the package open and handed her two of the small cylinders. She handed him the old ones, wedged the new ones into place, and replaced the cover on the compartment.

This time, the remote control worked, and the little television came to life. Hanna smiled triumphantly at him and nestled herself more firmly into the couch. Then, as the action began on the screen, she dragged the heavy bowl of popcorn over to rest on the couch between them. Jon wondered if this was so they could reach it more easily or to help ensure that he kept his distance.

The movie was, as she had warned, very silly and romantic, but Jon found himself laughing and hoping for a happy ending—and watching Hanna from the corner of his eye. After a while, she tucked her feet beneath herself on the sofa and reached down to pull Mr. Bickles up onto her lap. Did that mean she felt unsafe with Jon there? A lock of hair slipped from behind her ear, falling across her cheek as she wrapped her arms tightly around the plush bear and propped her chin on top of its head. Jon felt a sudden urge to lean closer and brush the soft brown curl away from her face. What would she do if he did? Would she think the gesture a romantic advance? Would it *be* a romantic advance?

She was human.

What would it feel like to trail the backs of his fingers across her skin?

He shifted in his seat and turned his attention back to the movie. She was afraid of him. He should remember that and not do anything to give her reason to fear. But she didn't flinch when their hands collided in the popcorn bowl a moment later, just shot him an amused smile. Her currents were difficult to read.

They had been watching for about an hour, and all seemed lost for the characters in the movie, when someone knocked on Hanna's front door. The couch was tucked in front of a shallow bow window next to the door, and Hanna leaned over to tweak aside the curtain so she could see who stood on her porch. "It's Tiffany," she reported. "And Tomin." She picked up the remote and paused the movie. "They've probably come to drag you back and make you host your own party." She gave him a conspiratorial grin. "Are you done hiding, or do you want me to get rid of them?"

He smiled back. "I have placed myself under the protection of your sanctuary, Hanna. And I would like to see how the movie ends. Unless you wish me to go."

"Here," she said, "hide behind Mr. Bickles. They'll never find you." She tossed the pink bear at Jon as she got up. It was lumpier than he would have expected. And it smelled like Hanna.

Hanna unlocked the door and pulled it open a crack. "Hi, Tiff," she said. "Hello Tomin. What's up? How's the party?"

"We're looking for Jon. Tiffany thought he might be here." Tomin's voice held an edge of disapproval. He undoubtedly had a list as long as his arm of reasons Jon should not have come. And he was probably right about all of them.

"He did drop by," Hanna said. Maybe she wanted him to leave after all.

"So he's here?" Tiffany asked.

"Yes, Tiffany," Hanna said, and Jon started shifting to get to his feet. But Hanna continued, "There's a huge, semi-aquatic alien ex-soldier sitting on my couch as we speak, eating popcorn and cuddling Mr. Bickles while we watch chick flicks together."

Tiffany laughed. "It does sound a bit far-fetched when you put it like that."

"It does, doesn't it?" Hanna laughed too.

Tomin didn't sound amused. "If you do see him, could you please tell him we were looking for him? It isn't urgent, just a small fire, and—"

"A fire!" Jon lurched to his feet. "In my house?" A few steps took him to the front door. Hanna sidestepped out of his way as he flung the door wide open.

"Jon!" Tomin looked taken aback. "You *are* here."

"Explain!" Jon ordered.

Tomin took a step back. "We put it out! It's not that bad. Maybe you should just come see for yourself."

"Perhaps I should." Jon turned to Hanna. She looked up at him, laughter in her dark eyes—the same shade of brown as her cake he realized. Chocolate eyes. Distracting. The laughter in them vanished when he stepped toward her, replaced by something closer to alarm. But she didn't look away.

He handed her the pink bear. "Thank you for allowing me to share your evening with you, Hanna. I had a very good time."

Hanna smiled uncertainly. "Sure, Jon. Maybe we can do this again sometime."

Did she mean that, or was she just being polite? He hoped she meant it.

Chapter 6

I T WAS THE LIGHT FROM the full moon spilling through her bedroom window that woke Hanna. It should've been something else—a
sound, the sense of a foreign presence in the room—something. But
when she shifted sleepily in her bed to get the moonlight off her face, *he*
was just there, standing in the shadows behind her closet door, watching
her. His red electronic eye gleamed wickedly in the darkness. The rest of
him was hidden in shadow.

She should've screamed. Should've run. Should've fought. Should've
done *something*. Anything. But she just lay there stupidly, half turned
sideways, frozen in her bed as he stepped closer.

She knew what would happen next. A heartbeat . . . and a heartbeat .
. . and he would step in front of the window. The moonlight would glare
stark white across his black half mask. Across his manic eye. Across
the contorted mouth, drawn down on one side by the scar that ran the
length of his face and drawn up on the other by a predatory sort of glee.
He would make no sound as he leaned over her bed. As his cold fingers
brushed her cheek.

She knew what came after that too. A sharp sting against her neck.
Bright lights. Voices. That odd smell, like watermelon taffy mixed with
furniture polish. And then he would take her again and . . . and what
always happened would happen. Again.

He took a step. Her heart seized. Her breath went ragged.

But . . .

This *wasn't* happening. Not really. Not this time. This time it was only a *dream*. And sometimes, when she knew it was a dream, she could wake up.

She drew a steadying breath and willed herself to wake.

He took another step.

She closed her eyes. Clenched her teeth. Focused. She would wake up. She *had* to wake up. *This was not happening!*

But when she opened her eyes, he was still there.

Another step. She couldn't breathe.

The moonlight shimmered, as it always did, across the fur-textured darkness of the half mask, along the multitude of black needle teeth that curved down the man's cheek below the staring red eye. It slid inexorably over his jaw to his leering—

No.

Wait.

The mouth was full and friendly. And the rest of the face was . . . wrong. He stepped closer. A clear, high cheekbone. A deep hazel eye rimmed with dark lashes.

Jon smiled as he leaned over her.

The terror lodged in Hanna's throat tore free in a flailing shriek! She flung herself sideways, away from his reaching fingers. Hit the floor hard in a tangle of sheets. Scuttled backward until she crashed into the bedroom wall.

She sat there, eyes wide and searching, every muscle tense, chest heaving.

She blinked.

Sucked in a great gulp of air.

Nothing was there. No Jon. No glowing red eye. No moonlight. It wasn't even the same bedroom. She'd sold her childhood home after her mother died six years before, used some of the money to buy this place, and invested the rest.

It was only a dream.

The same dream.

Again.

She scrubbed at her face and stood. Wrapped her robe tightly around herself and went into the dark kitchen, where she shakily put a mug of water into the microwave to heat and got out a box of herbal tea. While the tea steeped, she checked the locks on the kitchen window and the door that led to the back yard. She went into the living room and checked the front door and the bow window. She checked her bedroom window and the one in the little guest room.

She wasn't kidding herself. She knew the locks were completely useless. *He* wouldn't even be slowed down by a lock. But somehow, the ritual of checking the locks made her feel a little better anyway. There were other things in the world that a lock would keep out, and the idea that *some* bad things could be stopped comforted her.

The three windows in the studio provided a lot of good light in the daytime and looked out into the picturesque copse of trees beyond the side yard. As she checked the lock on the last window a movement flickered among the trees. For half a moment she saw *him* stepping between one tree and another, and she choked on a blistering flash of panic. But of course it was just the bright moonlight casting the shadow of a wind-blown tree branch, and when she made herself look once more, carefully, searchingly, nothing was there.

Again.

She sighed. First the nightmares were back and now the hallucinations.

It was going to be a long night.

Chapter
7

HANNA WOKE LATE THE NEXT morning to the blaring sound of Tiffany's ringtone. She groped on the bedside table and brought her phone to her ear. "Hi, Tiff," she mumbled.

"So, what happened?" Tiffany sounded chipper today; the party must have ended well.

"What do you mean?"

"Come on, Hanna. What happened with Jon last night?"

"He came over and watched half a movie. Then he went to see how badly you burned down his house with your party." Hanna sat up and slung her legs over the side of the bed, rubbing at her eyes with her free hand.

"And . . .?"

"And I watched the end of the movie alone and went to bed. Why, what did you think happened, Tiffany?"

There was silence for a beat on the other end of the phone. "Are you all right, Hanna? You sound a bit cranky."

"Sorry. I didn't sleep well." Hanna scrubbed a hand through her tangled hair. "And you know as well as I do that nothing could've happened between me and Jon." Where had she put her robe?

"Don't play stupid. Everyone knows humans and Talessanins are anatomically and genetically compatible. I saw this thing on TV a couple of weeks ago where they did a spotlight on the Lopez twins. They're going to be starting kindergarten in the fall, and they're happy and healthy and cute as little hybrid buttons."

Hanna groaned. "The Lopez twins? Seriously, that's where you're going with this? The Lopez twins?" She found the robe tangled among the blankets on the floor in her closet and shrugged it on.

"No, that's not where I'm going with this. I just thought my new friend Jon seemed a bit taken with my old friend Hanna last night, that's all. And I thought you liked him too. I thought maybe . . . I don't know."

"What are you talking about?"

"Didn't you notice how he looked at you at lunch? And then there he was at the party, sitting on the front porch gazing longingly over at your house."

"So naturally, you sent him right over? Give me a break, Tiffany. He probably just needed some air."

"Hey, I didn't drag him over there. And you did let him hold Mr. Bickles."

Hanna snorted. "Just for a minute while I answered the door." She wandered down the short hallway to the kitchen.

"Still," Tiffany pressed, "you have to admit the guy is easy on the eyes."

"Yes, he's very good-looking. For an alien."

"And he's nice, too, isn't he Hanna."

"Oh, he's charming." She thumped a glass onto the counter and went to the fridge for some orange juice.

"And you like him. Admit you like him."

Hanna sighed. "Fine. You win. I like him."

Tiffany squealed. "I knew it!"

The triumph in her friend's voice made Hanna's gut clench. She tried to keep the bitterness out of her voice but didn't succeed. "I'm pretty sure that's why I spent most of the night in my closet with the door locked."

Silence weighed on the other end of the phone for a moment before a more subdued Tiffany said, "The nightmares again?" She sighed, knowing the answer. "But it's been months since the last time. I hoped maybe—"

"Tiffany, this is my life," Hanna snapped. "This is how it is."

Silence again. A clumsy, awkward silence. Then, "Was it bad this time?"

"It's bad every time." Hanna drew a slow, deep breath and reminded herself that her frustration wasn't really Tiffany's fault. "It's worse when there's a guy I'm actually attracted to."

"Are you okay?"

Hanna scrubbed her free hand over her face and pushed back her hair. "After the sun came up I crawled back in bed for a while, and I'm feeling a lot better now. But I really wish you'd leave me out of your matchmaking." Hanna remembered the orange juice and poured some into her glass while she waited for her friend to say something.

"I'm sorry, Hanna." Tiffany sounded honestly contrite. Then she rallied. "But you need somebody. You're not good alone."

Hanna huffed. "I'm fine alone. I like alone. Alone works for me." She fished around in the spice cupboard until she found some Tylenol.

"No it doesn't." Tiffany insisted. "You think it does, but it doesn't. Remember the eighth grade job fair?"

"Tiffany—"

"Ms. Fuola asked you what you wanted to be when you grew up, and you said you wanted to marry a doctor and have ten children."

Hanna snorted a sour laugh. "She turned three shades of purple and said any girl as smart as me should never joke about things like that. And then she lectured the entire class for ten minutes about how we live in an enlightened era when women can have any job they want, and no woman should ever be told that all she has to contribute to society is menial labor and making babies. I got detention for that, Tiffany."

"Yeah." Tiffany's laugh was more genuine. "Only you meant it. Not the part about the doctor, maybe, but a nice husband and lots of kids to stay home and bake cookies for. Some people are fine alone, Hanna, but you're not one of—"

"Tiffany," Hanna interrupted. "Just stop. I can't. I've tried. Twice. You know what happens."

"Hanna, Jon isn't even the same species as those guys."

"Do you even hear yourself, Tiffany?"

Tiffany was silent.

"Alone is better." Hanna shook her head and rubbed tiredly at the back of her neck. "It's just better. My mortgage is paid off, the investments from Mom's life insurance mostly keep the bills paid, and my art usually fills in the gaps—the gallery sold three of my paintings last month. I've had a lot fewer panic attacks since I stopped waiting tables, and the nightmares . . . well, I'm working on that. Maybe it's not what I wanted in eighth grade, but it's a good life."

Tiffany sighed. "You mean it's safe. It's not really a life, Hanna. Not for someone like you. For you, it's more like a way to pass the time until you die."

"Well, call me crazy, but I like being safe. And there are worse things than dying."

For a moment, Tiffany was silent again. Then she said softly, "There are better things too, Hanna. And you scare me when you say things like that. Okay, maybe Jon's not the one. And I'm not saying you have to run out and jump back into the dating pool tomorrow. All I'm saying is . . . you know . . . leave the door open, just in case. Okay?"

Hanna sighed. She put the lid on the orange juice and shoved it back in the fridge. "Look, Tiffany, you're my best friend. I know you mean well. But you really don't understand this. Can you just leave it alone? Please?"

"Sure. Okay. I'm sorry." Tiffany sounded disheartened. "You know, if you ever want to talk about it . . ."

"I know. Thanks Tiff." Hanna rubbed at her forehead. "Look, I need to go. I'm driving over to Fairview this afternoon to talk to the new buyer at the gallery; that'll help clear my head. And if I can avoid seeing Jon for a couple of days, that will help too. I'll talk to you later, okay?"

"Sure, Hanna. Sorry."

The call disconnected. Hanna set the phone on the counter, turning to take her juice to the table.

And froze.

Jon's jacket still hung over the back of the chair.

Adrenaline surged through her. Orange juice sloshed over her hand. The Tylenol bottle dropped from her suddenly numb fingers. For several heartbeats Hanna just stood there, staring at the thing that lurked like a snake in her kitchen. During the night she'd been so focused on checking the locks that she hadn't even noticed it there in the shadows by the wall.

She'd have to take it back to him. Otherwise, he'd show up unexpectedly on her doorstep wanting it back.

She reminded herself to breathe, crossed to the table, and carefully set the juice glass down. Moving deliberately, she went to the sink for a dishcloth and wiped up the spilled juice. She retrieved the Tylenol, poured herself a bowl of cereal, and sat grimly down in the other chair at the table.

The nightmares were *not* going to win.

He was not going to win.

Chapter
8

THE SUN HAD BEGUN TO set, but it wasn't yet dark when Hanna returned home. The new gallery buyer liked her work and had taken three more of her pieces. The gallery's owner had written her a check for the canvases that had already sold and had given her contact information for a man who might be interested in using some of her paintings for a calendar. Hanna felt buoyed up by the experience, and the long drive home from Fairview had been soothing.

Jon's jacket, of course, still waited in her kitchen, but she expected it this time, and when she peered hesitantly in from the living room doorway, she found that it had lost a good deal of its menace. It still meant she'd have to see Jon, though.

Maybe she should just wait until he came for it. She stepped forward and reached out a tentative hand to touch the black leather. Its buttery softness reminded her of the way the webbing between Chance's fingers felt when she shook his hand. What would it be like to hold Jon's hand? His fingers had brushed hers a couple of times in the popcorn bowl during the movie, sending little shivers of panicky pleasure through Hanna's heart. Tiffany was right; Hanna did like Jon. More than she wanted to. It would be best to get the jacket out of her house as soon as possible.

She went into her bedroom and changed out of the business suit she wore when she wanted to feel professional, trading it for soft capri pants and a loose top. Then she went into the kitchen and, taking a deep breath, lifted the jacket off the back of the chair. It was heavier than she'd anticipated. And big. Like Jon was big. It carried a warm, spicy scent on top of the earthy leather smell, and Hanna couldn't help wondering if it had been left by some kind of alien personal hygiene product, or if that was just the way Jon smelled close up. To stop herself from thinking too far in that direction, she whirled and headed for the door. If she went now, it would be over, and she could be back before dark.

By the time she thumbed Jon's doorbell, Hanna's hands were shaking, and her heart was throbbing in her throat. Relief flooded through her when it was only Tomin who came to the door; she could just give the jacket to Tomin, and she wouldn't even have to see Jon.

She cleared her throat. "Hi, Tomin. Um, Jon left his jacket at my house last night. Would you mind giving it to him for me?" She held out the jacket expectantly.

Instead of reaching for it, Tomin grinned and gestured for her to enter. "You can give it to him yourself. Jon's just out back building a treehouse for his niece."

Panic welled up in Hanna's stomach, worse than before. She didn't want to see Jon. Why couldn't Tomin just take the jacket? But he only stood there looking at her like he expected some kind of response.

She blinked. "His . . . um . . . niece?" Somehow, it was strange to think of Jon having a niece.

Tomin's grin widened, and he reached out to take her elbow and guide her into the house. "Jon's brother is bringing his little girl for a visit. It'll be good for them to get away from the embassy for a while. Especially Tala. She hasn't been out much the past couple of years since her mother died."

"The embassy?" What was wrong with her? Why could she only parrot back what Tomin said?

Tomin shrugged. "Kamm has an important job in the Talessanin government. Come on, let's go find Jon."

Hanna's feet moved numbly forward while something in the back of her mind screamed at her to drop the jacket and run. Tomin kept talking as he steered her through the house toward the back, but Hanna couldn't make herself focus on what he was saying because she was trying frantically to think of a rational excuse she could give Tomin for not seeing Jon.

She hadn't come up with anything when Tomin stopped in front of the wide French doors that stood open at the back of the family room off the kitchen. "Jon will be just down there by that big oak."

Hanna's eyes followed Tomin's gesture. The French doors opened onto a broad flagstone terrace scattered with clusters of tables and cushioned patio chairs. Natural stone pillars pushed up through the flagstones, supporting a sloping roof that curved over half of the terrace, leaving the other half open to the evening sky. The roof also sheltered one end of what must be Jon's "hot tub"—a small, man-made hot spring grotto edged with smooth stone ledges and surrounded by decorative arrangements of boulders with greenery tucked artistically into crevices. A miniature waterfall trickled into the pool where it curved out into the tidy lawn beyond the terrace.

The sweep of the lawn drew Hanna's eyes back to the trees at the far end of the fenced yard, and she easily spotted the one Tomin meant. A new set of stair steps spiraled around the trunk of a large oak, leading to a platform nestled among the branches about eight or ten feet off the ground. She didn't see Jon, though.

"Look, Tomin, I don't want to bother him." Her mouth was dry, but to her relief, her voice came out steady enough. "Why don't I just leave this with you, and—"

"I'm not taking that jacket, Hanna." Tomin grinned, and his eyes danced with mischief.

"What?" Hanna frowned. "Why not?"

"Because Jon didn't forget it."

Hanna gaped. How else did Tomin think she'd gotten Jon's jacket? "Yes, he did." Hanna held the jacket up again, hoping Tomin would take it. "He took it off to help me in the kitchen, and then when you and Tiffany came to tell him about the fire, he left so fast he forgot it."

Tomin shook his head. "I'm sure that's what it looked like, but I've known Jon a long time, and he doesn't forget things. I think he left it on purpose so you'd return it, and he could see you again."

Quiet as it was, the suddenness of Jon's laugh behind her made Hanna flinch and gasp. Heart hammering, she turned to face him. "Tomin said you were in the back yard." She hadn't intended it to sound like an accusation.

"I came in only a moment ago. I am sorry to have startled you." Jon stepped forward, joining them at the French doors, and Hanna felt his closeness like a thrum of electricity in the air. "Tomin's fondness for conspiracy is the reason he joined the diplomatic corps. However, he does sometimes imagine ulterior motives where none exist." He shook his head and directed a heart-stopping smile at Hanna. "But I am very happy to see you again, and I am grateful you returned my jacket. I am afraid I left you rather abruptly last night."

"You did." Hanna forced a smile. "Speaking of which, I'm so sorry about my friends and their party. I hope there wasn't any permanent damage. Was there really a fire?"

Jon gestured toward the terrace. "The caterers placed scented candles on the tables to ward off insects. A guest accidentally tipped a candle onto a patio chair and the cushion caught fire. It was easily extinguished. The guest was kind enough to purchase a replacement cushion and now, as you see, all is well."

"I'm glad it wasn't anything worse," Hanna said.

"As am I." Jon paused a moment, then continued in a tone that seemed almost bashful. "I thought about returning to see the end of the movie, but I decided I had imposed too much on your kindness already. As you can see, however, I took your very good counsel to bang around with tools in order to restore my damaged manliness." He gestured out at the treehouse. "There is much work yet to do," he said softly, "but I am rather proud of my little staircase. Will you come out and see it? It is for my niece, and I would value a woman's opinion."

"Tomin mentioned that your brother is bringing his daughter to stay for a while," Hanna said, attempting to make her voice cheerful and friendly. "How old is she?"

Jon glanced away, his lips moving as if he were counting, then looked back at her. "In Earth years, Tala is seven years old. And she has an opinion about everything." He smiled, as if at an inside joke. "Will you not come look at my treehouse and tell me whether you think my niece will like it?"

His expression was so eager that Hanna couldn't help nodding. Jon took his jacket from her and handed it to Tomin, then led the way out across the terrace and down the lawn to the oak tree, where he bounded, two at a time, up the narrow steps he'd anchored into the tree trunk.

Hanna lagged behind until he came out on the alarmingly skeletal platform above her head.

He grinned down at her between the joists. "Please come up, Hanna. I need your advice about where to put the windows."

Well, if the stairs would support a man Jon's size they'd certainly hold her weight. She took a deep breath and started up. The steps felt sturdier than they looked, and the banister that curved up the outer edge of the staircase helped her feel—not safe, but close enough. At the top of the stairs, however, she discovered a gap between the last step and the first of the floorboards on the unfinished platform. The hole was only a couple of feet across, certainly less than a yard—just one big step. But it seemed much wider when she looked down.

"I will build a landing there." Jon explained from the other side of the platform. He motioned for her to join him. "The lake is visible from here. Come see."

He stood only a few steps away, but with that chasm gaping in front of her feet the distance seemed much greater, and Hanna felt like a frightened child. She probably looked like one too. She ordered herself to move before Jon noticed her fear, but when she looked down to see where to place her feet, all she saw was that long drop to the ground. She couldn't make herself do it. Her hand clenched more tightly around the banister.

She was taking too long. Jon would be laughing at her. She let out a shuddering breath.

"Hanna," Jon's voice was suddenly close. And gentle. "May I help you cross?" He wasn't laughing.

She looked up to find him standing just across the gap, webbed hand extended, lean body turned to allow space for her to step over beside him. Hesitantly, she reached out.

He took her hand slowly, tentatively, as if worried she'd snatch it away from his alien touch. When she didn't, he smiled and gripped her hand more firmly. His hand felt warm and strong, and his finger webbing folded around her hand, making his grip feel even more secure. "I will not let you fall. Are you ready?" Hanna nodded, took one more deep breath, and stepped forward, heart pounding.

It was less than three feet, after all, and of course she landed safely on the other side, feeling foolish. The platform measured maybe ten or twelve feet across, but only slightly more than half of it had floor planks attached to the framing. She felt a little safer standing on the flooring than on the stairs, but there were no walls or railing, and it was still a long way to the ground. She kept a firm grip on Jon's hand.

Jon guided her carefully across the platform. As he'd said, she could see the water of the lake sparkling between the branches, reflecting the rosy light from the setting sun. It was a lovely view, and she told Jon so.

"I had thought to show you the view from the far end as well," he said softly, "but that would require walking across the framing joists. Perhaps you would prefer to return when the floor is complete."

"And the safety rail," Hanna added emphatically.

Jon chuckled. "Shall we go back down?"

"Could we please?" Hanna wished she didn't sound quite so relieved.

Still holding her hand, Jon led her back across the unfinished floor to the top of the stairs. The gap had been frightening from the other side, but coming that direction she'd at least had half a floor to land on. Going back the other way, all she had to aim for was the narrow top step, and just looking at it made her insides twist into a knot.

Jon gave her hand a reassuring squeeze. "My honor, Hanna, you will not fall." He straddled the gap with his long legs, one foot on the platform, one on the top stair step, and guided her forward.

Her first foot came down firmly on the top step, and Jon steadied her with his hand. But when she began to step across with her other foot, her heel caught the edge of the platform, and she stumbled. Jon's grip on her hand tightened, and his other arm wrapped around her waist, pulling her against his chest.

White lightning went off in Hanna's brain. Hot blood scalded through her body. She choked on her own breath, and her knees buckled. She had a vague impression of motion, but tunneling vision and the ringing in her ears kept her from making sense of what was happening.

She couldn't move. She couldn't breathe. She could only squeeze her eyes shut and let the wave of panic crash over her.

At last, she caught a gasping breath, and the wave began to recede. Dimly, she became aware that she was sitting firmly on the hard earth, leaning against Jon's chest like a child as he knelt on the ground beside her, his arm supporting her back. He must have carried her down those narrow steps.

"You are safe, Hanna," Jon murmured. "You are safe, Little Mouse." And for a heartbeat she almost *felt* safe, enveloped by his strong, protective presence, with his soothing voice in her ears, his spicy scent filling her nose along with the smells of the soil and trees.

Then he lifted his hand to brush a lock of hair away from her cheek, and the gesture triggered the surge of panic again. She cringed away from him, scrabbling backward until her spine pressed up against the rough bark of the oak tree. Breath shuddered in and out of her body. Her heart raced wildly.

A jagged fragment of her mind feared he'd follow her, touch her again. A softer part wished she could hold on to his hand again to keep from falling apart. He stayed where he was, however, kneeling and still.

She watched him warily and forced herself to begin the sequence of calming exercises her therapist had taught her. She made her breathing slow and deep. She focused on relaxing her feet. Then her calves, her thighs, her hips, working her way up her body until she could unclench her jaw and allow her forehead to drop to her drawn-up knees. Hot tears threatened, but she was determined not to cry. Not now. She'd cry when she got home. The nightmares would come for her in the night, and she'd certainly cry then. But she would *not* cry now. She sucked in more slow breaths, eyes closed, until she stopped shaking. Then she raised her head and opened her eyes.

He still knelt in the same spot looking at her. "Better?" He asked, his voice deep and gentle.

She nodded. "Better. Sorry about that. Sometimes I have panic attacks."

Jon shifted to a sitting position. "I understand." The earnest way he said it made her think maybe he did understand. He'd been a soldier. Sometimes human soldiers had panic attacks after being in combat. Did that happen to Talessanins? He tipped his head a little sideways as he regarded her. "You look very pale, Hanna. Have you had anything to eat?"

"Not since lunch," Hanna admitted.

Jon nodded, appraising her solemnly. "We have a quantity of food left from the party. Will you come back to the house and have some? It would help you feel better, I think."

She considered.

"Perhaps I shall make it a condition for showing you my treehouse," he added, a mischievous smile playing with his lips. "The first condition is that you must eat party food, even if you do not like it. The second condition is that you must teach me how to make strawberry slushies. And the third condition is that if you wish to have a date, you must invite Mr. Bickles. There will be no funny business." His hand made that odd gesture again—forehead, lips, heart.

Hanna laughed despite herself. "But you already showed me your treehouse. It's too late to set conditions."

Jon shrugged. "I can hope you will accept them anyway."

Well, she was already going to have nightmares, Hanna reasoned. She might as well stay and eat something. "All right, I accept your terms. But I think Mr. Bickles is otherwise engaged this evening, so I might have to attend by myself."

"Very good." Jon stood and dusted himself off. He hesitated a moment, looking down at her, then slowly stepped closer and offered a cautious hand to help her up.

Hanna took a deep breath and put her hand in his.

He smiled as his fingers closed around hers again, and he steadied her when she rose shakily to her feet. "Better?" he asked.

"Better."

Holding Jon's hand was oddly comforting. And intensely disconcerting.

Chapter 9

HIS HAND TIGHTENED ON HER throat. His scarred face hovered too close, his sour breath burning against her open lips as she struggled to breathe, to move, to scream. Her arms and legs were dead. Frozen. Useless. He had done something to her—she couldn't move, but she could feel everything. *Everything.* His other hand slid up her body to her face as he held her pinned like a dead insect between his body and the wall of the shed. His cold fingers nudged a loose strand of hair off her cheek. She couldn't stop him from touching her. Couldn't scream for help. It was going to happen. Again.

Her vision started to swim, and a red haze crept over everything. Maybe this time she'd be unconscious. But his hand relaxed its grip on her throat ever so slightly. Her breath wheezed out, and she sucked in another one through her half-constricted airway. The air tasted of old wood and gasoline. Before she could even attempt to scream, his grip tightened. His free hand moved from her cheek down her neck, down her naked, bleeding chest, and his body pressed harder against her. She couldn't move. Couldn't scream. Couldn't stop it from happening. Again.

Again.

Hanna choked shudderingly awake. Frantically, she fumbled for the lamp on her bedside table and switched it on.

She was in her own house.

She was alone in her bedroom.

Mr. Bickles lay tangled in the sheets next to her pillow. She snatched him to her chest and buried her face in the top of his head as she began to sob. The nausea came in a boiling rush, and she stumbled out of bed and into the bathroom. After she emptied her stomach of all the left-over party food, she sat on the bathroom floor and finished the crying jag. When she could think somewhat rationally again, she turned on the shower and methodically scrubbed every inch of her body. Twice.

She needed to stay away from Jon.

Chapter 10

HANNA WIPED THE LAST PAINTBRUSH dry and tucked it into its loop in the roll-up brush case. The light had shifted too much toward noon; the shadows were pallid, stunted things, and the colors had all gone flat in the high glare of the sun. She frowned at the canvas on the portable easel trying to decide if she should come back for another session tomorrow morning when the light was right again and try to fix it, or if it was just time to admit she'd botched the thing, re-prime the canvas with gesso, and start over. Maybe both, if it would keep her out of the house longer. So far, she'd managed to avoid seeing Jon for three days in a row, and the nightmares were beginning to recede.

The ringing of her cell phone startled her, and she dragged her daypack closer to the rock she was sitting on so she could fish her phone out from under the tightly closed palette case and the sweater she'd removed after the sun came up.

"Where are you?" Rachel's excitement vibrated over the uncertain connection, making Hanna smile.

"Sitting on a rock under a tree staring at a ruined canvas. Why?"

"Tell me you don't already have plans for dinner tonight."

"Nothing I can't get out of." Picking up take-out on the way home didn't really count as dinner plans. "Where are we going?"

"She's in." Rachel's voice was muffled as she spoke to someone else on her end; Tiffany must have stopped by Rachel's office for lunch. Then, to Hanna, "It's a surprise. We'll meet you at your house as soon as Tiffany and I get off work." She hung up without waiting for a response.

Hanna shook her head as she finished packing up her things and considered trying to catch the afternoon shadows at another location. She'd planned to stay out painting until after dark so she wouldn't accidentally run into Jon, but having dinner with her friends could serve the same purpose—and keep her from mutilating another canvas. She wiped at a smudge of burnt umber on her forearm and realized it ran all the way up under her sleeve. Someday she'd learn not to scratch mosquito bites with paint on her fingers. She'd scratched at one on the back of her neck, too, she remembered. If she was going out tonight, she'd better go home and get herself cleaned up.

By the time her friends knocked on her front door, Hanna had showered and changed and filed the paperwork from the gallery. She also had three batches of gingersnaps cooling in the kitchen. Baking helped her think, and Tiffany was always happy to take extra cookies to the salon for her clients. When she answered the door, however, it was not Tiffany who had come with Rachel, but Tomin.

"Surprise!" Rachel beamed at Hanna. She glanced back toward the street, and Hanna followed her gaze to see Tiffany waiting there, along with Jon, Chance, and a clutch of rounded objects that floated a foot above the ground. "Tomin wanted to treat us to a picnic by the lake as a thank you for helping with their party."

Hanna gritted her teeth. So much for avoiding Jon. She managed a smile but just barely. The nightmares would come for her again tonight. "Sounds fun," she said. It didn't, but the damage was already done, and she didn't want to disappoint Rachel. "I'll bring some of the cookies I made this afternoon. And my sketchbook." Maybe she could use her art as an excuse to sneak off after dinner and hide in the woods somewhere.

Rachel helped her scoop gingersnaps into a couple of cookie tins, and they went to join the others. Up close, the floating objects looked like large baskets made of woven vines. Tomin opened the top of one and tucked the cookie tins inside. A faint green shimmer clung to the inside surfaces of the basket, giving off enough heat to keep the food inside warm. "Delicacies from across the galaxy," Tomin explained in his tour guide voice, when Hanna peered into the basket. "You generously shared your culture with us, and it is our pleasure to return the gesture."

"Don't worry." Chance's amber eyes glinted in his dark face. "We didn't cook it. Tomin had it all sent in from the embassy kitchens."

Tomin shot his friend a glare, then turned with a sheepish grin to offer Rachel his arm. "Shall we go?" The two started moving toward the trees on Jon's side of the road, and the baskets trailed along in a line behind Tomin like obedient ducklings, seemingly of their own volition.

Tiffany caught at Hanna's elbow. "I'm really sorry, Hanna," she murmured softly. "Rachel and Tomin had this all planned before I knew anything about it, and I couldn't figure out a way to stop them without—" she cut off as Jon joined them.

He offered his arm to Hanna, as Tomin had to Rachel. "May I escort you?"

Something in the tone of his voice snagged on Hanna's pulse and set it racing with the memory of leaning against his chest on the ground below the treehouse with his arm curved comfortingly around her shoulders. And the memory of another arm clenched around her waist, crushing her naked body against . . . *him*. Hot flickers of impending panic licked up her spine to the base of her skull. "Um . . ." she stammered, "thanks, but I'm f-fine. I bet Tiffany could use a hand, though, she . . . um . . ."

Fortunately, Tiffany took her cue as Hanna floundered for an excuse. "Yes," she enthused, "if you don't mind. I didn't realize we'd be walking so far, or I would have worn different shoes." She pouted prettily down at her sandals.

Jon's brow furrowed slightly, but he smiled and said, "Of course. I am glad to be of assistance." Tiffany tucked her hand into his elbow, and the two of them set off to catch up with Rachel and Tomin and their trailing row of picnic baskets. Hanna looked over once at Chance, who frowned and stuffed his hands into his pockets. He moved beside her in uncomfortable silence as the two of them followed the others.

Chapter 11

TIFFANY WAS TALLER THAN HANNA, and her longer legs easily kept pace with Jon. He slowed anyway, hoping Hanna might catch up and walk with them.

Why had she passed him off to Tiffany? From a Talessanin woman, that would have meant rejection, and possibly a hint that her friend was interested in forming a romantic relationship with him. Did it mean the same from a human? Had he offended her? Frightened her? Perhaps, as she'd said, Hanna truly only thought Tiffany had greater need for an escort. Or perhaps it meant nothing at all. She was human; who could tell what humans meant by anything they did?

Tiffany prattled. She talked about her shoes. About the weather. About a woman's hair arrangement of which she did not approve. Jon tried to pretend polite interest in what his companion was saying, but he had never been very good at such talk. Hanna had not required it of him when they walked back from the treehouse. She had only held his hand and smiled shyly up at him once.

She had held his hand on the treehouse platform, too—had hardly hesitated to take it when he offered to assist her. Most humans hesitated. They were not accustomed to interacting with off-worlders, and finger webbing made them nervous. But Hanna had offered her hand to

Chance at lunch that first day without so much as thinking about it. And in the treehouse, she had . . .

Still, perhaps it had been a mistake to take Hanna to the treehouse. Perhaps that was why she avoided him now. She had been frightened of falling, but she had been more frightened when he'd caught her after she stumbled; the suddenness and intensity of her fear had surprised him. But she'd clung to him as he carried her down the steps, and the memory of Hanna's soft curves pressed against his body made him impatient with her lanky friend. Holding Tiffany would be like embracing a sack of sticks.

Of course, when the second wave of terror had struck, Hanna had moved away from him quickly enough. But she'd left her hand in his on the way back to the house, and she'd laughed with him when he discovered he owned not a single strawberry for making slushies. What did it mean? He'd thought it meant . . . well, something. But he hadn't seen her once in the three days since the treehouse, and he was beginning to think she was intentionally avoiding him.

In spite of Jon's slower pace, Hanna remained behind him. She must be lagging on purpose. He could hear her soft footsteps, and Chance's even quieter ones, behind him on the footpath. Had she accepted Chance as her escort? It would be rude to turn and look.

The walk to the lake seemed much longer than Jon remembered, but at last the footpath they followed through the trees meandered into a small, grassy glade near a place where the lake curved between two large outcroppings of rock, forming a private cove deep enough for diving. Unlike the gravelly verge that surrounded most of the lake, the shoreline here was a sloping stretch of grass and sand.

When Jon and Tiffany emerged from the trees, Tomin was fussing over the panniers, and Rachel stood near the edge of the water, stripping off her t-shirt and shorts to reveal one of the bikini bathing suits some human women wore for swimming. Tiffany patted his arm and said something he didn't quite catch before scampering off to join Rachel, pulling her shirt off over her head as she went; another bikini. Jon wondered how well the women could swim without fins, but had to admit there was something exotic and alluring about their streamlined silhouettes.

A small quiver of anticipation ran up his dorsal fin. What would Hanna look like wearing nothing but a bikini? But when she joined her friends, Hanna only shifted her small net bag a little higher on her shoulder and scratched absently at her elbow. And when the other women splashed, laughing, into the clear water of the lake, Hanna settled onto a rock the size and shape of one of Jon's beanbag chairs, and drew a sketchbook from her bag.

Chance laid a hand on Jon's shoulder. "Are you planning to help, or do you want to stand here and gape at her all evening?"

Jon turned to find both Chance and Tomin watching him speculatively. He scowled at them, then nodded to Tomin. "I am at your disposal. How can I be of use?"

Tomin gave him one last penetrating look, then shrugged. "The rugs and cushions are in that pannier. You could start by laying those out, if you like."

Chance joined Jon as he set briskly to work. "She's a human, Jon." Chance said pointedly as he took the other end of one of the broad picnic rugs and backed away, tugging it out to lie evenly on the grass.

"I noticed that about her." Jon's voice came out wry and more clipped than he intended.

"That doesn't bother you?"

"Should it?"

Tomin cleared his throat. "You have been somewhat outspoken in your disapproval of Lord Trakanaleth and his human woman."

"It is her circumstances that I object to, not her kinship." Jon flipped the end of the other wide rug toward Chance, and the two of them tugged it straight.

Tomin frowned. In Talessanin, he said, "And what circumstances did you imagine creating with Hanna?"

"English, Tomin." Jon pulled a cushion from the pannier and tossed it on the rugs. "How else will I learn?" He lobbed another cushion after the first. "It does not matter what I imagine. I do not know how to properly court a human woman. And she does not want me anyway."

"Court?" Tomin's frown deepened. "That could be . . . complicated."

"She wants you," Chance said quietly, glancing over to where Hanna sat on her rock. "She watched you all the way here."

"She is frightened of me." Jon followed Chance's gaze. Hanna's head was bent studiously over her drawing. As he watched, one of her hands drifted up to push a lock of hair off her cheek. He'd done that himself as she nestled against him beneath the treehouse. He shouldn't have; it had triggered her panic again. But her skin had been warm and smooth beneath his fingers. And she'd smelled of something sweet baking, mixed with the sharper scents of a maker's workshop.

Chance snorted. "*Everyone* is frightened of you, Jon."

"There would be repercussions," Tomin mused. "Your mother could probably be persuaded, and your brother might even be pleased, but your sister would be appalled, and your stepfather would be furious."

"I do not care what my stepfather thinks." Jon snapped.

"That's obvious." Tomin chuckled grimly. "Of course, the Council—"

"I retired," Jon interrupted. "The reaction of the Council no longer concerns me."

Tomin shrugged. "I suppose not. The Assembly, on the other hand—"

"Also does not concern me."

"If you say so."

"She passed me off to her friend." Jon spoke to Chance, turning his back on Tomin.

This time Chance laughed aloud. "I don't suppose that's ever happened to you before."

"Once or twice." Jon pulled one of the telescoping support poles from the pannier and pointed it at the ground near the edge of the rugs. "But not when it mattered." He pushed the trigger and braced his arms as the end of the pole thudded deep into the sandy ground. He tugged it to be sure it would hold and extended the top end before taking another one from the case. When he looked up, Chance was watching him, a thoughtful expression on his face.

"And this time it matters?"

"I do not know." Jon anchored the second support pole. "She is different. She does not obsess over her clothes. She does not need to fill every silence with empty words." He shrugged sheepishly. "She bakes very good cakes."

Tomin laughed a little mockingly. "You know she'd have done that for any new neighbor, right? It wasn't really personal."

"That is the point." Jon reached for another pole. "She did not want anything from me; she is just the sort of person who welcomes a new neighbor." He took aim and pulled the trigger. "It is . . . appealing."

Chance's grin grew broader. "And of course it doesn't hurt that she's such a pretty little thing."

"I did notice that about her too." Jon ran a hand back through his hair pushing it out of his face. "And sometimes, when she looks at me . . ." After a moment, he cleared his throat. "Yes. It matters."

For a while no one spoke. Jon placed the remaining support poles and began hanging the brightly colored shade cloth and the gauzy curtains that would keep the local insects at bay with their clinging particle fields. Chance and Tomin set up the low table and began arranging containers of food down its length.

Finally, Tomin broke the silence. "It would certainly have some interesting diplomatic implications. It might be fun to see it all play out."

"I don't think Jon is playing, Tomin." Chance popped open one of Hanna's cookie tins, releasing a delightful aroma of exotic spices. "Jonantathinel of Kanestelan Ehr has already waded boldly into the shallows of a mysterious alien ocean." He took out one of the cookies and sniffed it. "You should watch your step, though, Jon. Something is hiding beneath her surface. You wouldn't want to get too entangled."

Jon straightened. "Perhaps. But I have not told her everything either."

Tomin shook his head and muttered, "I should hope not."

Chance bit the cookie and chewed thoughtfully. "Never mind," he said after a moment. "Forget what I just said. Court her, troth her, wed her, and bed her if it makes you happy. You have my blessing as long as she keeps making these." He popped the rest of it into his mouth and reached for another one.

Chapter
12

H ANNA DARKENED THE WATER BELOW one of the stone outcroppings in her sketch and paused to sharpen her pencil. A movement at the corner of her vision startled her, and she jumped, twisting toward it, heart pounding, breath crowding in her throat. Her pencil clattered against the rock and hit the sand with a soft thump.

Jon hesitated a pace or two away, watching her carefully. *How had he come so close without her hearing him?*

"Forgive me, Hanna. I did not mean to alarm you. I am sent to tell you all is ready for the picnic."

Hanna swallowed hard and drew a shaky breath. "It's not your fault," she said. "I wasn't paying attention." She turned to look for her pencil, but she could still feel his eyes on her.

"Allow me?" he asked softly, and when she looked up at him again he added, "Please." But he didn't move until she gave a slight nod. As he had that night at the treehouse, he seemed to understand her need for distance.

He stepped closer and dropped smoothly to one knee next to her, bracing a hand against the rock beside her thigh. As he bent to retrieve the pencil, she caught his spiced leather scent, and her heart pounded even faster. He was so close. He brushed the sand off the pencil and offered it to her on his open palm. Her fingers brushed against his as she took it, and her face warmed.

"Have you finished, or would you like me to wait a few moments before I call the others?" He didn't stand or move away, just stayed there on one knee, webbed hand resting beside her, face turned up slightly. In this light his hazel eyes looked the same deep brown-green as the shadows the rocks made in the water of the lake.

She hadn't finished, but she couldn't remember now what she'd been about to change in the drawing. And it no longer seemed important. "Um . . ." She cleared her throat. "I think I'm done. It's only a sketch anyway." She began to close the book, but his fingers brushed the back of her hand, and she stopped.

"Might you allow me to see?"

Hanna hesitated for a heartbeat. It wasn't a very good sketch. What if he laughed? But he hadn't laughed at her in the treehouse when she was afraid of a little gap. She nudged the book slightly toward him, and he carefully lifted it off her lap, turning fluidly as he did so to sit cross-legged on the ground with his back leaning against the rock, his shoulder nearly, but not quite, touching her knee.

He held the book gently by the edges, careful not to touch the drawing as he studied it. After a moment, he said, "The shadows are very nice. And I very much like the way the lines of the flying birds echo those of the swimmers. It is as if the birds are swimming in the air—or as if the women are flying through the water."

Hanna's eyebrows rose. Not many people noticed that sort of thing. She wouldn't have expected it from a soldier.

Jon tilted his head thoughtfully. "You have added a tree."

"There used to be one there—a big oak with a rope swing hanging from one of the branches out over the water. It got some kind of wilt a couple of years ago and the owner—the previous owner—cut it down and burned it to keep the disease from spreading. But I liked that tree, so sometimes I still put it in."

Jon shifted to look more fully at her. "And thus defy the Destroyer." He grinned. Hanna only blinked at him in confusion. After a moment, Jon shrugged and shifted his attention back to the drawing. "I like it too," he mused. "Perhaps I should plant a new one there. You have sketched this place before, then?"

Hanna hesitated. "I used to come here a lot; the lake is one of my favorite places. But the last time, a guy came around and said the property had been sold, and the new owner didn't like trespassers."

"My land agent." Jon turned his head to regard her seriously. "I am sorry, Hanna. There are reasons for the security."

"Your brother?"

Jon shrugged one shoulder. "Among others. But of course you must come whenever you like. I will have Chance amend the security system's protocols immediately to allow you access to the grounds." He turned back to the sketchbook. After a moment he said softly, "Two women in the water, two birds in the air." He hesitated. "And one little bird with its wings spread, standing on a rock by the shore." He looked at her over his shoulder again. "Do you not swim, Hanna?"

Hanna blinked at him. He'd understood that from the sketch? "Um . . . no."

He looked back at the book. "I could teach you." His voice was low and a little breathless; it sent a thrill chasing down Hanna's spine. "If you wish."

What would that be like? The lake, and the stars, perhaps, and Jon's gentle webbed hands keeping her safe as the water closed over her head—her heart lurched sideways at the thought, and she gagged a little as the back of her throat spasmed shut. She swallowed back the panic. "No." It came out sharp and brittle.

He tensed and closed the sketchbook.

"Forgive me." His voice had gone flat. "I should not have—"

"No," Hanna interrupted. "I mean . . . I'm sorry, I didn't mean it to come out like that. I only meant . . . I already know how to swim, I just don't do it anymore. Deep water isn't a good place to have a panic attack. And . . . and . . . I can't be where I'm not able to breathe. I just . . ." her voice trailed off, and she shrugged, turning her head to look out over the lake so he wouldn't see her face. Tiffany had seen them talking and was urging Rachel back toward the shore.

After a moment, Hanna heard Jon shift again against the rock. "Do I make it worse for you?" His voice was gentle. Regretful. He made it a question, but he knew. She could tell he knew.

Hanna swallowed hard and looked back at him. She could fall into those eyes and never find the bottom. She looked away. "Yes," she said softly. "But it isn't your fault."

"I would like to be your friend, Hanna." Jon held the sketchbook out to her. "But perhaps it would be . . . better . . . if I stayed away."

Hanna's eyes darted to Jon's face. He would do that? A torrent of relief washed through her. That *would* make it easier. Her fingers closed on the sketchbook. But would it really be better? She remembered his delight over the cake, his bemused smile at lunch, his self-conscious fascination with her nail polish, and his subtle humor. And she remembered the way it felt to hold his hand; the way he'd cradled her so tenderly against his chest. "*You are safe, Little Mouse.*" And she'd almost felt safe. When was the last time she'd felt that safe? A small, desolate ache formed in the pit of her stomach at the thought of never feeling that way again. But that feeling came at a high cost. And it couldn't last. If he stayed away, the nightmares would fade, and that would make her feel safer too. Wouldn't that be better?

She heard herself whisper, "No." Because it would mean the nightmares had won. That *He* had won. And he did not get to win. Hanna cleared her throat, and said more firmly, "No. It would not be better." And the truth of that settled through her like sunlight through water. A small, slow smile crept across Jon's lips, and his eyebrows rose in pleased surprise. He opened his mouth to say something, but that was when Tiffany and Rachel joined them, dripping and chattering.

Jon rose smoothly to his feet and greeted them with a small bow. "All is ready for the picnic." The smile had gone, replaced by an expression of solemn formality. "I believe Tomin brought warm towels and robes in one of his panniers." He indicated the cluster of baskets that still hovered near the small pavilion the men had erected a little way up the slope.

Rachel set off immediately, but Tiffany hesitated, directing a questioning look at Hanna. Hanna drew a deep breath and smiled in response, gesturing slightly with her chin in the direction of the pavilion. Tiffany's eyes flickered to Jon and back. Then she raised a knowing eyebrow and followed Rachel.

Hanna looked down, busying herself with tucking the book back into her bag and gathering up her pencil, the blob of kneaded eraser, and the small craft knife she used for sharpening pencils.

Jon waited for her, as she slid off the rock and dusted herself off. When she looked up, his eyes met hers, searching. "May I escort you, Hanna?" He held out his arm as he had before.

Hanna frowned. Telling him not to stay away was one thing. Touching him, walking with him—that was different. Frightening. Alluring. She cleared her throat. "It's not very far."

He shrugged one shoulder. "The distance is not important." Still, she hesitated. After a moment, his gaze dropped, and he nodded slowly once as he stuffed his hands dejectedly into his pockets.

She hadn't meant to hurt him. She was going to have the nightmares either way. And it would not be better if he stayed away. Hanna drew a deep breath. "All right," she said softly. She closed the few steps between them and tucked her hand into the crook of his elbow.

Jon turned his head slowly to look at her, and the crooked grin that spread across his face made her realize just how carefully controlled his expressions usually were. She found herself grinning back at him and looked down at the sand as the fingers of his other hand brushed lightly over her wrist.

"Thank you, Hanna," he murmured.

Hanna cleared her throat. "So what does Tomin have lurking up there in his picnic baskets," she asked, trying to lighten the mood. "Anything I should be warned about in advance?"

Jon's hand came to rest over Hanna's fingers on his arm as the two began walking slowly toward the pavilion. "There are several kinds of fruit," he said musingly, "and some pastries I think you will like. There are small sausages made from elecha meat. Elecha are like lizards but with feathers."

"That doesn't sound so bad," Hanna said uncertainly.

"I quite like them," Jon said, warming to the topic. "And you will like one of the beverages he brought—it is creamy, and tastes somewhat like strawberries. There are small spore capsules floating in it that pop between your teeth, and the spores inside are very sweet."

Hanna frowned. "Spores?"

"You will like them." Jon smiled reassurance. "Tomin has also brought a dish of *peleng nanth*. It is expensive and meant to impress you and your friends."

"What's that?" Hanna asked warily.

"They are the pickled brains of insect-like creatures about the size of a house cat. They live in caves in the deserts of a distant planet and can be difficult to obtain due to the inhospitable atmosphere and their venomous stings."

Hanna stopped walking and stared at him. "You *eat* that?"

Jon grinned and patted her hand. "Not personally, no. I find *peleng nanth* repulsive. But some people quite enjoy them. Possibly more because of the price than the flavor."

She regarded him skeptically. "And Tomin thinks that will impress us?"

He chuckled softly and leaned toward her. "If you do not wish to eat it," he whispered conspiratorially, "give me a signal, and I will distract Tomin while you hide it among the cushions."

Chapter 13

THERE WAS SOMETHING IN THE water—a vaguely bitter flavor that left behind a taste of metal and grass. *He* tilted her head and poured a little more into the side of her cheek. She wanted to spit it back at him, but her body no longer obeyed her; the stuff trickled to the back of her throat and triggered a swallow reflex.

Why couldn't he just let her die?

She lay unmoving on the sticky, stinking blankets feeling a rush of vitality spread through her body as he poured more of the stuff slowly down her throat. Her disused muscles began to prickle and burn, protesting the influx of unusable energy, and a garbled whimper clawed its way free of her throat.

He hissed something that sounded like words, but made no sense. A foreign language? Or was her brain as paralyzed as her body?

Flask emptied, he went back to rummage in the bag he'd dropped on the floor at the edge of her range of vision. Then he rose, taking a step back toward her. His boots made no sound on the dirty plywood floor of the shed. He took another step, and her heart began to pound faster in dreadful anticipation of what she knew came next. But halfway through his next step, he was gone. Not gone through the door. Not gone by ghosting through the wall as she'd seen him do before. Just gone—like a candle flame that had flickered out. Her breathing sped up, and her pulse pounded in her ears. What was this?

Silence settled through the still air, like the dust motes drifting through the slices of sunlight that stabbed through cracks between the planks in the walls. Time began to settle too, from the erratic, off-center whirl that crashed over her whenever he arrived, to the numb, half-conscious slog through which she drifted in the betweens. Her pulse slowed, and her breathing returned to a steady, rhythmic in and out, in and out, beyond her ability to control.

She heard his low, rasping chuckle half a heartbeat before she felt his boot against her leg, his knee against her thigh on the other side. *Invisible!* He'd been there all along, watching her. He'd just gone invisible. His weight settled across her hips, and his hands slid, unseen, up over her belly, and higher, tracing the lines of her breasts. Her heart surged into her throat. Inside, she shuddered and screamed, but her body remained motionless, and a small, strangled moan was all the protest that could claw its way free. He chuckled again at the sound, and she felt the soft kiss of his sharp blade as he traced it across the skin just above her navel, followed by the biting sting of nerves newly exposed to the air and a warm trickle of fresh blood.

It was going to happen again, and she couldn't stop him. Couldn't even see him. He was a phantom; the sunlight mocked her. But she felt the tickle of his breath, warm against her belly, and the flick of his tongue as he bent to lap at her bleeding skin. She heard his contented sigh and smelled the sweet copper of her own blood. She couldn't see him, but she knew what he was doing. She knew what was going to happen.

Again.

Hanna woke with the scream still raw in her throat and wondered whether anyone across the street might have heard. She'd liked it better when there were no neighbors to worry about. She staggered to the bathroom and emptied her belly between fits of sobbing.

Why hadn't she told Jon to stay away from her? She was an idiot. The nightmares had already won. *He* had already won. A long, long time ago. He had broken her, and she couldn't be fixed, and it did no one any good to pretend otherwise.

It was a long while before she dragged herself into the shower and picked the vomit out of her hair as she scrubbed the feel of him off her skin. Again.

Always and forever, again.

Chapter
14

H ANNA SPENT THE NEXT SEVERAL days clearing her head by driving down obscure, winding back roads, where she marked scenic locations on a map, took snapshots, and made notations in a sketchbook describing the interesting landscape features and the times of day that would produce the best lighting in each location. She made small exploratory sketches, and sometimes she got out her watercolor pencils and a paintbrush to create quick color studies.

Letting her mind get lost in the landscapes helped. The nightmares came only every couple of nights, and she imagined seeing *him* outside her house only once during that time.

She spent most of the following two weeks painting a formal oil portrait of a saucy tortoiseshell Persian cat. She could've finished faster, but it was a relief to be out of her own house, and Mrs. Bedella was so enraptured with having a real artist under her very own roof painting her beloved Miss Mattie that she kept inviting her friends over to observe. Hanna collected three potential commissions from other cat lovers, and Mrs. Bedella seemed to feel she'd gotten her money's worth. She even added a generous "bonus" to the price Hanna had thought almost too exorbitant to ask for.

Hanna didn't see much of her new neighbors during that time. Tomin came to her door once to return her cake plate. She saw Chance taking measurements in the yard across the street one morning and waved to him on her way out. He regarded her solemnly for a moment, then inclined his head. When she returned home from Mrs. Bedella's one day, a sleek black flutter craft sprawled jauntily across the road, but it didn't block the driveway to her detached garage, and it took off shortly after she returned home, so there was no need to talk to anyone about it. She assumed it meant Jon's brother had arrived, but she saw neither Jon nor the brother.

The nightmares receded, and Hanna's anxiety began to ease.

The day after she finished with Mrs. Bedella and Miss Mattie, she drove the hour into Fairview to stock up on some essentials at the warehouse store. When she returned home, a thick white envelope lay in ambush, wedged into the crack between her front door and the doorjamb. Her name was printed neatly across the front in a careful, unfamiliar hand. She tucked it into the top of one of the shopping bags she carried and took it into the kitchen, where she stared at it for several minutes before working up the courage to open it.

The envelope contained an elegant invitation, its message professionally printed with metallic silver ink in what must be Talessanin on one side and in English on the other. Evidently, Jon and his brother were hosting a formal dinner the day after next, to which their friends and family were cordially invited. Included with the invitation were a small white response card with a silver envelope, and a personal note from Jon, handwritten in English with the laborious precision of someone writing in a foreign alphabet:

Hanna,

I must apologize for the short notice. I had hoped to deliver your invitation in person, but you come and go so quietly on your little mouse feet that I have been unable to find you at home. Kamm and Tala are eager to meet our only neighbor. Please come, Hanna, or I shall be alone in a sea of party people with no one to make me laugh.

Jon

Hanna stood in the kitchen for a long time staring at the note before she went back outside to retrieve the rest of her bags. Moving mechanically, she put her purchases away, folded up her shopping bags, and weighed the risks. If she saw him again, the nightmares would almost certainly return. But then, the man lived across the street from her. It was impossible to avoid him forever; sooner or later she would see him again. She couldn't keep running away, making excuses to be anywhere but home; home had always been her refuge. And she needed to spend some time in her studio. Besides, if she saw Jon more, if she let him be her friend—which, after all, was all he'd said he wanted from her—maybe the electric breathlessness she felt when he looked at her would wear off. She didn't feel that way with Tomin or Chance, and most of the human men she encountered no longer bothered her. Much. But then, she didn't daydream about any of them holding her hand. She didn't ache for them to pull her close and tell her she was safe.

The thought of seeing Jon again made her pulse speed in anticipation, and her stomach clench in dread. If she went to this dinner party, what would it cost her? How many times would she have to live through the nightmare again? She turned the note over in her hands. *Please come, Hanna . . .*

The truth was, she *had* lived through it—the first time, when it was real, and every time since, when it wasn't. The truth was, the nightmares would come sometimes whether she saw Jon or not; they were just a fact of her life. The truth was, she wanted to see him again. Wanted maybe more than that, if she was perfectly honest, though she knew she could never have it. Not really. Still, how many people did she know who had been invited to a Talessanin dinner party? None, that was how many. Even if she wasn't really a party person, how could she pass up an opportunity like that? For one thing, Rachel would never let her hear the end of it. And if she'd see him sometime anyway, and would have the nightmares anyway, she might as well experience a Talessanin dinner party as part of the bargain.

Right?

She picked up her phone, hesitated only a moment longer, then selected Rachel's number from the contact list and hit send. Rachel answered after the second ring, and Hanna spoke quickly before she could change her mind. "What do you know about formal Talessanin dinner parties?"

"What? Why?"

"Jon has invited me to a dinner party at his house. The invitation says it's formal. I know you're into party planning, and I thought maybe you'd read something about Talessanin etiquette or something. I don't want to go and do something stupid or rude. He's my neighbor. If I go, I have to be able to look him in the face the next day."

Rachel was silent for a heartbeat, then chortled, "What do you mean, *if* you go? Of course you're going to go! And then you're going to come home and tell me every detail. *Every detail*, Hanna."

"Okay, coach. So what do you know about etiquette for formal Talessanin dinner parties?"

"Absolutely nothing. But I have a good source. I'll call you back." She hung up.

Hanna put her face in her hands for a few minutes, then picked up the phone again and called Tiffany.

"Hi Tiff," she said when her friend picked up. "Are you working tomorrow?"

"I don't think so, why?" Tiffany asked.

"I wondered if you could drive up to Fairview with me. I think I'm going to be having a major wardrobe crisis. And Mrs. Bedella gave me a nice bonus."

Chapter 15

"SIT STILL!" TIFFANY COMMANDED.

Hanna fidgeted. "You're pulling my hair."

"Shush. It's all in a good cause." Tiffany jabbed her with another rhinestone hairpin.

"Ouch!"

"I'm almost finished."

Rachel came back in from the living room. "Another limo and two flutter shuttles," she reported. "This is so exciting! Also, Tomin just gave me the signal. You're on, Hanna."

For a heartbeat, Hanna thought she might hyperventilate. She took a deep breath, stood, and had a final look at herself in the mirror. The three of them had ransacked all five formal wear stores in Fairview the day before in search of the perfect dress. They'd made her try on every gown they could find in her size, from frothy Cinderella confections she kept tripping over to form-fitting bits of nearly nothing that would probably have required glue to keep in place.

Their final choice pleased Hanna. The gown had a simple, but elegant cut with ruched cap sleeves framing the sweetheart neckline, and layers of filmy fabric that draped cleanly down to just graze the floor. The deep midnight blue of the bodice set off her pale skin without making her look sickly, and the subtle, layered shading of the skirt from midnight through indigo and into a deep, subtle violet at the hem gave the dress personality without making it gaudy. Rachel's pearl necklace, and Tiffany's dangling silver and sapphire earrings provided an elegant finish.

Hanna was relieved to see that Tiffany's excessive fussing over her hair had resulted only in a sophisticated chignon with a few curls "escaping" artistically down her neck, and tiny sparkles of light where the rhinestones nestled in the arrangement. And she was amazed at how much more grown up she looked with a little makeup skillfully applied. She didn't feel very grown up, though; she felt like a little girl playing with her mother's things.

Tiffany did a bouncy flutter-clap dance and beamed at Hanna, but she did refrain from actually squealing, which Hanna appreciated.

Rachel just grinned and said, "Jon won't know what hit him."

The thought of Jon almost made Hanna reconsider going. She wished Rachel and Tiffany were going too; then she'd at least have somebody to talk to. But according to Tomin, the guest list was an unfortunately exclusive mix consisting primarily of diplomats, dignitaries, and a small number of very close friends of the family. He'd startled Hanna by winking at her when he said that; remembering made her even more nervous. What had he meant by it?

Tomin and Chance would be there, but as part of the household staff, not as guests, and she wasn't supposed to talk to them other than to announce her name to Tomin when she went in. He had been over yesterday evening to instruct her in proper protocol, and he'd dropped by again earlier this afternoon to make sure she hadn't forgotten anything vital and to practice the steps of the dance he'd taught her for after dinner.

Hanna had been dismayed to find that Tomin was Rachel's "good source" for information about Talessanin etiquette—what must he think of her? But as it turned out, he was flattered to be called upon to train a new protégé in the finer points of Talessanin custom and culture. And, disturbingly, he seemed to join Tiffany and Rachel in regarding the project as some kind of secret surprise for Jon. Again, the thought of Jon made Hanna's stomach turn over, and part of her begged to be allowed to stay home, hide under the bedcovers, and forget the whole thing. This was a mistake. A terrible mistake. But Rachel and Tiffany were already herding her out the front door and into the night.

Alone.

As she lingered outside her front door, a purring vibration rippled through the air, a sound she felt more than heard. A dozen or so feet in the air above the road, a sleek Talessanin flutter shuttle flickered into being, descending gracefully until it settled to the ground. A hatch glided open at the front of the vehicle, and a man in a dark uniform stepped out. He stalked to the back of the shuttle and stood smartly at attention as another hatch skimmed open and two exquisitely gowned Talessanin women emerged. They swept gracefully across Jon's front lawn without even glancing at the uniformed bodyguard who trailed behind them. The shuttle lifted off the ground again and, with another nearly silent pulsing throb, flickered out of existence.

A loud rap on her bow window made Hanna start, and she glanced over to see both Rachel and Tiffany making shooing motions at her. She rolled her eyes at them and set off across the street, walking slowly to give the women ahead of her time to get inside. Her knees were shaking, and her palms were sweating, and she didn't want to have to stand on the porch with them and try to make small talk.

They had entered, but the door hadn't yet closed when Hanna arrived. As promised, Tomin manned the door, and seeing his familiar freckled face eased Hanna's nerves just a little. He eyed her with solemn approval, giving her a slight nod, which she took as encouragement. Beyond him, the Talessanin women were stepping forward to greet their hosts; their bodyguard had disappeared into the house.

A tall, dark-haired man was first to greet the women. He wore a calf-length robe—a style Tomin had called a longcoat—in a deep shade of green, with elaborate silver and gold embroidery spilling down the long lapels and winding up the sleeves. At first, with his face turned away, Hanna thought this was Jon, but when he turned, she saw that he was a slightly smaller, somewhat younger version of Jon, with a friendly, open face. He must be the brother. Kamm.

Hanna watched as the copper-haired Talessanin woman, who had entered first, offered the man her right hand in the manner Tomin had taught Hanna was the traditional Talessanin form of greeting between good friends—raised to shoulder height, palm turned sideways as if offering to arm wrestle. The man placed his right palm against the woman's, and they clasped hands, then swayed toward each other like courtly medieval dancers, forearms pressing together, until their shoulders met. They held this pose for a moment, beaming at each other and speaking together softly, before the man placed a welcoming kiss on the woman's cheek, which she returned, and they swayed apart again, each moving to greet the next person in line.

As Kamm greeted the dark-haired Talessanin woman, the redhead bobbed a jaunty curtsy, and Hanna saw, behind the man, a pretty little girl with long, dark hair and big, dark eyes, who returned the curtsy with rehearsed solemnity.

And there was Jon.

He'd been bent down on one knee, speaking to the little girl, but when the woman stepped in front of him he rose smoothly to meet her. Standing, he was at least half a head taller than anyone else in the room. He wore a sleek, black Talessanin military uniform that looked like a seriously upgraded version of what the bodyguard wore. Every inch of the leather had been tooled into complicated textures and patterns that rippled in the soft light of the living room like water, or wind, or sinuous reptilian scales, and here and there glints of silver highlighted the patterns. His hair was pulled back into an intricate arrangement of braids as it had been when she first met him, and black feathers and ebony beads had been woven into some of the braids. He looked like a primeval war god—regal, and exotic, and more than a little bit menacing. Hanna caught her breath.

The copper-haired beauty turned her radiant face up to Jon, and he smiled down at her as he clasped her hand. It took Hanna a heartbeat to register the subtle difference in this greeting. With Kamm, the woman had leaned in elegantly to touch shoulders and engage in light banter, laughingly receiving his friendly kiss on her cheek. With Jon, she glided sinuously close, pressing not just her shoulder and forearm against his, but also her hip and thigh, and her left hand went to his waist. She gazed coquettishly up at him as he spoke to her, and when he leaned to kiss her cheek, she turned her face so his kiss landed nearly, but not quite, on her mouth. It was a much more intimate greeting than she'd given Jon's brother.

After their hands parted, the woman's fingers slid across Jon's chest and down to rest possessively in the crook of his elbow as she moved to his other side, and they both turned together to greet the dark-haired woman. It was easy to see that they were a couple—that Jon *belonged* with this gorgeous woman. They might've been created for each other, he a fierce shaft of midnight, and she a dancing flame, light glinting off her copper hair and sparking in the orange and gold gems that studded the rich embroidery of her tailored, mahogany-colored gown.

Hanna suddenly realized why Jon had laughed when she stipulated "no funny business" as a condition of watching the movie with her. Compared to this woman, he probably thought of Hanna as some kind of amusing little alien forest creature. What had she been thinking? She wasn't even the same species as Jon. He just wanted to be her friend—that was what he'd said, and it was clearly all he'd meant. She shouldn't have let Tomin's winks, and Tiffany's giggles, and her own silly, schoolgirl daydreams convince her there could ever be any more to it than that. But she'd wanted it to be more—hadn't realized how much she wanted it until she saw the proprietary way this enchantingly exotic woman touched Jon.

If she hadn't already been standing in the open doorway, she might've turned around and gone home. But she *was* standing in the doorway. And she was an invited guest. And while her new dress wasn't a custom-tailored one-of-a-kind designer evening gown, it was certainly the most elegant article of clothing she'd ever owned, and she wasn't going to let it go to waste. She was going to attend a fancy Talessanin dinner party, meet interesting new people, taste exotic alien food, and pretend for one night that she belonged here. Then at least she'd have something new to think about over her third cup of herbal tea after she'd checked all the locks. Again. Hanna squared her shoulders.

Chapter 16

"ARE YOU READY?" TOMIN WHISPERED, and when Hanna looked at him, he winked. "You look lovely. Just remember what I told you, and you'll be fine."

Hanna started breathing again.

"Well?" Tomin asked, a mischievous gleam in his eyes.

Hanna bit back a nervous giggle. "Miss Hanna Bradley," she said softly as he'd instructed.

He winked again before he turned and announced, "Miss Hanna Bradley!"

Faces, human and Talessanin, glanced toward her briefly, and then away, as she stepped into the room. They didn't know her. She didn't matter.

The one familiar face in the room was Jon's, and it broke into a delighted, boyish grin when he looked up and saw her. She stopped breathing. He stepped away from the two Talessanin women and moved toward Hanna so swiftly that she involuntarily took half a step back and drew a quick breath as he stopped in front of her. She collected herself and offered her hand, shoulder height, palm turned, as the Talessanin women had. She even managed to keep her voice from shaking when she said, "Hello, Jon."

Jon tilted his head slightly, his gaze intensifying as his webbed fingers folded gently around her hand, sending warm shivers down her spine, and he stepped even closer to her, bringing their clasped hands to rest in the center of his chest. Hanna's shoulder came only halfway up Jon's leather-covered bicep. She felt small and ridiculous. Jon's spicy leather scent enfolded her, and his breath brushed warm against her neck when he leaned down to murmur in her ear, "I am so very glad you came, Hanna. Tomin would not tell me whether we had received your response, and I was afraid you had very sensibly abandoned me to my terrible fate."

Hanna grinned in spite of herself. "I almost did," she murmured back. "After all, you brought it on yourself this time."

Jon chuckled. "So I did. But I am very happy to see you. And you do look delightful this evening."

Hanna blushed and whispered conspiratorially, "It's because I left the rainbow trout oven mitts at home with Mr. Bickles."

Jon laughed and straightened. He looked searchingly down at her for a moment. Would he kiss her cheek? What would she do if he did. This was not a good time for a panic attack. She must have stiffened a little or something, because he gave a slight nod of his head as if in assent, and only said, "Please come and meet my family." Instead of releasing her hand as she expected, though, he gently transferred it to his other hand, and led her over to the group he'd been standing with.

"Kamm," he said, "may I present our neighbor, and my very good friend, Miss Hanna Bradley. Miss Bradley, this is my brother Kammanalithen of House Kanestelan Ehrat."

"Miss Bradley, we've heard so much about you," Jon's brother said with a friendly smile. He held out his hand, low and straight as if for a handshake. Hanna had to tug slightly to free her hand from Jon's in order to perform the mutual wrist-clasping gesture that Tomin had taught her was proper for a first meeting. Kamm noticed the tug and gave his brother a teasing glance before saying, "It's a pleasure to meet you at last, Miss Bradley. You must call me Kamm."

"And I hope you'll call me Hanna," she responded. "I've been looking forward to meeting you, too." She felt a small hand pluck at her skirt and looked down into the enchantingly eager face of the little girl.

Kamm smiled indulgently and said, "Tala, this is our neighbor Miss Bradley. Hanna, please meet my daughter, Talasanesta of House Kanestalen Al Ahnat. You may call her Tala. She is playing hostess this evening."

Tala still clutched the skirt of Hanna's dress. "Miss Bradley," she chirped, "You are the kind neighbor who brought Bahta Jon a chocolate cake when he came here?" Her English was more or less correct but heavily accented.

Hanna nodded. "Yes, Tala, I did bring a chocolate cake when Jon moved in."

The child's face turned reproachful. "Why did you not bring a chocolate cake for Baba and me when we came here?"

Hanna wasn't sure how to answer, but Kamm stepped in. "Tala, please remember your manners. Miss Bradley is very busy, and she does not owe you a chocolate cake."

Tala freed her hand from Hanna's dress, stepped back, and curtsied. "I regret my impertinence, Miss Bradley," she said in a more subdued tone. "It is only that I have never had a chocolate cake before."

Hanna returned the curtsy solemnly. "That is a terrible state of affairs, Tala. We must see about fixing it as soon as possible."

Jon's hand found hers again, and he steered her over to the two Talessanin women Hanna had observed before. "Hanna," he said, indicating the darker of the two women, "I would like to introduce my sister, Naristanalana of House Kanestelan Ahn. You may call her Narista." Jon released Hanna's hand, moving his to the small of her back, which made her stomach turn over and clench and her heart begin to pound. She hoped it didn't show on her face. "Narista," Jon continued, "this is my very good friend, Miss Hanna Bradley."

Hanna smiled. "It's nice to meet you, Narista."

Jon's sister eyed Hanna speculatively. Up close, Hanna could see the woman's resemblance to her brothers. She was probably younger than both of them, but her eyes were hard, like bulletproof glass, not friendly and open like Kamm's, or deep and enigmatic like Jon's. Hanna stood there a moment, feeling awkward, unsure what to say, while the woman's hard eyes dissected and discarded her. Finally, Narista inclined her head without offering her hand. "Miss Bradley," was all she said.

Jon turned to the woman with the gorgeous copper hair, the one who was flame to his midnight. He kept his hand on Hanna's back, almost possessively—or protectively. "And this is Narista's good friend, Saleniastanelen of House Trakanaleth Ahnat. Please call her Salenia."

If Narista's eyes were bulletproof glass, Salenia's eyes were cold poison. Jon had introduced her as *Narista's* good friend, not his. Why? They were obviously well acquainted. "I'm pleased to meet you, Salenia," Hanna offered, heart pounding in her throat.

Salenia glanced at Hanna and gave her a brief nod. Then she reattached herself to Jon's elbow, turning him slightly to look back in the direction of Kamm. "Is that the Canadian ambassador speaking with your brother?" she purred.

Jon scowled. "I thought all the guests had arrived." He gave Salenia's hand a friendly pat that, seemingly quite by accident, dislodged the woman's grip on his arm, and guided Hanna a few steps farther into the room. He took her hand again and looked earnestly into her face. "I apologize for abandoning you so soon, Little Mouse, but I must go play host a few minutes longer. Will you wait for me near the French doors?"

Hanna felt off balance. What was going on between Jon and Salenia? "I . . ." she began. Then, "Yes, of course."

He grinned. "Very good," he said, and started to turn away, but his brow furrowed, and he turned back. "Hanna . . ." He hesitated. "I do not wish to be presumptuous . . ." He stopped again, as if trying to think of the right words.

Hanna thought of about a thousand things he might say. She'd bungled the greeting. She'd offended his sister. Her mascara was smudged. Her dress was inside out. The invitation had only been a formality because she was his neighbor, she wasn't really supposed to actually show up. She swallowed hard. "Whatever it is, Jon, just say it."

"It is just . . ." he began again. He gave his head a slight shake and said, "Just please do not let someone else walk out with you to dinner?" His intonation made it a question. "You will wait for me?"

Relief flooded through her, making her smile perhaps a little too animated when she said, "I will wait for you. By the French doors."

"Very good." He gave her a parting grin and went to greet the Canadian ambassador.

As he strode away from her, she saw the back of his exquisitely tooled leather dress uniform for the first time. Across his broad shoulders and down his entire back, mouth gaping, hooked fangs bared, forked tongue lashing out and writhing around the side of his hip, curved a ghastly image of the striking head of a snake. The leather was finely tooled and subtly padded in strategic places so the snake's head appeared to be emerging from Jon's back. Silver edged the ridged scales, red venom hung suspended, sparkling like rubies, from the cruel tips of the fangs, and where the light struck the flat, merciless eyes, they seemed to actually glow. It was a terrifying effect.

"I've never seen him like that," said a soft, alto voice just behind Hanna. She started just a little and turned. A plump, white-haired human woman sat on one of the high-backed chairs that had been lined up for the event along the walls of the cleared-out living room and dining room. She was looking right at Hanna, her brow gently furrowed, and her lips slightly pursed. "You'll want to be careful," she added.

Hanna was confused. "I beg your pardon?"

The woman rose and came to stand next to Hanna. "Miss Bradley, was it?" Hanna nodded, and the woman continued. "Miss Bradley, I'm Mrs. Miriam Milgram. My husband is an advisor to House Kanestelan on matters of planetary trade."

"It's nice to meet you, Mrs. Milgram," Hanna said. "But I'm afraid I don't understand you. What did you mean?"

Mrs. Milgram's gaze shifted from Hanna to where Jon and his family were receiving their guests. "How well do you know our hosts, Miss Bradley?"

Hanna hesitated—after all, this was really none of the woman's business. But her question made Hanna realize how little she did know about Jon, and this seemed an opportunity to learn more. "Not as well as you do, I'm sure," she said with an encouraging smile.

Mrs. Milgram eyed Hanna appraisingly. "Very diplomatically answered, my dear," she said.

"What is it you think I should know?" Hanna asked.

Mrs. Milgram frowned. "I don't mean to speak out of turn, Miss Bradley. I should really have kept my thoughts to myself. But since I did say some of what was on my mind, I suppose I ought to explain myself."

She paused, as if gathering her thoughts, then continued. "My husband has worked for House Kanestelan for a number of years now," she said. "Almost since the first ships landed. He consults with Kammanalithen Ehrat regularly and knows him well. I've not been as closely associated with the Family as he has, of course, and he doesn't tell me anything confidential, but he does mention little things, and I've attended several events over the years at which members of the Family have been present. So I'm better acquainted with them than some, but not as well as others."

Hanna nodded, and the woman continued. "Over the years, I've understood Kammanalithen Ehrat to be an unfailingly steady, intelligent, and highly capable man. My husband says he'll make an excellent and honorable leader when he inherits. He has already taken on a great deal of responsibility." Mrs. Milgram looked appraisingly at Hanna, as if determining whether she was paying proper attention to the older woman's assessment of Kamm.

"I haven't met him before tonight," Hanna said, "but he does seem nice."

"Nice." Mrs. Milgram frowned slightly. "Yes. He greeted you as an equal. This does not seem to have pleased the Ahn."

"The Ahn?"

"Oh my, you *are* new at this," Mrs. Milgram said with a smile. "The Ahn is the sister, Naristanalana Ahn. Talessanins put certain kinds of titles at the end of their names, you see, not at the beginning like we do. In English, saying 'Miss Bradley' indicates that you're an unmarried woman from the Bradley family. For Talessanins, Ahn means a woman is the daughter of a Head of House. Ehr is the son of a Head of House. An Ehrat or Ahnat is first in line in the inheritance order. In House Kanestalan we say *the* Ahn because there is only the one daughter, you see."

"Yes, I see," Hanna said, wondering why Tomin hadn't explained all this to her. "I did wonder why Narista seemed offended."

Mrs. Milgram looked at Hanna sharply, her cheeks flushing. "It's not proper to use short form names for the Family, Miss Bradley." Hanna fumbled for something to say, but Mrs. Milgram smiled wryly and shook her head. "No, of course you must if you were introduced as the Ehrat's equal. Please forgive me." The woman dipped her head slightly and took a deep breath, eyeing Hanna uncertainly before she continued. "The

Ahn is very conscious of social proprieties. That would be a good thing to remember if you deal with her often."

"Thank you, I'll try to remember that," Hanna said. "And what do I need to remember about Jon?"

The older woman didn't answer for a few frowning moments. Then she said softly, "You need to remember that he's dangerous."

Hanna studied the woman's face. "Yes. You said before that I should be careful. Will you please explain what you mean? I haven't known Jon very long, but he's always been kind to me."

Mrs. Milgram looked back again to where Jon's family greeted their guests. "There isn't much I can tell you, I'm afraid. I was introduced to him once at a ball given in his honor when he visited his brother's household at the North American Embassy a few years ago. I've dined in company with him several times at the embassy but was not presented to him then. So you see, I have very little first-hand knowledge of your friend to share and can only tell you that on those occasions when I have observed him myself, he spoke little to anyone, and everyone in attendance seemed too frightened of him to seek out his company. His dance partners and dining companions were, I believe, arranged by his sister.

"But, Miss Bradley, it's common knowledge that he served as Commander of the Nine Winds for at least a dozen years. That means he's dangerous, even if only half the stories are actually true. And, of course, he has the ear of the Empress—perhaps even more so than his brother—which is not a thing to take lightly. So that's why I say you'll want to be careful. Jonantathinel of Kanestalen Ehr isn't a man to be trifled with. From the way you spoke with him, I was uncertain whether you knew that. I thought you should be aware."

Hanna followed Mrs. Milgram's gaze to where Jon and Kamm stood. Kamm's face bore a broad smile as he conversed enthusiastically with a portly gentleman in a black tuxedo. Jon stood beside his brother, face hard and expressionless, eyes focused intently on the human man, lean body poised in a stance of unconscious military readiness, but utterly, breathlessly still—a panther eyeing its prey. Jon looked . . . dangerous.

Except then, as if he felt Hanna's eyes on him, he glanced toward her. When he met her gaze, his face relaxed, and his stern mouth quirked up in a boyish half-smile as he inclined his head a little in her direction.

Hanna felt the blood rush to her face and looked to see if Mrs. Milgram had noticed the exchange.

She had. She studied Hanna's face, eyes narrowed, lips pursed. "Yes," she said. "He did that when you first came in, too. And what's more, he went to welcome you as a personal friend and then offended his sister by introducing you as a social equal. I heard him ask you to be his dinner companion myself. And in my admittedly limited experience I'd never seen him behave like that. It rather surprised me, and I'm afraid I spoke without thinking. I hope you'll forgive me. I imagine you must have known all this already, and I've interrupted your evening unnecessarily."

It took Hanna a moment to think how she could respond without revealing just how deeply ignorant she'd been. She needed to have a long chat with Tomin when this night was over. "Not at all, Mrs. Milgram. I appreciate your concern on my behalf, you've been very kind." She attempted to produce an understanding smile.

Mrs. Milgram smiled back. "Thank you, Miss Bradley." She paused thoughtfully for a moment, then added, "Perhaps you'll indulge me in one more intended kindness that might be thoroughly misplaced?"

"What do you mean, Mrs. Milgram?"

"Only that if any of this information is new to you and has caused you concern, I hope you're also aware that Talessanin custom allows a woman to change her mind at any time without repercussion. And as my husband wasn't available to attend with me this evening, I've brought my son David along as my escort. I'm sure he'd be happy to walk out to dinner with you if you should find yourself in need of a companion."

Chapter 17

RELIEF WASHED THROUGH JON WHEN Tomin, who had insisted on playing steward tonight, came to discreetly inform him that all the expected guests had arrived and dinner was ready to be served. As host, Jon gave his official leave for the chimes to be sounded. Tala, delighted with her role as hostess, claimed her father as her dining companion and happily led the way out to the back lawn where the meal was laid out.

Narista plucked one of the hopeful-looking young men out of a hovering cluster and followed Tala and Kamm, directing a dark look at Jon on her way out. Narista objected to eating outdoors at night, a practice she considered barbaric. But none of the rooms in Jon's new home were large enough to accommodate all of his brother's most essential guests; he hadn't intended to host state dinners when he'd had the house built. In fact, part of his design in building a house here in the first place had been emphatically to avoid the odious things.

Jon had quite enjoyed the picnic at the lake, however, and Hanna had not objected to outdoor dining. Unlike her friends, she had not said very much, curled up on her cushion across the low table from him, but her eyes—her sweet, chocolate eyes—met his several times as they ate, and she directed a playfully defiant tilt of her chin his way when she sampled a sliver of the *peleng nanth*.

Salenia flowed gracefully to Jon's side, assuming, as Kamm and Narista undoubtedly did, that Jon would walk out with her tonight as he had so often before. But none of them had consulted him on the matter. He forced a polite smile to his lips and detached Salenia's fingers from his elbow again. "You will excuse me, of course, Salenia. I have petitioned Hanna's companionship for the evening and must go learn whether I am accepted." He offered Salenia a small bow and took a sour sort of pleasure in the outraged gleam in her eyes as he straightened. It was even more satisfying than the look on Narista's face had been when he asked Tala to fill the role of hostess. Tala, on the other hand, had looked as if he'd swum the galactic ocean and handed her a moon.

Jon threaded his way through the press of guests as they finalized social arrangements and made their way toward the back of the house. Would Hanna be there? She had said she would wait for him, but after conversing with that white-haired woman, Hanna had left the living room on the arm of a young human man.

Jon tried to remember who Kamm had said those people were. Hanna had certainly appeared interested in whatever the woman had to say, and they had looked in Jon's direction several times as they spoke. Had the woman told Hanna something that would make her change her mind about dining with him? That thought made his mind begin whirling with all the things Kamm's guests might say to Hanna. He went cold. She would never want to speak to him again, let alone dine with him.

Maybe he should have listened to Chance, who'd advised against inviting Hanna this evening in the first place. But as Tomin pointed out, she would be able to tell they were having a party, and she might interpret the lack of an invitation as a social slight. And Jon had been longing to see her again. He'd watched for her the morning after the picnic but had not seen her all that day. Nor the next. After that he'd been called to the embassy to help Kamm prepare for this visit, and every dragging day there he'd found himself wondering what she might be doing and imagining what he might say to her the next time they met. If he had been able to hand deliver her invitation as he intended, he might have had a chance to prepare her. But she had proven elusive, and he'd had no opportunity to speak with her. And now Kamm's guests might be saying anything at all to her. His pulse began to throb somewhere deep in his belly. She had only been here a few minutes; maybe it would be all right. *Please let it be all right.*

When he came at last within sight of the French doors, he paused, scanning the area. He didn't see her. She hadn't waited. Of course she hadn't waited. Why would she wish to dine with a man who triggered her terror fits? He was a fool and worse than a fool.

Then a tall man near the doors bowed to a lady who had evidently just accepted him as her companion, and Jon caught a glimpse of Hanna standing behind the man, closer to the wall. He lost sight of her again as the man straightened, but she was there. She *had* waited.

Warmth flooded through Jon, and he took two long, buoyant strides forward before the tall man moved out through the doors with his companion, and Jon halted. Hanna was not alone; the young human man who had escorted her from the living room stood against the wall next to Hanna, leaning in to speak earnestly with her. She smiled and laid her hand on the man's arm, and Jon went cold all over again. But he had no right to be envious. He had no claim on Hanna; she was free to choose a companion she preferred.

He expected the couple to move toward the door, but instead, Hanna patted the man's arm as if reassuring him and turned away, looking out over the crowd. Her eyes met Jon's, and her smile widened. *She* had *waited for him!* Jon's heart surged and hot blood burst through his veins, and he barely noticed how quickly his guests moved out of his way, as he strode to meet her.

"There you are," she said softly when he finally stood before her. "I had begun to think you'd sneaked out the front again when everyone's back was turned, and I'd have to sit with David at dinner. I'm glad you decided to come for me after all." She moved to stand beside him and tucked her small hand into the crook of his elbow, smiling up at him. He would never get tired of seeing her smile.

Jon's relief crept out as a chuckle, and he placed his hand over hers, leaning down to speak confidentially. "Alas, I cannot creep out when everyone's back is turned this time. As host, I am required to wait until last to walk out to table, and the staff must not serve dinner until I arrive. It is all very tiresome, but Kamm and Narista insist that everything must be done properly, and it would be ungracious of me to leave my guests standing up all night while their food got cold. I am very happy you are here, Hanna. Thank you for waiting for me."

She eyed him seriously, "I said I would."

"You did. And I should have trusted your word. But when I came in, I did not see you hiding there by the wall, Little Mouse. I feared you had tired of waiting or had found a less disagreeable companion and walked out already."

Hanna laughed. "And I was afraid you'd walk in with Salenia on your arm and not be able to even remember who I was."

"Salenia?" Hanna was perceptive. Jon scowled. "Salenia talks too much and says too little. And she is forever sticking to my elbow."

There was an awkward pause as they both looked down at his hand resting atop hers on his arm. Hanna giggled softly. "Like this?" she asked, wiggling her fingers. She attempted to remove her hand, but he caught it before it could escape and tucked it back into the crook of his elbow, holding it firmly in place with his own hand. Hanna's small, webless fingers felt as if they belonged there.

"Not at all," he murmured. "She is a great deal stickier than that. I think you had better keep practicing."

Hanna blushed rather fetchingly and laughed.

Looking around the room, Jon saw that the last of the guests had paired up and moved out through the French doors. "Are you ready, Miss Bradley?"

"I'm ready, Jonantathinel Ehr," Hanna responded. He must have looked surprised, because she smiled and said, "I've learned several interesting things about you this evening, Jon."

Jon took a deep breath and tried not to let his mind linger on the possibilities.

Chapter
18

HANNA CAUGHT HER BREATH AS she and Jon stepped through the French doors. Jon's back yard had been transformed.

On the terrace, the patio furniture had been replaced by a long, ornately carved table, where light from glass-shielded candles glimmered and danced over elaborate, fanciful place settings lined up along a velvety black tablecloth that glittered with gold embroidery. More tables stood on the lawn, arranged in two long rows perpendicular to the terrace. In the grassy space between the rows, directly in front of the high table, a cluster of musicians bent and swayed, seducing lilting harmonies from instruments made of twisted glass. Hundreds of softly luminescent lamps that appeared to be made of intricately folded paper gleamed in the air, floating above the guests' heads like white water lilies on the still surface of a pond. It was magical.

Jon paused just outside the door while the unobtrusive attendants showed the last few dinner guests to their seats, and Hanna had a moment to recall what Tomin had taught her about the significance of the seating arrangements. Tala, the darling hostess, stood near the center of the head table, with her father standing at the place to her right as the hostess's honored dining companion. Narista occupied the place to Kamm's right as a guest of honor, and a young man stood behind the chair at the end of the table, presumably Narista's companion for the evening. Two empty places waited to the left of Tala's seat, one for the host, and one for his companion. The remaining guests would be seated based on the rank of the socially superior member of each dining companionship, with the highest ranking closest to the head table. Hanna found it all rather intimidating, especially once all the guests were standing behind their seats, eyes turned toward Jon, waiting for the host to take his place.

As Jon led Hanna across the terrace, the musicians produced a dramatic, rippling flourish of sound and then went silent. Jon escorted Hanna to her seat and took his place next to her, smiling down at his niece. "Are you ready, little Tala?" he asked.

She gave him a wide-eyed smile and nodded.

Jon spread his arms wide, palms up. "Honored guests," he said in a voice loud enough to carry to the far ends of the long tables, "we welcome you to our home, and we offer tribute on behalf of this company and in gratitude for your friendship during this time of change."

He looked down at Tala. She picked up something small, like a marble, from a delicate silver tray on the table in front of her, then held the object above her head, stretching her arms up as if offering it to the stars. Her hands lowered, and she touched the thing solemnly to her forehead, to her lips, to her chest over her heart; then she placed it carefully in the flame of a small brazier nestled among the candles on the table in front of her. After half a heartbeat, a trickle of white smoke drifted upward from the offering, giving off a rich, spicy scent that reminded Hanna of the way Jon smelled up close. Jon clapped his hands loudly three times and swept his arms out to the sides again.

The guests apparently recognized this as a signal to take their seats, and the musicians resumed playing softly. Servers began to appear, one by one, out of the shadows by the trees at the back of the lawn, and Hanna remembered what Tomin had said about the catering arrangements. She squinted at the tree line to see if she could make out where the self-contained kitchen flutter pod squatted, hidden behind its mask shielding, but she couldn't detect so much as a ripple in the scenery.

Jon turned with his shy half-smile to hold Hanna's chair for her, and by the time he took his own seat, the servers were placing water basins on elegant stands between the chairs. Tomin had instructed Hanna in their use, of course, but she was still glad when Jon demonstrated by swishing his fingers slowly in the two basins on either side of his chair before drying them on one of the soft towels that hung from the stands. Hanna followed his lead, then turned to examine the place setting laid out in front of her.

The plate and knife, at least, were recognizable, though the plate was narrow and oblong in shape, and the knife blade arced through several sinuous, decorative curves before rounding out into a handle. The other utensils would've completely baffled Hanna if Tomin hadn't educated her in advance.

Tomin had cheerfully asserted that no matter what planet one was dining on, most of the implements used would perform one or more of a small number of common functions: slicing, scooping, impaling, pinching, or drinking. So she knew that one sliced with the knife, but never impaled. She understood that the array of jeweled metal beetles with long, pointed antennae were used more or less like forks—one impaled food on the antennae and transported it to one's mouth. The graceful porcelain sea shells were scoops, like spoons with short handles and broad bowls. And the veritable garden of crystal flowers would hold various beverages. Talessanins, according to Tomin, used their fingers if something needed to be pinched. He'd said that in a tone that made it sound ever so slightly suggestive and winked at her.

Servers bustled along the other side of the table for a few minutes, placing tidbits of food in neat rows along the length of the oblong plates and using vessels with long spouts like watering cans to fill a few of the little crystal flowers. Hanna was glad Tomin had taught her that the shape of a flower's petals could be used as a clue as to whether the beverage in it would make her tipsy or not. Even under the best of circumstances she didn't like the floating, disconnected sensation alcohol produced in her; it made her feel too vulnerable. And she knew she'd need all her wits in place to navigate this evening without making any embarrassing mistakes—especially since her newly, rapidly, and incompletely acquired Talessanin table manners were going to be on display at the head table right next to the host.

Hanna's concern turned out to be unnecessary, however. Tomin had prepared her well. He'd taught her the pattern in which the utensils were laid out, so she always knew which one to use, and he'd explained how to eat each of the more exotic dishes. She even remembered to never leave a beetle on her plate belly up and to clean her fingers in the basins between courses.

Actually, that part turned out to be rather entertaining. Between the first and second courses, Hanna felt Jon's hand brush gently against hers in the water and looked over to see him smiling at her in a mischievous, questioning way that made her think maybe he'd timed it that way on purpose. She smiled back at him.

Between the second and third courses he tangled his webbed fingers with hers, capturing her hand in a caress that sent chills down to her toes and left her momentarily breathless. But Tala playfully flicked water at him from the basin on his other side, and he let go of Hanna's hand so he could shift to a better angle to retaliate.

Between the third and fourth courses, Hanna's poor fingers were abandoned to their own devices, as Jon was engaged with his brother in an animated discussion about the quality of lumber harvested from places she had never heard of. But after she dried her hands, she felt several water droplets patter against her elbow and looked over to see Jon wiping his fingers on his towel. He was saying something to Kamm about teaching someone new forestry management techniques, but Kamm was looking past him at Hanna and appeared to be trying not to laugh.

Between the fourth and fifth courses, Jon's hand waited for hers in the basin, but Hanna pretended to be engrossed in watching the musicians until he gave up and began to withdraw; then she reached quickly out, catching the tips of his retreating fingers and pulling his hand back in. He chuckled softly and gave her hand another spine-tingling caress in the water. And after that, her fingers always found his waiting.

Between these interludes, Hanna and Jon talked of many things as they ate. He told her about his recent trip to the embassy enclave to help Kamm prepare for his extended visit. She talked about her work, and he laughed at her descriptions of the measures she and Mrs. Bedella had taken to coax Miss Mattie to sit still while she had her portrait painted. He told her about animals and insects he'd seen on his travels to other worlds.

There was one awkward moment when Hanna asked Jon what the Nine Winds were and how one became their Commander. He looked at her sharply and asked where she had heard about that. She told him Mrs. Milgram had mentioned that he'd been the Commander of the Nine

Winds for some time but hadn't explained what it meant. Jon scowled and looked away as he told her that was the name of the specialized military unit in which he'd served and then changed the subject.

Hanna decided not to mention anything else Mrs. Milgram had said and, instead, asked about his progress building the treehouse. Jon assured her that although he hadn't had as much time to work on it as he'd hoped, the platform had been completed, including a sturdy safety rail, and he had constructed a good, solid landing between the stairs and the platform. Tala heard them talking about it and begged her indulgent uncle to tell her again about his plans for the little house that would be built on the platform.

Hanna found she also enjoyed the breaks in conversation as Jon spoke with Tala or Kamm. Since her seat was at the end of the group at their table, there was no one on her other side to converse with, and Hanna had time to look around at the floating lanterns, watch the musicians, and observe the other guests. David Milgram sat about halfway down the table to her left, sandwiched between his mother on one side and a pretty young woman in a low-cut gown on the other. He caught Hanna looking at him once and offered her a large smile and a small nod. She smiled back at him.

Her eyes shifted to the long table to her right. Salenia sat close to the near end between two young Talessanin men wearing elaborately embroidered longcoats. She was most emphatically *not* smiling, even though both of the gentlemen were obviously attempting to make her do so. The man Salenia had pointed out as the Canadian ambassador sat closer to the far end of the same table and seemed to be enjoying himself. Hanna had no idea who any of the other guests were, but she found it entertaining to watch their interactions anyway.

Hanna's supply of beetles, seashells, and flowers dwindled as the courses were served and cleared away, until she was left with a small, square plate, one tall, trumpet-shaped crystal flower, and a small golden beetle with ruby red gemstones for eyes. As the servers began distributing the sweet, fruity confection that constituted the final course of the evening, the lead musician rose to his feet, bowed to the head table, and announced, "With your permission, lords and ladies, a story to sweeten the entertainment, as you sweeten the ending of your feast!"

Tala bounced in her seat and clapped her little hands. She called out something in Talessanin that Hanna thought might be the name of a favorite story, and Jon waved his assent to the entertainer, who began an elaborate, theatrical telling of a story in which a brave warrior fought to rescue a fair maiden from a terrible beast deep in a forbidding forest. Hanna smiled, reflecting on the truly universal nature of fairytales and the little girls who loved them.

The man paced the story so it ended at just about the same time the servers began clearing away the last of the dishes from the tables and removing the finger basins. When he finished, the guests began rapping enthusiastically on the tops of the tables, creating a low rumbling sound that evidently expressed their approval of the tale. Several voices called out for another story, and all eyes turned to the head table as the rumble of applause died away. From the far end of the table, Narista called out, "Give us a tale of the Viper in the Night!"

A low murmur rippled among the guests, and the entertainer looked again to the host and hostess for approval. Hanna glanced expectantly at Jon and was startled to find that his face had gone pale and his brow was drawn into a dark scowl. The edge of his jaw rippled as he clenched and unclenched his teeth.

Seeing the host hesitate, the entertainer raised his arms theatrically, turned to face the other direction, and called out to the guests, "Let's offer His Lordship some encouragement!" Again, the guests began rapping enthusiastically on the tables.

Jon leaned slightly toward Hanna and asked quietly, "Do you dance?"

Not sure what to make of Jon's sudden shift in mood, Hanna replied softly, "Tomin taught me a dance he called the *aylencanat* in case there was dancing. He said if anyone asked me to dance something else I should just say I regret I'm feeling fatigued and smile a lot."

Jon nodded thoughtfully, then seemed to make a decision. He rose slowly to his feet, and the sounds of table rapping trickled into silence. By the time he spoke, his smile was back in place. "For me, one story is enough tonight," he announced loudly, "I am of a mind to dance with my enchanting hostess. Give us a *berantelcanat*, if you would, Master!"

The guests rapped on the tables again, with perhaps even more enthusiasm. The entertainer bowed deeply, turned, and waved a complicated series of hand gestures at his troupe. The musicians rose from their seats and began to play a gentle, merry tune as they marched around the perimeter of the grassy space between the tables until they stopped, all in a row, facing the high table. They stood frozen for a moment in silent stillness, and Hanna noticed that the servers had moved the musicians' seats from the center of the grassy space to the back of the yard, closer to where the servers disappeared into the invisible kitchen pod.

Abruptly, the music exploded into a wild, running melody with complicated harmonies flitting in and out and through it like little fishes. At the same time, the musicians burst into motion, leaping and whirling through the space between the tables, seemingly without pattern or plan, and apparently on the constant verge of colliding with each other or falling over a table. A flurry of giggles bubbled out of Tala, and the little girl leapt from her seat. She dashed around the far end of the head table and out between the capering musicians to stand in the middle of the dancing space. Jon rose from his seat as well and strode around Hanna's end of the table. He walked to the center of the table on the other side and offered a deep bow in the direction of his niece, who curtsied in return. When their dance began, it looked more to Hanna like a complicated game of tag, with Jon pursuing the child as she dodged in and out between the musicians like Little Red Riding Hood evading the Big Bad Wolf.

Hanna heard a low chuckle and glanced over to see Kamm shaking his head wryly. He caught her looking and grinned. "My daughter's favorite dance," he explained, inclining his head toward the chaos on the other side of the table. "She nags her dance instructor for it incessantly, the little tyrant. And since he has no children of his own, my brother takes every opportunity of spoiling mine. I'll be hearing about this nonstop for a week, at the very least." His indulgent expression showed Hanna that he was more amused than annoyed.

"Tala is utterly adorable," she said. "Every little girl should have an uncle who spoils her. And a father who doesn't." She smiled back at Kamm.

Kamm's gaze focused more fully on Hanna. He tilted his head and looked as if he were going to say something, but his attention flickered back to the dance.

Jon had captured one of his little dance partner's hands, and the musicians were moving back to line the sides of the grassy space as Jon and

Tala began dancing in earnest. The *berantelcanat* was quick and complex, and now and again Tala missed a step. But Jon always compensated, and the night's host and hostess whirled smoothly around the grassy dance floor in front of their guests. Tala giggled joyfully each time the dance required her partner to lift her into the air and twirl her around, and by the time the dancers separated and offered each other a final bow, the little girl's cheeks were rosy and her eyes sparkled, and Jon's smile looked genuine again. Jon swept his niece off the ground and carried her back to her seat, which he could now approach more easily, since the servers had unobtrusively folded up and removed all the tables during the course of the dance. Tala threw her arms around her uncle and kissed his cheek as he set her carefully on her chair.

The musicians moved to their seats at the back of the space and began a slow, sweet, lilting melody with rhythms that Hanna recognized from her dance lessons with Tomin as an *aylencanat*. Jon stepped in front of her and bowed. "Hanna," he said solemnly, "will you do me the honor of dancing with me?" She took his offered hand and walked with him to the center of the dance floor, where he claimed her other hand as well and began leading her through the slow, graceful steps of the dance.

After a few minutes he released one of her hands in order to make a sweeping gesture that invited the guests to join in the dancing, and other couples drifted out into the open area, moving with the rippling flow of the music. But instead of taking her hand again, Jon dropped his hand to Hanna's waist and pulled her closer. This wasn't how Tomin had taught her. Tiny flashes of panic sparked around the edges of her mind. He was so *close*. She drew a deep breath and pushed the panic back. He was Jon; she was safe. But she could feel the warmth of his hand through her gown, and her heart pounded faster.

She wasn't sure what to do with her free hand, and thinking about it caused her to miss a step in the dance. Jon shifted in a way that made her misstep seem more like an intentional variation, and took his hand from her waist to capture her lost hand and guide it to his shoulder, "It goes here." He bent his head to whisper, and his breath tickled down the side of her neck. "Or here." He moved it to rest over his heart, and his fingertips traced a tingling caress down the back of her hand before he left it there. He returned his hand to Hanna's waist, sliding it around to the middle of her back so he could draw her even closer. The spicy smell of him made Hanna feel giddy, and she was surprised to find she could feel his heart beating and the muscles of his chest moving under her fingers beneath the warm leather of his uniform as he shifted with the slow rhythms of the music. Practicing with Tomin had been nothing like this.

After a few more minutes, Jon tipped his head down again to murmur, "Are you having a good time tonight, Hanna?"

Hanna missed another step as she considered her response, so she settled for, "It's a very nice party, Jon. And so far nothing has caught on fire." She felt his low laugh vibrate through her fingers on his chest, sending shivers up her arm that made her catch her breath.

They swayed with the music. Jon said, "I am glad you are here tonight Hanna. I usually dread the dancing."

Hanna missed another step. "I'm glad too, Jon," she said. "But could you please stop talking? I have to count the steps in my head, and you're messing me up."

He laughed again and said nothing else until the dance ended and they were walking back toward their seats on the terrace, her fingers still twined with his. Then he said, "Hanna, if I could, I would dance with just you all night. But I am the host, so I must dance with my sister and her friend, and several of the other ladies, or I risk damage to my brother's reputation. And I owe my brother a great deal. Will you forgive me if I abandon you again for a little while?"

Glancing up at him as she walked, Hanna saw that his face had gone quite serious, even a bit grave, so she bit off the teasing retort she'd been about to give, and said only, "Yes, of course, Jon."

He gave a quick nod, then looked down at his feet. "And Hanna, . . ." he began, but stopped as they arrived at her chair. She gave his hand a gentle squeeze, and he shifted his gaze to look earnestly into her face as he continued. "Hanna, I have a reputation as well. Some of it is deserved. Some of it is just stories told by people who were not there and do not know. If . . . if someone tells you stories about me tonight, will you do me the courtesy of giving me a chance to explain?"

Jon's deep, hazel eyes held Hanna in place, refusing to release her until she gave an answer. She thought of his evasion earlier when she'd asked him about the Nine Winds, and of what Mrs. Milgram had said about him being dangerous. Then she remembered his shy uncertainty as he stood in her kitchen asking if he could stay. She remembered the sheltering comfort of his arm around her shoulders beneath the tree-house, and the way he'd kept his distance by the lake so as not to frighten her, and his crooked, unguarded grin when she'd taken his arm to walk back to the pavilion for the picnic. Her fingertips still thrummed with the memory of his heartbeat and the soft vibration of his laugh beneath the leather while they danced. But he had a reputation: *Dangerous.*

"Jon," she said carefully, looking into those penetrating eyes, "You're my friend. I trust you. If someone tells me anything that might change that, I'll ask you about it before I draw any conclusions. But you have to promise to tell me the truth."

"My honor, Hanna." Jon's quiet voice startled her with its intensity. "I will never lie to you." His eyes held hers a moment longer, imploring her to believe him. Then he raised her hand to his lips and pressed a soft kiss into her palm before striding off to where his sister waited, her face drawn into a disapproving frown.

Chapter

19

HANNA DECIDED TO GO FIND the powder room before someone else asked her to dance. She drew out her search for an absurdly long time—especially considering the fact that Tomin had pointed out its location the night Jon had showed her his treehouse—and took as much time as she thought she decently could before wandering slowly back to the French doors.

Stopping just outside, she saw that many of the guests who weren't dancing had abandoned their seats and stood in groups scattered around the lawn and terrace. Servers circulated among them, offering beverages and other refreshments. Here and there, a dark-uniformed bodyguard or two lurked in the shadows. The floating lamps had been dimmed and now drifted in slow, swirling eddies above the guests' heads.

It took a moment to find Jon among the dancers, but he was there, his movements lithe and disciplined, muted lamplight sliding over the subtle textures of his uniform and glinting from the silver detailing as he swept through the patterns of the dance with his exquisite partner. Salenia. His partner was Salenia. The soft light that slipped off Jon caught in the tall, slender woman's coppery hair and glittered from the gems on her gown like flying sparks as Jon's hands caught her hips, drawing her close in the dance. The two of them looked so right together—fire and darkness, grace and gallantry, danger and desire. Jon *belonged* with

Salenia. Two sides of the same coin. Matching bookends. Peas in a pod. Every stupid, cloying cliché that Hanna could never be part of.

A spasm of senseless jealousy clutched at Hanna's insides, and she ruthlessly squashed it. She had no right to be jealous. She had no right to be *here*. Why had she come? What was she thinking? There was something magnetic about Jon that drew her like a cat to a sunny windowsill. He made her feel alive. And wanted. And almost safe. And it had been an achingly long time since she'd felt any of those things. But it was wrong for her to be here. Wrong to be pretending that a happy ending was possible. That Jon could really want to be with her. That *any* man could want to be with her. That she'd ever be able to truly love and be loved. The truth was, she didn't know how, and she was too broken to be able to figure it out. Some broken things just couldn't be fixed.

And Jon was too nice to play these games of pretend with. He deserved something real. He should be with someone like Salenia—someone whole, and beautiful, and so very obviously right for him. He shouldn't be getting mixed up with a damaged cast-off like Hanna. She was using him. She had to stop. Had to at least be honest with him about what she was. What he had put his foot in. And then he wouldn't want her anymore. Not even a little. If he ever really had.

"Don't be absurd." Almost as if in response to her thoughts, a voice drifted from behind the nearest of the large stone pillars on the terrace—an angry, raised whisper, as if the speaker had become too agitated to continue speaking softly. ". . . cannot possibly be saying you approve!"

Another voice answered, also in a raised whisper. ". . . saying it's not my decision to make."

The voices evaporated back into the night for a moment, and Hanna began to move away to give the speakers privacy. But the first voice hissed out again from behind the pillar, catching at her. ". . . first female he trips over after he leaves the Winds! It isn't even Talessanin!"

"*She* makes him happy!" The pronoun was laden with emphasis.

"It's obscene!" the first voice retorted.

A furious rustle of movement startled Hanna, and she reflexively backed into the shadows to the side of the brightly lit doorway as a woman stalked from behind the pillar. Narista. A moment later, Kamm followed, shaking his head.

Hanna watched them from the shadows and shivered at a sudden chill. Narista paused at the edge of the terrace, straightened her shoulders, smoothed her dress, and went to join one of the knots of conversing guests. Kamm walked back to where little Tala, perched primly on the edge of her seat, waited all by herself on the row of chairs that remained where the high table had been.

After a moment, not knowing what else to do, Hanna went back to her own seat. Kamm and Tala glanced up at her as she approached, and both of them smiled. Hanna smiled back, but her smile felt shaky and artificial. The three of them sat there for a few minutes, Jon's empty chair between them. And in front of them, Jon and Salenia turned, and swayed, and touched in perfect, elegant synchrony among the other couples, as if they'd always danced together. Hanna felt awkward—lost and a little afraid, like an inadvertent imposter about to be unmasked.

Tala leaned over and whispered something to her father. Kamm looked appraisingly at Hanna, then nodded to his daughter.

Tala hopped off her chair and walked over to stand in front of Hanna. "Miss Bradley," she said shyly, "would you like to see my treehouse?"

Hanna suddenly felt a great fondness for this little girl with the big dark eyes. "Thank you, Tala," she said, trying to keep the relief out of her voice. "I'd love to see your treehouse."

Tala slipped her hand into Hanna's and led the way around the dancers and across the lawn. For a moment, Hanna thought Tala was leading her in the wrong direction, but then she saw the streaks of light that now spilled across the grass from open doorways on either end of the shielded flutter pod kitchen and realized the little girl was just leading her around it. As they passed, Hanna looked inside. Several servers rested on padded benches that lined the walls of a small anteroom, chatting with a handful of black-uniformed guards who were evidently also taking a break. One of the guards looked up as Tala led Hanna past the doorway, and Hanna recognized Chance. She waved at him, and he soberly inclined his head in return.

Moments later, Hanna stood at the bottom of the treehouse stairs, watching as Tala gathered up her skirts and dashed joyfully up the spiral steps. Hanna followed, carefully holding the hem of her own gown out of the way. At the top, she was relieved to discover that a solid landing did indeed connect the stairs to the platform, and that both the landing and the platform were encircled by a waist-high safety rail. A mesh of woven rope filled the space between the rail and the floor to prevent small people from falling under the rail. Tala bounced up and down on the other side of the platform, beckoning for Hanna to join her there. Hanna walked across the sturdy floor and helped Tala admire the view of the moonlit lake. Tala took Hanna's hand again to tug her to the far end of the platform. From that side, the view through the branches was of an open glade among the trees, where the moonlight shone through the canopy of leaves onto waving grass and wildflowers. When that view had been sufficiently appreciated, Tala began skipping merrily around the platform, showing Hanna where her Bahta Jon had said there would be a bench, and a flower box, and where the little house would be. Hanna sat with Tala in the spot where Bahta Jon had promised a table would stand, and the two of them had a delightful—and extravagantly mannerly—imaginary tea party.

Just as they were finishing their non-existent chocolate bundt cake, a soft chuckle interrupted from the top of the stairs, and they both looked up, startled. Jon stood with his back against the tree trunk, watching them. "Tala," he said, "your father is looking for you."

Kamm appeared on the stairs behind Jon, and Hanna was grateful for the darkness as she felt herself blush under the weight of both pairs of eyes.

Tala scolded her Bahta Jon for making them drop their cups, waved goodbye to Hanna, and squeezed past the men to scamper back down the stairs, chattering rapidly in Talessanin. Her father nodded solemnly to Hanna and followed.

For a long moment, Jon and Hanna just looked at each other. Jon blended into the shadows the moonlight cast on the oak, gazing out at Hanna like some kind of mystical tree spirit. Hanna thought she must look silly, sitting there in the moonlight on the bare wooden platform in her evening gown. After a moment, she said softly, teasingly, "You made me break my cup, Jon. Shame on you, sneaking up on people like that."

Jon's mouth quirked into that boyish half-smile of his. "I am very sorry, "he murmured. "May I help you sweep up the pieces?"

She laughed. "I might need you to help me up first. This dress wasn't really designed for treetop tea parties."

He stepped out of the darkness and across the moonlit platform, holding out his hands. She slipped one hand into his, and he steadied her as she used her other hand to untangle her skirt from around her legs. As she stood, he brought his other hand up to the small of her back and pulled her close as if they were dancing again. "Better?" he whispered.

She couldn't interpret his expression, but those dark eyes had again become bottomless pools of lake shadow. A soft, breathless glow started to throb in the pit of her stomach, and every inch of her skin began to tingle.

A stray breeze tickled a loose strand of her hair across Hanna's cheek, and Jon released her hand to caress it away. As his fingers touched her skin, white-hot terror lanced through Hanna's body, and she flinched back from his touch, breath hissing through suddenly clenched teeth.

"Hanna?" He pulled away from her, snatching his hand from her back. "Hanna, I am sorry, I did not intend . . ."

She clutched at him. "Wait!" she gasped, trying to catch her breath. "Please stay. Just . . . need a moment." A shudder passed through her body, and she squeezed her eyes shut, holding the tears in check.

Her breathing steadied as Jon cautiously returned his hand to her back and tucked his other arm slowly, carefully, around her shoulders. Relief flooded through Hanna, and she leaned her forehead against his chest, forcing herself to breathe slowly and deeply. The scent of him settled into her, shored her up as the torrent of fear washed around her. His strong arms steadied her. She had never felt so safe.

But it wasn't right for her to use him this way. As sweet as it was to make believe, this was no more real than the tea party had been, and it was time to put an end to the pretending before someone got hurt. When she felt she'd regained sufficient control, she took one more deep breath and pushed away from him. He let her go without resistance.

She straightened and looked up into his face. "There's something you need to know."

This time, Jon's expression stayed carefully neutral, but his voice was gentle when he said, "Tell me, Hanna."

She hesitated. She couldn't think how to say it. She didn't often talk about these things. "This isn't going to work."

He didn't respond; just tilted his head inquiringly.

Hanna cleared her throat. "I don't really do romance, Jon. I can't. It . . . it doesn't work. I'm sorry."

"Hanna . . ." Jon's expression didn't change, but her name was a throaty, coaxing caress when he said it. Then he stopped, and his lips pressed together. He nodded once, and looked away, shoulders stiffening. "You promised me an opportunity to explain." His voice had gone brittle.

For a heartbeat, Hanna was confused; then she remembered. "Nobody told me any stories about you, Jon. I just can't do this."

He looked at her again. His expression was still carefully controlled, but his eyes searched her face intently. "Then"—he slowly raised a hand, palm up, webbed fingers spread—"it is because I am not human."

Hanna choked on a bitter laugh. "No. It's nothing to do with you. You're amazing." One of her fingers strayed out to skim the edge of the webbing between his long fingers. "I just can't."

"Hanna . . ." The caress was back in Jon's voice again as his hand closed around hers.

She jerked away as if he'd burned her. "Please don't do that. This is hard enough already." She turned away and moved the short distance to the railing, clutching it with trembling fingers as she looked through the trees at the rippling water of the lake. After a moment he stepped up beside her. She tensed, but he didn't touch her again, and he didn't say anything.

Finally, Hanna drew a deep breath. "There was a man," she began, keeping her eyes fixed on the lake so she wouldn't have to see his face when she told him. "A long time ago. I was seventeen. And I was still . . . such a child." She stopped, trying to find the right words. Jon didn't say anything. After a moment, Hanna swallowed and went on. "He came into my room one night and took me . . . away." She stopped again, and again Jon just waited for her to continue. "He . . . um . . . he hurt me. And . . . and . . ." she couldn't say it. She couldn't. She let out a long breath and made a helpless gesture with one hand before pressing her fingers to her forehead.

She couldn't look at Jon. The silence dragged out between them.

"I understand," Jon murmured finally.

"No," Hanna said bitterly. "You don't."

Jon shifted. "Hanna—"

"He kept me in a shed," Hanna interrupted. "Like an animal. For days." Jon was silent again, and after a moment, Hanna went on. "He came back . . . I don't know how many times. And every time, he . . . he hurt me, and he . . . touched me, and . . . and he used my body. And I couldn't stop him. I couldn't even scream. He kept me drugged, and I couldn't move, I could only . . . watch." Hanna looked down at her hands, ran a finger along the smooth wood of the railing. "I made it partway to the door once," she whispered, "when he was late, and it started to wear off. But . . ." she shook her head. "He always came back." Hanna took a deep breath, gripping the handrail again, watching the backs of her knuckles turn white as she clenched her fingers around the wood. "There wasn't even a lock on the door."

Jon turned, facing out across the lake with her, and after a moment his hand came up to clasp the railing next to hers—not touching, just there.

Hanna stared at it for a long minute, wanting . . . wanting . . . she wasn't sure what she wanted. She took another deep breath. "Whenever I try to be . . . close with someone, or if someone touches me in a way that . . . that reminds me"—she swallowed hard—"I have panic attacks. Flashbacks. Nightmares. It's as if it's happening to me all over again." She shook her head. "Sometimes I think I see him outside my house."

Jon's hand slid a little nearer to hers on the railing, and Hanna stopped talking to stare at it again. But he stopped before he touched her. And Hanna didn't move her hand away.

"I don't think I can give you what you seem to want from me," she said, still not looking at his face, still watching his hand warily. "It isn't that I don't want to. Tonight has been . . ." Hanna's voice got stuck halfway up her throat, and she stopped to choke it back down again. She sighed. "I just can't, Jon. I don't know if I will ever be able to have that sort of relationship with someone. With . . . anyone."

Hanna was quiet again for a long time, until Jon shifted and cleared his throat. "I understand."

"I thought you should know." Hanna's voice was hardly more than a whisper. "So you could make an informed decision about . . . this."

Jon's hand tensed on the railing, and he drew a quick breath. He didn't say anything yet, but Hanna knew what was coming; she'd been down this road a few times before.

"So you could stop before you got in too deep with me and my . . . my wreckage," she said. "It wasn't fair of me to let you think that this was . . . something it isn't. Something it can probably never be. I'm sorry." She shrugged one shoulder slightly. "Please don't tell anyone else."

Jon shifted again, taking his hand off the railing this time, sliding his other hand to take its place close to hers as he turned to face her. "Hanna . . ." Jon's whisper held an almost painful intensity. "You speak of an informed decision, as if I have a choice. What if I do not wish to stop? Would you allow me to . . . to continue?" His hand slid slowly closer to hers, still not touching, but close enough that she could feel the warmth from his skin.

Hanna stopped breathing. Her pulse throbbed in her throat. She drew a shuddering breath and shook her head. "Why would you want to do that?"

"I like having you with me," he said quietly. "You make me laugh. You make me feel that the universe is full of good and beautiful things. I like who I am when I am with you." One of his fingers closed the gap, tracing the side of Hanna's hand as gently as a breath. "But I want only what you are able to give and only when you are able to give it freely. I will not pursue this if you do not wish it."

Hardly daring to breathe, Hanna turned her head to look up at him.

Jon's deep hazel eyes were solemn, intense. "You do me great honor in telling me these things, Hanna. If you ever wish to tell me more, I will listen. If you do not, I will not ask. Some wounds are too tender to uncover overmuch; I understand. If I do something that frightens you, you must tell me to stop, and I will stop. If I can do something to help you feel safe, tell me; I will do it. And if ever you wish me to leave you forever, I will do that too. This I swear to you. But I hope that will not happen."

Hanna's heart began to pound in earnest. Jon's hand shifted on the railing, and he brushed two fingertips across the back of her hand, sending a delicious, tingling shiver through her body. He knew. He knew, and he still wanted to touch her.

Hanna turned toward him, away from the railing, and his face fell as her hand pulled away from his. Disappointment?

He *knew*. Could he really still want her? She raised a tentative hand to trace the line of his cheekbone, and he closed his eyes, tilting his face toward her touch, letting out a soft sigh. She left her hand where it was, cupped against his cheek. "Jon," she whispered, "I . . . don't know how."

Jon opened his eyes and lifted his hand tentatively, cautiously, to lie against the side of Hanna's neck, his thumb gently skimming her cheek. "There is no hurry, Little Mouse," he whispered. "We can discover how together." His shoulders rose and fell slightly. "There are other things we must come to know of each other. And there will be challenges to overcome. But given the choice, I would very much like to continue . . . this." His thumb stroked the edge of her jaw once. "Would you allow it?"

His other hand came up to her waist and slid around to her back. She let him draw her gently closer to him as his eyes searched hers, seeking, asking. The feathers and beads in his braids skimmed against her hand on his cheek as he bent his head down to whisper in her ear, "Please say yes, Hanna."

His voice held a longing that brought tears to Hanna's eyes. Her fingers drifted around to the back of his neck, tangling in his braids, and her cheek brushed lightly against his as she whispered, "Yes, Jon. I think I would like that very much."

Jon breathed out a sigh that tickled down Hanna's neck and pulled back just enough to look into her eyes. "You are sure?" he asked.

In answer, Hanna brought her other hand up to trace the line of his jaw. Then she leaned forward, upward, until tentatively, hesitantly, ever so carefully, her lips met his.

He drew a small, startled breath but didn't pull away. He didn't move toward her either, though she felt his fingertips press lightly into her waist as if he wanted to pull her against him but feared she'd bolt. His lips responded, though. Tenderly, trembling a little, they moved with hers, warm and soft, sending a shiver down Hanna's spine to her toes and making her pulse pound in her ears.

He remained still for a breathless moment after she leaned away, his eyes studying her. Then a slow, sweet smile dawned across his face, and he straightened, trailing his fingers up her neck until his hand cupped her cheek, and his thumb brushed across her lips as softly as a butterfly wing. "Hanna . . ." he breathed, and this time her name sounded like a prayer.

She felt the blood rise to her face, and she looked down, her hands sliding from his face down over his shoulders and chest, as if her fingers were reading the braille of his tooled leather armor. "I'm sure," she whispered.

"Jon!" Chance's voice pierced the moment from below, and Hanna jumped and pulled away from Jon, stumbling back a few steps, suddenly self-conscious and a little frightened by what had just happened.

"A moment!" Jon called back. He was watching her, wary and tense.

Hanna reminded herself to breathe.

"You are wanted at the house, Honored Ehr." Chance's voice was dry and stiff. "Something about hosting a dinner party."

"Yes! A moment!" Jon called back. Then, to Hanna, he murmured, "Are you still sure?" His head tilted as he said it, and the words held an undercurrent of pleading that washed around Hanna's heart and started it beating steadily again.

She drew a deep breath and smiled at him. "Yes," she whispered.

He held out his hand, and she took it, and the two of them went down the steps together.

Chapter 20

HIS MOUTH GROUND LIKE STONE against hers. She felt his teeth again and tasted more blood. When he relaxed his grip on her throat enough for her to suck in one more half-lungful of the air he exhaled, his breath had a bitter, chemical smell to it. Everything seemed somehow distant, detached, as if she were watching it happen in slow motion to someone else's body. It wasn't real. Couldn't be real.

His body shuddered against someone else's body, skin sliding against blood-slick skin, the body's back pressed against the rough wood planks of the shed's wall. She wanted to close the eyes, but they wouldn't respond. They weren't her eyes. This wasn't happening. Not to her.

At last, he released his grip, and the body slumped to the floor. Air flooded into the lungs in a gush, and her body started coming back to her again. She still couldn't move. She felt lightheaded. Blood trickled into her throat; not much, just enough to half choke on. Her body spasmed in great, wracking coughs, and she saw droplets of red spittle dance through the air, felt it trickle down her chin. But she couldn't turn her head enough to keep the blood from draining down her throat. He stood over her, looking down, enjoying her pain, her fear, his ownership of her body. She looked up into his face—at the jagged scar that drew the outside corner of his left eye downward and contorted that side of his mouth, at the unblinking red electronic eye set in the black half-mask that covered the right side of his face.

Her body retched, and she tasted bile. The man's mouth twisted in disgust, and he used his foot to shove her over onto her side. She couldn't see him anymore, but as her body continued to convulse, she heard sounds coming from his direction; a clicking and a thud, an electronic whine followed by several sharp taps. An antiseptic smell drifted to her nose. Her body stilled, and she sucked in more precious air. She felt him grab her by the wrist and drag her back to the pallet of blankets on the floor in one corner of the shed. His hands were cold. His hands were always cold. And something about their shape felt odd, but they always seemed to be just out of her range of vision, and she couldn't say what it was.

That icy touch prickled against her skin as he inspected her body, top to bottom on the back, then rolled her over to check the front. He pressed something cool and metallic against her bleeding lip, and she felt the familiar sharp sting that preceded a lessening of pain and staunching of blood. She felt the same sting in other places as his hands moved down the front of her body, repairing the damage he'd just finished perpetrating. Tears leaked out the corners of her eyes. Again. He rolled her back onto her side, and she felt the burning sensation at the back of her neck that always brought oblivion—or at least dull torpor—until next time.

There was always a next time.

Chapter

21

HANNA LURCHED UPRIGHT, GASPING AND clutching Mr. Bickles to her chest. The clock on her bedside table said it was almost ten o'clock. That meant she'd slept a solid seven hours before the nightmare woke her up, even though it had taken her so long to fall asleep.

She heard a thump in the kitchen, followed by a loud clatter and a low curse. Tiffany. Rachel's voice murmured in indistinct, conciliatory tones. Hanna smiled. When she came in last night after Jon walked her home, she'd found Tiffany camped out on her couch and Rachel asleep in her guest room. She wasn't sure if they'd slept over to help ward off nightmares or because they didn't want to have to wait an extra minute to hear all the details of the dinner party, but either way, she was glad they'd stayed. It helped.

Hanna went to her closet and lifted her robe off the hook on the back of the door, exposing the formal gown from last night, which hung on a hanger from the same hook. It made her think of the warmth of Jon's hands on her skin through the fabric of the dress while they danced. Of the way his fingers had tangled with hers in the water basin.

How could Jon's gentle hands be so different from *his* icy webbed fingers? At least, she thought *his* hands had finger webbing. She had only felt them, not seen them, and at the time no one had ever heard of

Talessanins or of any of the other sapient races that inhabited the intergalactic empire. It wasn't until later, when the embassy ships came, that she realized what, exactly, was odd about the man's hands—and why he had such advanced technology. And it had taken some time after that to really convince herself that the Talessanins weren't all like *him*. But it was as unfair to fear all Talessanins based on one man's actions as it would be to fear all humans on the same basis. She hadn't met another Talessanin in person until Jon and his friends, but in the media reports they all seemed peaceable enough. And it wasn't as if they'd charged in and taken control of everything—with the exception of a few carefully implemented improvements in medical care and agricultural technology, not much had changed on Earth since humanity found out it had neighbors.

And then there was Jon. Hanna reached her own hand out to skim her fingers over the gown. As the fabric stirred, Hanna caught a faint whiff of Jon's spicy scent. She pressed the material to her nose and inhaled deeply, letting the fragrance seep into her where it could help displace the remnants of the nightmare. She thought of the look on his face after she kissed him. That had been rather impulsive . . . but it had worked out well. What might have happened next? Maybe it was a good thing Chance had come to prod Jon back to his duties as host.

She'd danced with Jon one more time last night, but there had been no more private moments between them. Even when Jon walked her home, Chance walked a few steps behind as Jon's socially necessary bodyguard, while Kamm and Narista pretended to be engaged in lengthy farewells with Salenia on Jon's front porch, so Jon had only kissed Hanna's palm and given her another of those bottomless gazes that twisted her stomach up in knots.

Hanna wrapped her robe tightly around her body and walked down the hall to the kitchen. Rachel and Tiffany were sitting at the table, heads bent over one of Hanna's cookbooks. They looked up as Hanna entered the room.

"Oh no!" Tiffany exclaimed. "I knew I woke you up. It was bad enough when I dropped the cookbook, but I almost went through the roof myself when it hit that crock by the stove and all your cooking utensils went flying. I'm sorry, Hanna."

Rachel looked disappointed too. "We were trying to find your recipe for sticky buns," she explained. "We wanted to have them ready when you woke up."

Hanna laughed. "You won't find it in there. It's on a card in the recipe file."

"But we already looked there!" Tiffany wailed.

"It's under C for Caramel Pecan Rolls, not S for Sticky Buns," Hanna told her. "They take a couple of hours, though, because the dough has to rise."

Tiffany looked crestfallen, but Rachel said, "That's okay, we'll just call them lunch instead of breakfast. It's going to take at least that long for us to interrogate you about last night, and it looks like it might rain, so you're not going to get any painting done today anyway."

Rachel was right. There was no point in driving out to any of her recently marked scenic locations to paint, as she'd intended, if it was just going to rain. And after all the help her friends had given her in preparing for the party, it was only fair that they should hear all about it.

It took three ham and cheese omelets in addition to the entire batch of sweet rolls for Hanna to recount the details of her evening to the satisfaction of her friends—even though she skipped from Tala's tea party straight to the kiss, glossing over the conversation in between. And then, of course, there followed an in-depth analysis of those details. It was late afternoon by the time Rachel and Tiffany packed up their overnight bags and went home.

And it wasn't until she finished cleaning up and went to take a bag of trash out to the bin that Hanna found the note. It was pinned to her back door with a long knife. Or a short dagger. Stuck to the envelope, skewered through by the blade, hung the cold, stiff corpse of a little brown mouse.

Chapter
22

F OR A WHILE, HANNA JUST stared, stunned. At the mouse. At
the dagger. At the note in its thick, white envelope. What kind of
person did this sort of thing? What if *he* was still out there? She
took a cautious step outside, searching in the gray light, but saw no trace
of anyone.

She couldn't help thinking of the nights she'd imagined seeing *him*
outside in the trees. Of course, she'd had that hallucination many times
after waking from the nightmares, and he was never actually there. But
what if he was this time? Should she call the police?

That was probably a bad idea. She'd called them a couple of times
shortly after buying this house when she thought she saw someone in
the trees. The officers hadn't been very sympathetic when it turned out
to be nothing. She was probably in their crazy person file. This was not
nothing, though; someone had stuck a dead animal to her door with a
knife. Then again, if she *was* in their crazy person file, they might think
she'd put it there herself.

But it was most likely just some punk teenagers playing a practical
joke. Or for all she knew, the note was from Jon, and the traditional way
for a Talessanin to deliver a love note was to stick it on the beloved's
back door with a dagger.

That seemed unlikely. But who, then? And why?

She decided it would be best to at least see what the note said before she did anything drastic. And she couldn't just leave that dead mouse hanging there, it was disgusting.

She took a picture with her phone first, in case she needed to show the police. Then she fished a couple of paper grocery bags and a pair of yellow cleaning gloves from the cupboard under the kitchen sink and pried the knife out of the door. A little putty and paint would take care of the damage to the wood. She picked the envelope off the end of the knife and scraped the dead mouse into a grocery bag. Then she wrapped the knife in another paper bag and tucked it into a back corner of the cupboard under the sink in case the police wanted to see it.

Cautiously, still wearing the cleaning gloves, she extracted the note from the envelope and was relieved to see that the thick paper of the envelope had prevented anything nasty from leaking through to the note. She tossed the envelope into the bag with the mouse, wrapped them up, and put them outside in her trash bin. If the police wanted to see those, they'd just have to fish them out.

The few lines of handwriting on the inside of the folded paper were completely unintelligible, but after looking at it for a few minutes Hanna thought she recognized some shapes that looked a little like the letters on the Talessanin side of the printed party invitation. Could this be something like a cursive form of written Talessanin? Jon would be able to tell her if it was. She tucked the note in the pocket of her cargo shorts.

The darkening clouds had been indulging in fitful bouts of drizzle all day, and there were puddles on the road. Hanna didn't want to ruin any of her good shoes, so she just stuck her feet in some old flip-flops and hurried across the street before she lost her nerve.

"Hi, Tomin," Hanna said when he answered the door. "Could I talk to Jon for a few minutes?"

Tomin's freckled face looked grim. "You can, but I wouldn't recommend it. Jon has an old battle wound that bothers him when it rains, and he's been in a temper all day, when he hasn't just been sulking."

Chance spoke from somewhere behind Tomin. "You're going to tell Jon that Hanna came to see him, and you told her to go away?" He chuckled sardonically. "You're a braver man than I am."

Tomin scowled. "You make a good point." He eyed Hanna. "Maybe you'd better come in after all. Jon's out back soaking his aches in the hot tub."

Hanna followed the two men to the back of the house, where the three of them peered out the French doors. Jon lounged in the roofed end of the hot tub with his back to the door. His hair, unbound again from the numerous braids of last night, clung loose and wet down the back of his neck and over his hunched shoulders, which was all Hanna could see of him.

"Don't say I didn't warn you," Tomin whispered as Hanna reached for the door handle.

Jon's shoulders stiffened as he heard the door open. "Out!" he barked. "In the name of all the Gentle Gardeners, why can you not just let me be?"

Hanna froze halfway through the door. She'd never heard Jon raise his voice before. He sounded fierce. Wild.

When Jon didn't hear the door close, he bellowed, "I said go!"

"I'm sorry," Hanna said quickly. "I didn't mean to disturb you." She turned to leave.

Behind her, she heard a splash and a surge from the water, and Jon called out, "Hanna! Wait!" His voice had lost its savage edge and now sounded a little forlorn. "Please wait. I am sorry."

Hanna turned around again. Jon stood in the thigh-deep water now, facing her. Dressed only in some kind of breechcloth, hair loose, water streaming off his muscled body, the big man looked primitive. Frightening. Every bit as dangerous as Mrs. Milgram had hinted at. And Hanna could see the lines of his Talessanin fins folded along the outsides of his forearms. She caught her breath, her heart suddenly pounding. He'd always worn long sleeves before, and it had been easy not to think about how alien he really was.

She drew a slightly shaky breath. "It's all right, I can see it's a bad time. I just wanted to ask you something, but I'm sure Tomin can help me."

She turned back into the house, but again his voice caught at her. "Please stay, Hanna. Please. I am sorry." This time his tone was soft and beseeching, and when she looked back, he said, "I thought you were

Tomin. He has been nagging me about one thing or another all day. I am very glad it was you instead."

"You're sure I won't be bothering you?"

"I am always happy to see you, Hanna. Please do not go." His voice held the same note of longing as it had the night before in the treehouse when he asked her to say yes.

Hanna's heart skipped a beat, and her cheeks warmed with the memory of kissing him. She released her tight breath and stepped out onto the flagstones, pulling the door shut behind her. "Tomin said you were soaking an old battle wound."

Jon's smile held relief. He shrugged. "One or two of them ache sometimes when the weather changes. The hot water feels good. But if you wait a moment, I will get dressed, and we can do something else."

"Oh," Hanna said hesitantly, "no, I just wanted to ask you about something. We can talk while you soak." She waved a hand at him and, after a moment's indecision, he sank back down to his seat in the water. "Maybe I'll sit by you and warm up my feet, if that's okay," Hanna added.

"Please do." She could hear the smile in Jon's voice, even though she could no longer see his face. "I would enjoy the company of your little mouse feet very much." He patted a spot on the smoothed natural stone edge of the pool with his webbed hand.

Hanna kicked off her flip-flops and sat in the place he'd indicated, swinging her rain-chilled bare feet over the edge. The water felt very hot against her cold skin, and she took her time lowering her feet into the pool.

Jon watched curiously for a moment, then slowly reached over and caught one of her feet in his big hand, glancing up at her face to make sure it was all right before tugging it over to where he could study it more closely. He chuckled, and running a careful finger along the line of her toenails, he asked, "Lemon slices?"

Hanna grinned. "Tiffany painted them for me this afternoon," she said. "I wondered if you'd notice."

Jon's hand continued to trace the lines of her foot and ankle until he ran a finger softly up the arch of her foot; she jumped reflexively and yelped, "Stop!"

Jon released her foot immediately. "I am very sorry Hanna." His voice was a misery of self-reproach. "I did not mean to hurt you."

For half a heartbeat, Hanna was confused. Then she laughed. "You didn't hurt me, Jon, it just tickled."

Relief washed over his face, followed by something close to fascinated curiosity. "Did it truly?" he asked. He eyed her speculatively up and down. "I wonder what else would tickle."

Hanna laughed again and scooted a little away from him along the edge of the pool.

Jon shook his head regretfully and said, "You are probably right. It is a line of inquiry best left for another day." He settled back into the water, watching her feet as she swished them around. "I find it curious sometimes," he said, "how many similarities there are between Talessanins and humans. And yet how many differences."

Hanna straightened one leg until her toes poked up out of the water and looked at them analytically. "Are my feet so very different from yours?" She asked. "Apart from the lemons, I mean."

Jon shrugged, "Yes," he said, "and no." He levered himself up onto the ledge beside her and stretched one long leg out next to hers until his foot also rose out of the water.

Hanna saw what he meant. For the most part, the structure of their feet was the same, but his toes were slightly longer and webbed. The ball of his foot was a little wider in relation to the rest of his foot than hers. But the biggest difference was the fin that ran up the outside edge of his leg from ankle to knee. As she studied it, he flexed a muscle in his leg, and the fin slowly unfolded like a Japanese fan. Three long, slender spines of bone curved out from his ankle; a sturdy web of skin stretched between them, and connected to a fourth, shorter spine that unfolded from his knee. After a moment, Hanna let her leg drop back into the water and turned a little to gaze quietly out into the night.

Jon released the fin to fold against his leg and slid back into the water. "Forgive me, Hanna," he said, sounding more subdued. "I have been told that most humans find our fins unsettling. I am sorry if I have upset you."

Hanna turned an annoyed scowl on him. "Stop apologizing for everything. I'm not upset, I was just thinking . . ." she stopped. "Wait. Is that why you always wear long sleeves and bow instead of shaking hands with people or using the regular Talessanin greetings? So you don't upset the humans with your fins?"

Jon shrugged. "It is the protocol we are taught for interacting with humans, yes. Especially outside the embassy enclave."

"Hmm . . ." Hanna mused.

They were both quiet for a time. Then Jon asked, almost shyly, "What is it like to not have fins?"

The question startled Hanna. "Um . . . I don't know," she said; then took a moment to think about the question before asking, "What is it like to not have horns?"

"Horns?" Jon asked, surprised. Then he grinned. "I suppose I have never given much consideration to my lack of horns."

Hanna grinned back, "That's what it's like for me to not have fins." After a moment she added, "But I've recently developed an interest in other people's fins. Yours especially. Are the ones on your arms built the same as the ones on your legs?" She frowned. "Is it rude to ask things like that?"

Jon lifted an arm out of the water, extended his forearm fin, and presented it to Hanna for her inspection. "You may ask me whatever you like, Hanna."

Hesitantly, Hanna grasped his wrist, drawing his arm gently out until it lay palm down across her knees as she sat on the edge of the pool, so she could study it more closely. The webbing of the fin stretched between three slender wrist spines and a folding nub at his elbow, much like his leg fins. She traced the bones of his arm and fin with her finger and carefully touched the webbing. Then she turned his arm over so she could look at the other side. The skin was slightly paler on this side and showed a subtle mottled patterning. About halfway to his elbow, a thin, purple line snaked across the underside of his forearm and up onto his fin. Where it crossed one of the spines, the bone seemed slightly bent.

"Why is this one crooked?" she asked, touching the bent place delicately with one finger.

"Ah." Jon said. "I broke it, and it was set incorrectly when it began to heal. The doctors tell me they can fix it, but they would have to break it again. A broken fin spine is very painful, and the misalignment does not bother me, so I tell them to let it be."

"And this," Hanna traced the thin purple line with her finger. "Is this a scar? I thought Talessanin doctors could heal wounds without leaving scars."

Jon shrugged. "They can, if they are able to treat the wound soon enough, and it does not require much complicated reconstruction. In a planned surgery, the tissue can be prepared in advance, and it leaves no mark at all. It is more difficult if the wound has already begun to heal, or if some of the tissue is missing or severely traumatized. This wound had mostly healed closed by the time the doctors were able to treat it, but it had not been tended to properly. They were able to repair the damage to the tendons and muscles well enough and healed most of the damage to the skin too, but it did leave a scar."

Hanna frowned. "Is this another scar?" She traced a barely perceptible white line across the inside of his elbow and up his bicep. Just before it reached his shoulder, it branched several times, sending pale threads out to twine around to his back and across the skin of his chest. Hanna scooted closer to Jon so she could trace one of the branches up onto his shoulder and along his collarbone. His fin retracted as his arm curved around her knees, tucking them close to his warm side as she bent over his shoulder.

Jon watched her from the corner of his eye with a musing expression. "Yes, that is a scar too," he said. "I have several."

Hanna's fingers found a small, slightly puckered spot on Jon's chest close to the line she'd been tracing, then another just like it a couple of inches away, and a third and fourth in a neat arc. "These look like tooth marks," she joked, "did something try to eat you?"

"They look even more like tooth marks if you line them up with the ones on my back," Jon said, and Hanna leaned back to find a matching arc of faint, puckered scars curving across the back of his shoulder almost directly behind the ones on the front. As she traced the line of them, Jon said, "I do not think there is a word for the creature in English yet. It is a bit like a thing I saw in an Earth zoo called a sloth, only much larger, and venomous. I do not think it would have scarred if there had been no venom." He shrugged, and his muscles rippled beneath his skin under Hanna's fingers.

"You're serious," she said.

"I would not lie to you, Hanna."

Hanna's fingers drifted toward the middle of Jon's back, following another thread-thin purple line, then veering off onto an intersecting band of paler skin. When she spoke again her voice was solemn. "You have more than several scars, Jon."

Jon was quiet for a minute before he said softly, "Difficult jobs often leave marks. And when a difficult job needs to be done, the emperor sends his best men to do it."

Hanna's fingers found another line to trace. "The Nine Winds?" she asked, then bit her lip, remembering his reluctance to talk about that at dinner the night before. But Jon just nodded.

Another fin ran down the center of Jon's back, and Hanna stopped tracing scar lines in order to inspect the fin more closely. The spines in the fins on Jon's arms and legs ended under the skin, but on his back, the fin spines ended in small, hard knobs. With the fin folded, the knobs ran down Jon's spine like a row of dark beads. Hanna reached out a finger and gently touched one of them. Smooth. Like a round fingernail. She ran her hand down as much of the row as she could reach, and Jon shifted a little in his seat.

"Does this one unfold too?" Hanna asked.

Instead of answering, Jon bent forward so his back no longer pressed against the wall of the pool and slowly raised the spines, making the fin stand up down the length of his back to his waist. The skin over the spines was dark, like the little knobs on their ends, but the webbing in between was lighter, with the same faintly mottled patterning Hanna had seen on his arm. The spines were longest in the middle of his back, about the length of Hanna's fingers, and tapered in length at both ends of the row. At the base of his neck and at his waist there were barely any spines at all.

Hanna ran her finger slowly down the top edge of the fin again, this time leaning her arm into the water to go all the way to the end at Jon's waist. Jon shivered. Hanna giggled.

Jon shifted quickly upright, folding the fin tight against his back again and leaning against the wall of the pool. "You are laughing." He sounded hurt. "You find my body comical?"

Hanna leaned down to whisper into his ear, "I find your body beautiful, Jon." She sat up straight again, and said, "But . . . different, like you said. I laughed because I thought . . ." She stopped, uncertain whether to say what she'd been thinking. "Please don't be angry, Jon. Sometimes these thoughts just come into my head."

He only looked at her, the hurt still showing in his eyes, so she continued. "I was thinking that these . . ." she touched one of the larger knobs not hidden by the wall, "were about the same size and shape as some wild strawberries I ate once. And then I couldn't help but wonder, if I sneaked into your bedroom at night when you were sleeping and painted all of them to look like little strawberries, how long would it take you to notice?"

Jon stared at Hanna, his face sliding into an expression she couldn't read. Indignation? Horror? "Strawberries," he said. His voice sounded a little choked. "Like the ones you made slushies with?"

Hanna looked down. "Sort of," she said softly. "The wild ones are a lot smaller. And really sweet."

Jon stood up in the water and waded a few steps farther into the pool to stare out into the rainy evening, hands on hips.

Hanna didn't know what to do. She'd made him angry. Of course she'd made him angry. *Strawberries?* What had she been thinking? She could almost hear her mother's voice reminding her that not every thought should be spoken out loud. She felt a hard, miserable lump form in her stomach. "I'm sorry, Jon," she said quietly. "I didn't mean . . . I think I'd better go."

But as she stood, Jon whirled and lunged toward her, catching one of her hands in his. "No! Stay. It is only . . ." he gestured helplessly with his other hand. "Strawberries," he said again in that slightly strangled voice. Then he started laughing, a low rumbling sound at first, breaking free into a great guffaw that echoed under the roof of the veranda. After a moment he caught his breath. "Weeks," he said, grinning. "It would be weeks before I noticed. Tomin and Chance would just laugh at me and not say a word. I find myself suddenly very happy that I am protected by Chance's excellent security system."

"You're not angry?" Hanna asked.

Jon raised her hand to his lips and kissed her palm, folding her fingers closed as if to keep the kiss from escaping. "I am not angry, Hanna. I am glad you are here to make me laugh at myself. I have had a very trying day, and I needed this. Thank you. You will stay?" Seeing Hanna hesitate, he said firmly, "You will stay. I will stop apologizing for everything, you will stop trying to run away, and we will talk about the question you came to ask me."

Chapter
23

STILL HOLDING HANNA'S HAND, JON knelt on the ledge he'd been sitting on in the hot tub. "Ask me your question, Hanna," he said, and some mischief in his deep voice made Hanna's cheeks warm, though she wasn't sure exactly why. Then, looking at him kneeling below her as she stood on the edge of the pool, she felt abruptly foolish like an awkward Juliet on a soggy balcony, and she pulled her hand away, stepping back.

She wiped her damp fingers on her cargo shorts and pulled out the note. "Someone left this for me," she said. I think the writing might be Talessanin, and I wondered if you could tell me what it says."

Jon's face grew serious. "May I see it?" He held out a hand.

Hanna shifted toward him, then hesitated. "Your hands are wet. I think the paper would tear."

"Ah," he said. "You are probably right. But that is easily remedied. Will you come inside?"

Hanna walked with Jon across the terrace and through the French doors into the family room where Tomin and Chance were setting up a board game on a card table.

"Chance," Jon said as he and Hanna entered, "I am going to my room to dress. I charge you, as my chief security officer, not to allow this woman to leave before I return." Chance looked from Jon to Hanna and back, a puzzled frown on his dark face. Jon grinned at him. "And under no circumstances are you to allow her to bribe you into divulging the codes to disable the security system for the house." Now Chance looked even more confused. But Hanna giggled and gave Jon's arm a playful shove.

After Jon was out of earshot, Tomin leaned toward Hanna. "Well, he's certainly in a better mood," he said. "What did you do?"

"I threatened him with strawberries," Hanna replied. "What are you playing?"

It was a Talessanin game called *jennan*—a lot like Chinese checkers, except its object had something to do with being the one to place the final piece on top of a pyramid built cooperatively in the center of the board by the players. Tomin was still explaining the rules when Jon came back in. Dressed in loose cargo pants and a snug, long-sleeved black shirt, with his damp hair still framing his face, he looked very nearly human. "May I see your note now?" he asked.

Hanna handed him the paper. "Is it Talessanin?"

"Yes," was all he said for a moment. His brow furrowed as he studied it. Then he asked, "Hanna, where did you get this?"

Hanna ignored his question. "What does it say?"

Jon refolded the note, a thoughtful expression on his face as he examined the place where the knife had passed through the layers. His jaw clenched, and his eyes narrowed. "How did this come to you?" he asked again, his voice tight.

"I'll tell you that," Hanna said calmly, "after you tell me what it says."

Jon looked at her, his eyes cold and hard. He opened his mouth to say something, but a series of electronic chimes cut him off.

Chance looked up from the game. "It sounds like Kamm and Tala are back from their shopping trip."

Jon tucked the folded note into one of his pockets and arranged his face into a pleasant expression.

Hanna scowled. "Jon," she said, "I want that back."

"Yes," Jon said. "Later."

Tala burst into the kitchen with Kamm trailing in her wake and another man in a dark uniform following behind with his arms full of bags and boxes. Tala skipped into the family room, her face beaming as she blurted out a rapid stream of Talessanin. Kamm was engaged in giving instructions to the uniformed man but stopped for a moment to say,

"Tala, you are in your uncle's home, and you will abide by his rules. English, please."

Tala stopped mid-skip, looking abashed. "Yes, Baba," she said quietly. "Bahta Jon, I am very sorry. I forgot for a minute."

"That is quite understandable, Tala," Jon said solemnly. "It is easy to forget. But I will learn faster if everyone here speaks English."

Tala frowned at him. "They will not let me use infusion to learn either," she said, a touch of petulance in her voice. "Is your brain still developing too, Bahta Jon?"

"No," Jon said, "but it is accustomed to my *enkalan*, so the synaptic infusion unit does not integrate with it as well as it does for most people, and I must learn some things the more traditional way." He smiled. "Contractions, for example. Isn't and aren't are apparently correct, but if I say amn't everyone laughs at me."

Everyone did.

Jon poked Tala's nose with one long finger. "Now, where are these wonderful shoes about which you are so excited?"

"I will get them," Tala said, dancing from foot to foot. "Baba says I may wear them to a restaurant tonight where I may eat pizza with pepperonis!" She dashed away in pursuit of the uniformed man, who had presumably gone to put her purchases away.

Kamm looked around the room. "You'll all join us for pizza, of course," he said with a grin. "There's a delightful shop in New York that I've been meaning to visit again."

"Kamm," Jon said solemnly, "will Tala be a few minutes?"

Kamm frowned. "Probably, why?"

Jon drew Hanna's note from his pocket and handed it to his brother. "Do you recognize the handwriting?"

Kamm opened the note and read it, his face drawing into a scowl. He refolded the note, turning it to look at the holes and handed it back to Jon, "Where did this come from?"

Jon tucked the note back in his pocket. "Hanna brought it to my attention just now."

Kamm looked grave and said something in Talessanin. Jon nodded once.

In English, Kamm said, "I'm sorry this happened, Hanna. Please be assured that this matter will be addressed. Will you join us this evening for pizza? Perhaps we can make this up to you by visiting the new exhibit at the Metropolitan Museum."

Hanna blinked. She had always wanted to see the art at the Met. But what, exactly, did Kamm think they needed to make up to her *for*? Was anyone going to tell her what that note said?

Jon spoke before Hanna could think how to answer. "I am sure that Tomin and Chance would welcome a trip to New York," he said. "I believe I will remain at home. I have spent all afternoon soaking the aches from my leg, and I have no desire to put them back again traveling by flutter drive tonight. Hanna must do as she likes, of course, but I had hoped she might stay and keep me company."

Kamm's frown deepened, and his eyes flicked between Hanna and Jon. He said something else in rapid Talessanin. Jon didn't respond, only met his brother's gaze steadily. After a moment, Kamm gave a resigned nod.

Tala burst back into the room chirping, "You see, Bahta? They have rainbows and lights!" Tala wore chunky white sneakers with pearlescent rainbows decorating the sides. Each of her bouncing skip-steps caused tiny red lights embedded in the shoes to flash. She stopped abruptly and sat on the floor by her uncle's feet, and he stooped to admire her new shoes. "And look!" Tala continued, "There are no laces because this part," she unfastened one of the Velcro closure tabs, "sticks to this part!" She replaced the fastener. "So I will not even trip on them!"

Jon exclaimed over the rainbows, and lights, and lack of shoelaces enjoying his niece's enthusiasm. After a moment, Tala looked up and seemed to notice Hanna for the first time. The little girl hopped to her feet and clapped her hands. "Miss Bradley!" She exclaimed. "Have you come to bring us cake? Are you coming with us to eat pizza with pepperonis?"

Hanna couldn't help laughing just a little. "I'm very sorry, Tala, I haven't had time yet to make your cake. But I haven't forgotten." Tala's face fell.

"And I think Miss Bradley will stay here with me this evening," Jon interjected.

"Yes," Hanna said. "Your uncle has promised to read something to me tonight. Maybe I can eat pepperonis with you another time."

Tala smiled again. "Bahta Jon is very good at reading stories," she assured Hanna. "You will have a fun time, even if there is no pizza."

It took only a few minutes after that for Kamm to herd everyone out the door to the waiting flutter shuttle, leaving Hanna alone with Jon again.

Chapter 24

JON STOOD LOOKING AT THE closed front door. Maybe he should've gone with them. Maybe Hanna would've gone too. Maybe there could've been one more magical evening in which he was still just her new friend, Jon, and she didn't think he was a monster. Didn't *know* he was a monster. But she deserved to know.

He turned to face her. Hanna stood with her arms folded across her chest. Her face was tight and her body tense. "I didn't give you permission to show that note to Kamm," she said. "What 'matter' are we talking about, and what does he mean that it will 'be addressed'? I want an explanation, Jon. What does that note say?"

He wanted more time. He wanted to reach out to her, to touch her face, to hold her, to feel the tantalizing softness of her body pressed against his, to kiss her one more time—could she even know what a gift that had been? But she was angry with him now. And would be worse than angry later. And there was no more time.

He waved vaguely at the couch and said, "You are right, Hanna. I am sorry. Please sit, and I will show you what it says."

Hanna relaxed at his capitulation but still eyed him a little warily as she perched stiffly on the near end of the couch. Jon wanted to sit by her, to put his arms around her and draw her close, to tell her it did not matter. But, of course, it *did* matter. It would matter a great deal to Hanna.

And it was not right for him to sit beside her on the couch and pretend it did not. He lowered himself to the floor next to her feet instead, so she sat above him looking over his shoulder as she had at the soaking pool. He would seem less threatening this way. He took out the note, carefully unfolded it, and held it up with one hand where she could see.

"First," he said, "you should know that the handwriting is recognizably that of my sister, Narista."

"It's from Narista?" Hanna didn't sound entirely surprised. *What did she know?*

"Yes," Jon said gravely. "And before I read it, you should also know that this is almost certainly nothing more serious than a harmless prank intended to frighten you."

"I see," Hanna said, even though she could not possibly.

"This is what it says." Jon pointed to each line as he read it aloud.

> *"The Mouse may play*
> *In the Viper's den,*
> *But she is a mouse still,*
> *And he is a viper still,*
> *And Death may come to dinner."*

"Except," Jon added, "in Talessanin the grammatical constructions are slightly different, and it rhymes." He paused only a moment before asking, "Will you tell me, now, how this message came to you?"

Hanna held out her hand for the paper, and she relaxed a little more when he gave it back to her. Then she pulled her phone out of her pocket and thumbed some icons on the screen before handing it to him. "I found it stuck to my back door with a big knife," she said. "And a dead mouse."

Jon stared at the photograph. What had Narista been thinking? He nodded once and handed the phone back.

"Hanna . . ." he began, but couldn't think what to say. He had expected the knife from the shape of the holes in the folded page. But a dead mouse? That was extreme, even for Narista.

"Mrs. Milgram told me before dinner that Narista was angry," Hanna said musingly. "She said it was because you introduced me as Narista's equal."

This was not the line of questioning Jon had anticipated. "There *was* a slight irregularity in the introductions," he said, grateful for the detour, "but your Mrs. Milgram was not entirely correct as to its nature."

He paused, deciding how best to explain. "The way I greeted you surprised my family. I do not have many good friends—especially not female friends. My work has not been easily compatible with such relationships. And I have not known you very long." He shrugged. "But as my good friend, you were entitled to be introduced as an equal to all who are my own social equals, at least for the duration of my party.

"So," Hanna said, still sounding confused, "Narista was upset that I claimed to be your good friend?"

Jon frowned. "More surprised than upset, I think."

"Maybe Tomin should've taught me a different greeting," Hanna murmured.

"No." Jon met her gaze. The hot anger was gone from her eyes, replaced by curious interest. "He taught you the right ones. You *are* my good friend, and I was most pleased when you greeted me that way. The greeting between equals was proper for my family and would make you seem gracious if used with those below my status. As none of the guests held higher social standing, there was no need for you to know how to greet a social superior. Tomin taught enough for you to make a very good impression."

He cleared his throat and looked down at his hands. "But perhaps he should have taught you some of the variations."

Hanna frowned. "There are variations?"

Jon turned a little and smiled up at her, warming to this topic. "Yes. A good friend might greet me as Tomin taught you, which you did very nicely. A very close friend who has known me a long time and spent time with my family might kiss my cheek as part of the greeting."

"I saw that," Hanna said, "when you and Kamm greeted Narista and Selenia."

"Ah." Jon said. "Yes, it is the same for a sister and for a close friend of that sort."

He half turned away from her again, watching her face from the corner of his eye as he spoke. "A woman who has a romantic claim on me might kiss me on the mouth instead. And we might . . . lean into the greeting rather more as well."

Hanna frowned. "Like Selenia did," she said.

Jon turned toward her and met her eyes. "Selenia attempted it." He shrugged." She missed."

"Not intentionally," Hanna said, her scowl deepening. "You dodged. Does she have a romantic claim on you that I should know about?"

Jon grinned at her. *Could she be jealous?* His heart skipped joyfully— and then seized up at the thought of where this conversation would end, and his grin went a little sour. "Not even a small one. My honor, Hanna," he said quietly. He searched her face, willing her to believe him. "We grew up together, and Salenia enjoys provoking me. That is all."

"I see," Hanna said, still looking a bit skeptical. "Go on."

John felt his face warm as he looked away from her. "When I saw you standing in the doorway I very much wanted to kiss you," he said softly. "I could not, of course, having never received permission, but you could have kissed me." Such an impertinent thing to say—but if he didn't tell her now, he'd certainly never have another chance.

Hanna laughed nervously. "I don't think I was ready for that at the time." She paused thoughtfully. "But what's the difference?"

Jon shrugged. "It is not honorable for a man to kiss a woman without her permission," he explained, "but a woman may kiss whomever she wishes."

Hanna looked at him quizzically for a moment. "Unless he dodges." She grinned.

Jon mimed pious solemnity. "It is not dishonorable for a man to dodge."

Hanna burst into giggles. "Well," she said, "I will certainly not stop you from dodging Salenia as much as you want. But I'll be very angry if you dodge me." She pouted prettily.

"I would never do that, Hanna." Jon's solemnity was no longer artificial, but he was not sure Hanna noticed the difference. It didn't really matter; after she finished discussing the sender of the note and moved on to its content, she would not wish to kiss him again. Ever.

Hanna sighed. "I still don't understand," she said. "What did I do wrong in the introductions that made Narista hate me?"

"You did nothing wrong. The irregularity was on my part, not yours." Jon shrugged. "It was in my positioning and the order of introduction. When there is a difference in status, the person performing the introduction places himself sideways, facing the space between the two who are meeting, but turned slightly toward the person of higher rank. This tells each person how to greet the other so there is no confusion. By standing to your side and slightly behind you during the introductions, I demonstrated that I considered you the social equal of those I was addressing. Do you understand this?"

Hanna nodded uncertainly, and Jon continued. "When I introduced you to Kamm, I acknowledged his place as Ehrat of our House by speaking first to him, telling him who you were, then telling you who he was. This indicated that I recognized him as the higher of two equals."

"Wait," Hanna said, "how can one be higher if the two are equals?"

"It is difficult to explain," Jon said. "But to a Talessanin it is an important token of respect."

"Okay . . ." Hanna said, still frowning.

"With Narista," Jon continued, "I spoke to you first, and told you who she was, then told her who you were. Do you see?"

Hanna stared at him. "You made me the higher of two equals, not Narista."

"Yes. And I placed my hand . . ." he trailed off. *What had he been thinking?*

"On my back," Hanna finished for him. *She had noticed.* "Why?"

Jon looked down at his knees. "I was being unforgivably presumptuous. It is the sort of thing a man might do if he has a romantic attachment to a woman, and it implied a kind of relationship between us that did not exist. I was annoyed at Narista for throwing Salenia at me again." He shrugged. "And also I very much liked the idea of such a relationship with you. I told myself it was more of an exaggeration than a deceit, and I harbored a fancy that if I played my pieces well it might become true by the end of the evening. It seemed a small thing at the time, but it was a liberty I should not have taken, and I am very sorry to have put you in that position, especially without your knowledge."

Silence settled between them for several long moments. Then Hanna said, her voice almost a whisper, "And was it true, Jon? At the end of the evening?"

Jon hesitated. "I am not sure," he said at last. "Human customs are so different. I was not always certain what your actions meant in that regard. But I had hope that it was, or at least could become, true."

Hanna's hand caressed his shoulder. "Jon . . ." she whispered.

The soft intensity in her voice tore at Jon's heart, but he didn't want her to say something she would undoubtedly regret in a few minutes, so he cut her off without looking at her. "That is why Narista was angry. She explained it to me very loudly early this morning before she left. My sister wishes me to marry a woman from one of the other Great Houses. Salenia is Ahnat of House Trakanaleth, which is a very wealthy and prominent house. If I married her, I would inherit with her and become the male Head of House when she became the female Head of House, which would expand the power of our own House as well.

"Narista at first believed that by placing you first in the introductions, I meant merely to annoy Salenia. However, by the end of the evening she was convinced that my romantic intentions toward you were sincere. Narista does not like the idea of a member of her family becoming romantically involved with a human."

Hanna's hand stilled on his shoulder, and Jon didn't dare look at her as he went on. "Humans are the first species we have encountered that is genetically compatible with Talessanins, and this has raised some new moral and social questions among our people. When humans are accepted as full citizens, they will become equal under the law with citizens of other sapient species that our empire has integrated. But the idea of accepting them as a new variety of Talessanin, so to speak, by intermingling with them, is . . . controversial. And Narista feels that a relationship with you would negatively impact my chances of marrying well."

Jon risked a look over his shoulder at Hanna's face but could not read her expression, so he turned away again before continuing. "Narista also felt that some of my behavior toward you was rather more assertive than is considered entirely proper for a man in Talessanin society, and the fact that I would behave that way toward a human was particularly offensive to her. But Tomin has given me to understand that in human society a man is expected to be somewhat more forward in pursuing a romantic interest. I wished to make my intentions clear to you, and I may have bent some traditional boundaries of Talessanin society in attempting to do so."

"And that's why Narista's angry?" Hanna asked.

"More or less," Jon said, shrugging sheepishly. "She will recover. I have always been somewhat unconventional in my choice of friends.

Tomin and Chance are the best sort of friends a man could ask for, but they are not high born and enjoy tormenting me by pretending they are my household staff. I asked them to come to the dinner party as guests, but Tomin insisted on playing steward so he could order everybody about, and Chance takes delight in skulking in the shadows and watching the security feeds. In truth, I rather prefer doing that myself, but it is my house, so I was required to play the part of host." He shrugged again and grinned at Hanna. "My family is accustomed to seeing me navigate by my own stars. When they know you better, they will like you as much as I do." *Would she allow that to happen?*

Hanna's fingers moved along Jon's shoulder as they had when she was tracing his scars, warm and delicate through the fabric of his shirt. When she spoke again, her voice was playful. "What boundaries did you bend, Jon? Besides exaggerating our relationship in your introduction, I mean." There was a smile in her voice, and he turned so he could see it on her face.

"Well," he began, "I asked you not to walk out with someone else to dinner. That was not quite proper. A woman might extract such a promise from a man, but for a man to ask it of a woman is rather brash."

Hanna's laugh reached all the way to her chocolate eyes. "I was glad you did," she said. "I would've had no idea what to do with myself otherwise." Her fingers brushed his still-damp hair away from the side of his neck and swept lightly across his skin.

Jon's smile was a little shy as he continued, "Also, it would have been more customary for me to dance the second dance with my sister. Dancing the second with you was somewhat forward. But it was an *aylencanat,* and you had just told me that was the only dance you knew. The third dance would have been more appropriate, but it certainly would not have been another *aylencanat,* and I feared that if I waited too long you might think I did not wish to dance with you."

Hanna laughed again, her fingers twisting and untwisting in the hair at the nape of Jon's neck, sending pleasant little shivers down his spine. She would never want to touch him that way again after tonight. He turned his face away from her and closed his eyes, savoring the sensation while he still could. "I also called you by a . . ." He hesitated. Shot a glance at her from the corner of his eye. "Perhaps it is a fault in my language acquisition."

Her fingers stilled. "What is?"

He frowned. The English term he knew for it was *pet name*. But Hanna was *not* a pet. "An informal name one gives someone for whom he feels a degree of . . . affection."

"Um . . . like . . . a nickname?" Hanna suggested.

"Nickname." He tested the word. It did not feel quite right. Not intimate enough. But he shrugged and continued. "I am not certain if Narista heard me do it, or if someone else heard and told her, and really it is no concern of hers, but in my culture . . . I should have waited. Particularly in public. I am sorry, Hanna."

She laughed. "Do you mean when you called me Little Mouse?"

Jon nodded.

Perhaps it was that movement of his head that nudged her fingers farther down his neck to start toying with the first *enan* at the top of his dorsal fin. She probably did not realize how close to the surface the nerves were at the tips of fin spines. Her soft touch sent a rippling sensation through his body that stopped his breath for a moment.

He caught Hanna's hand in his and pressed a kiss to her palm. *The last one?* "Please do not do that," he murmured without looking at her.

"I'm so sorry, Jon." She sounded very contrite. "I didn't mean to . . . to . . . did it hurt? Or was I just annoying you?" She gave a sad little sigh. "There's so much about you I don't know."

She was right.

Jon stroked the palm of her hand with his thumb. "It did not hurt, Hanna, and it was not annoying. It was very pleasant. But I think I found it a little more enjoyable than is good for me just now."

"I . . . oh." Hanna sounded a little lost. She was quiet for a moment, and her voice was contemplative when she spoke again. "But you called me that before," she said. "When you carried me down from the treehouse, you said, 'You are safe Little Mouse.'"

Jon ducked his head. "Yes. That was very improper. I did not think you heard me. A Talessanin woman would have slapped me soundly for being so familiar."

"I thought you were very kind." Hanna murmured. "Well, that definitely explains the dead mouse on my door. And the mouse in the note. What does she mean by the viper, though? Does she mean to warn me against associating with Talessanins in general, or does she mean you specifically? I mean . . . that *is* a pretty impressive snake on the back of your dress uniform."

And there it was—the question he had been dreading since he first read Narista's note. Jon's blood turned to ice. But Hanna deserved answers. She deserved to know what he was. He released her hand. "She means me," he said, his voice tight. "The viper is the totem chosen for me by my brothers of the Nine Winds when I became their Commander."

Hanna looked puzzled. "Isn't the viper an Earth animal, though?"

"The totem is chosen from among the creatures of the world on which the Nine are serving when the Commander is raised," Jon explained. "My brothers said at the time that they chose the viper because it waits quietly in the shadows, strikes without warning, and kills without mercy. My raising was somewhat unexpected, you see. I was the youngest of the Nine at the time, and the newest. I was not the leader they would have chosen."

"Then . . ." Hanna hesitated. "How does someone become the Commander?"

Jon stared out the doors to the terrace, where the damp twilight was giving way to darkness. He cleared his throat. "Usually the Commander is selected by his fellows after his predecessor dies in battle." Jon kept his voice carefully flat. "Sometimes he becomes Commander by killing the previous Commander himself in single combat before the Throne. In my case, the Emperor intervened before I struck the deathblow because the former Commander had been his friend since they were children. So I did not kill him, I only defeated him."

Hanna made a small noise in her throat, but Jon couldn't tell what it meant. Probably not something good. But she should know what he really was. He sighed. "In truth, I did more than defeat him. I thoroughly humiliated him. I . . . toyed with him. I taunted him. I wanted even his memory to be vanquished. But I took too long, and the Emperor intervened. I sometimes still think I should have killed him anyway."

Hanna was silent.

"The current Commander, of course," Jon continued, with a touch of grim humor in his tone, "was chosen by our brothers upon the somewhat unexpected retirement of the Viper in the Night."

"Wait!" Hanna exclaimed. "Narista said that last night. She asked for a tale of the Viper in the Night. Are you telling me she meant *you*?"

Jon sighed. "I do not even know anymore. The stories are so different depending on who is telling them. And most of them are no more than firelight tales. Within the empire, the Viper in the Night has become something of a folk hero who swoops in to rescue the innocent and punish the guilty. He is the silent hand of the emperor's justice—larger than life, more than a mere man, without fear, without limitations." He shrugged one shoulder. "No man could live up to those stories."

Behind him on the couch, Hanna shifted, and Jon went on before she could speak. "Among those who fear the empire, the Viper in the Night is a demon who stalks the darkness, striking hapless victims whose only crime is being in the wrong place at the wrong time.

"But my sister wanted a heroic tale, and she wanted all the guests to hear it with the Viper sitting among them as a symbol of the power of the Empire Among the Stars, and of House Kanestelan. She enjoys theatrics. But the stories . . . some of them are based on real events, and some of them are entirely fictional. A few come very close to truth. But only those of us who were there really know, and we do not often speak of these things."

"These things," Hanna said slowly. "You mean the 'difficult jobs' that have given you so many scars."

Jon inclined his head. "Yes, Hanna. The Nine Winds are the emperor's personal strike force. The only authority to which they are subject is that of the emperor and empress, personally. They operate outside the regular military structure and almost entirely outside the legal system. When the emperor needs something important done, whether quietly, or theatrically, and it must be done properly, he calls upon the Winds, and the Winds obey—without question, without hesitation, without thought for their own lives. Sometimes it is nothing more than standing around looking dangerous while some diplomat grovels before the Throne—but not often. Sometimes it is a rescue mission, or a particularly delicate piece of espionage or exploration. Sometimes it is leading a straightforward battle against insurgents or aggressors from outside the empire. Sometimes it is an assassination. Sometimes . . . well, there are things we do not talk about." He shook his head. "Whatever the duty is, the emperor commands, and the Winds obey. That is the way it works."

Hanna rose and walked across the room. She stood with her back toward him, arms wrapped around herself, pretending to examine the titles in Tomin's Earth music collection. "And that's why you asked me to allow you an opportunity to explain if anyone told me stories about you. Because sometimes the stories exaggerate or are made up."

"Yes," Jon said. "And because sometimes they are true." A bitter edge came into his voice. "I am not a good person, Hanna. There is a reason parents on some worlds tell their children that they must behave or the Viper may come in the night and kill them in their beds."

Hanna's back tensed. She stopped pretending to look at the music collection and stared down at her feet. "But you wouldn't, Jon." Her voice was soft, subdued. "I've seen you with Tala. You'd *never* hurt a child."

Jon said nothing for a moment. But he had promised her the truth. He spoke it softly, solemnly. "I would, though, Hanna. I have. More than once."

She spun to face him, a look of horrified revulsion twisting her features. A look he could not bear. Not from her. He looked at her feet instead. She had not put her shoes back on when they came into the house. She looked so small and vulnerable standing there, her feet bare except for the painted-on lemons, her legs bare even of fins. A little mouse caught unaware in the heart of the Viper's den.

"But, Jon . . ." Hanna's voice was hoarse, halting.

Jon didn't want to hear what she had to say now, so he spoke before she could find the words she sought. "The first child," he said, making his voice hard and flat, clearing all expression from his face, "the first time I killed a child, it was an accident. It was during my basic service before I was inducted into the Winds. I had recently been promoted to commander of my unit. We received reports of a band of insurgents in the ruins of a village near our position. My unit was one of three sent to kill or capture them. As we entered the ruins in search of our targets, shots were fired at us from behind a wall. I was first to see where they came from and returned fire. When we went to investigate, we found a young boy, no older than Tala is now. They had given him a weapon and were using him as a scout, but he was still only a child."

"Jon—" Hanna began again, but again he interrupted.

"The second child," he said to her feet, "I did not kill. It was after I had been brought into the Winds. A faction of fanatics on one of the outlying planets was causing a great deal of trouble. The Winds were sent to remove the leader of the agitators in the hopes of preventing a local civil war that seemed increasingly inevitable. We were commanded to eliminate the man, his wife, and their infant son. My commander sent me to do the job. A test, I think, because I was new."

Hanna made a small, strangled gasp. Jon still could not look at her, so he pressed on. "I stood in the dark looking down at the baby, thinking that he had done nothing wrong and did not deserve to die. So I took him with me. I gave him to a farmer and his wife on the other side of his world, and they were very happy to have a son. It was just like a firelight tale. But when his body was not found with those of his parents, rumors began to circulate of his survival. People began to come forward claiming to have found the lost heir. Three new factions formed where before there had been only one, and each faction claimed to have the legitimate heir, though not one of them did. The continental government destabilized, and the conflict cascaded, drawing in allies and enemies one after another. The war that followed was far worse than the civil war would have been. It spread to every continent on the planet, and eight million people died, including the farmer's family, because I could not move one infant boy quietly from sleep into death. My commander flogged me nearly to death for insubordination." He laughed bitterly. "Some of my most charming scars come from that. For a long time I wished they had just killed me outright. I wanted very much to die."

"Oh, Jon . . ." Hanna whispered. Then she cleared her throat. "Was that why you wanted to kill him?"

He closed his eyes and scrubbed a hand back through his hair. "Perhaps that was part of it. There were other reasons." He shook his head and went on. "After I became Commander of the Winds, this was not a test I wished to administer. The stakes are just too high. So when that sort of thing was required, I always went myself. My reputation for killing children quietly in their beds is not undeserved. I have done it a number of times, by choice, even though I could have sent someone else. As I said, Hanna, I am not a good person."

Hanna said nothing for a long time, and Jon let the silence settle around them like a cold fog. Then Hanna whispered, "But . . . how, Jon?"

Jon had not expected that and looked sharply up at her. Hanna's face was pale, her brown eyes big and frightened. Disgusted. And angry. Was she going to force him to tell her details? He had promised her the truth.

"As gently as possible." Jon kept his voice quiet, but it had a bitter edge. "Usually an inhaled toxin that brings death quickly and without pain."

"No," Hanna said, her face going a shade paler. "I meant . . . how do you do it? How do you stand there looking down at a sleeping child and just . . . kill it? How do you justify that to yourself in your head?"

"I do not." Jon's voice grew louder. Clipped. "There is no justification for killing a child. I did it because my emperor commanded it, and I am sworn to obey. I did it because the Council determined that the circumstances made it necessary. I did it because I could think of no better alternative. Because I am haunted by eight million people whose deaths I might have prevented. Because I will not send a man to do a task I would not do myself." He realized he was nearly shouting, and he drew a deep breath before continuing in a more measured tone. "Because I do not wish to create another monster like me. I am the Viper in the Night. So I did it. There are reasons. But there is no justification. There is nothing just about killing a sleeping child."

Hanna began to pace in quick, agitated strides, back and forth across the room. She was no longer looking at Jon, so he watched her, waiting. "So . . . what, Jon?" her voice was louder, high pitched, and pinched. "What am I supposed to do with that? I finally meet a man who's kind, and gentle, and funny, and isn't scared off by . . . by my past, and it turns out he's . . . what? An assassin? A serial murderer? The bogeyman in every child's dark closet?" She stopped pacing and turned to face him again. Tears streaked her cheeks now. "What am I supposed to do with that, Jon?" Her voice grew louder, more shrill with every word. She was edging toward a breaking point of some kind. Panic attack? Hysteria? Jon held very still, not wanting to make it worse for her. She turned away from him again, staring out into the night through the panes in the French doors.

Then she turned back to face him and the look in her eyes tore into Jon's soul. "What else do you do, Jon?" she asked plaintively. "Do you torture people?"

He hesitated. The truth. "Yes, I have tortured people," he said softly. "When it was necessary."

Hanna stared at him. Her next question wrenched its way out of her, twisting her mouth and cracking her voice. "Have you raped anyone, Jon?"

And he knew—this was how she saw him now. Not just as a monster who hurt children, but as a monster just like the one who had hurt *her* when she was still a child herself. He made his voice soft. Gentle. He put as much conviction into it as he could. He spoke the truth. "I am an assassin. I might be a murderer. I have done many things I am not proud of. But I am not a rapist, Hanna. I have not done that."

Hanna stared at him, searching his face, breathing in great, gulping gasps that were nearly sobs, nearly something worse than sobs. "And . . . what?" Her voice shook. "Do you expect me to just say, 'Oh, that's nice, Jon,' and go on as we were before?"

Jon could no longer look into her eyes. He drew his legs up to his chest and put the backs of his hands on his knees, looking into his palms as if he might find an answer there. "I expect you wish never to speak to me again," he said softly, his voice coming out a little hoarse. "I have been very selfish, Hanna. It has been a very long time since anyone looked at me and saw just a man. It has been a long time since anyone knew me just as Jon and liked me for who I am. It was like . . . it was like breathing again after diving too deep. But it was unfair to you, and I am sorry. I have no expectations, Hanna. You do not owe me anything. I am grateful for what you have given me. But of course we cannot go on as we were. I understand."

She just stared at him for a long, frozen moment. Then she choked out, "I need to go," and fled through the house and out the front door, her little bare mouse feet thumping across the hard wood of his floors before plunging out to where the sharp rocks and cracked asphalt of the street waited.

Jon wanted to go after her. To stop her. To hold her and kiss away her tears and think of something he could say to make her not hate him. To at least get her shoes for her and make sure she got home safely. But what would it look like to her if he came chasing after her? He was the Viper in the Night. And now she knew it. He leaned his forehead into his hands on top of his knees and listened as the sky opened up and the rain began to beat down.

Chapter
25

S HE WOKE GRADUALLY, FEELING STRANGELY rested in spite of the nauseating sense of dread that filled her empty stomach. Something was different.

Her eyelids drifted open. Sunlight crept between the planks of the walls. The air still stank of old wood and gasoline. Her hands were cold, her legs ached, and she itched everywhere the blood-soaked blanket had stuck to her skin as it dried. Nothing had changed.

Something moved—a spider picked its meticulous way across the blanket in front of her face. Why did there have to be spiders? The thing paused to poke exploratorily at a rank lock of Hanna's hair and then began to climb. It was in her hair. In her *hair*!

Why did that even bother her after everything else that had happened?

She wanted to scream and dance around the room, swatting herself all over. She couldn't, of course, so she didn't even try. She just lay there watching with horrified fascination as the thing crept over the hill of dirty hair and disappeared down the other side.

That was worse, knowing it was there but not being able to see it. Her heart began to pound in her chest as she watched for it to reappear. Surely it wouldn't just make a nest on the far side. Would it? And lay eggs? And make wriggly little baby spiders that would—

Movement. The spider wandered up a pale ridge on the far side of the dark spill of hair. Relief poured through her, ludicrous in its intensity—until her eyes refocused, and she realized that the pale ridge was her hand and that the spider was creeping up her index finger. Horrified revulsion flashed up her spine, stabbing into her brain, and she gasped as her hand convulsed, sending the spider scurrying for the edge of the blankets. The gasp stuck hard in her throat as time shrieked to a crushing stop. Her hand had moved. Her hand. Had *moved!*

For a long, still moment, she didn't dare believe. It was just her overstrained imagination. It was another of *his* tricks designed to torment her, to taunt her, to teach her a new and deeper shade of despair by layering it over a bright stab of hope.

Then she drew a deep, deliberate breath (*she could control her breathing!*) and told her hand to move. Slowly, her fingers uncurled, and her palm flattened against the blanket. Her heart surged, and a wretched trembling shudder passed through her body, forcing its way out in hot tears and a sobbing gasp.

Clumsily, she began testing other muscles. Her arms moved—weakly, but they moved. Her legs felt limp and rubbery, but they, too, moved. She rolled slightly and dragged both arms under her chest, bracing them against the floor while she lifted her heavy head to look cautiously around the shed. A few rusted tools lay in a heap in one corner. Three or four tattered leaves, blood red with autumn, were strewn across the floor. No invisible presence disturbed the lazy drift of the dust motes through the thin beams of sunlight; she was alone. And on the far side of the shed, the door hung ajar on its rusted hinges, taunting her.

If she could get there, could she call for help? Would someone find her? That thought chilled her in a new way. Did she really *want* to be found? How could she ever look anyone in the eyes again after this? She was broken. Contaminated. Disgusting. She would feel *his* hands on her body for the rest of her life.

The rest of her life . . . why wouldn't he just let her die? She'd come close to it more than once in the choking, blood-soaked darkness as he moved against her, but he kept forcing her to come back. If she could get out, maybe she could find a place to curl up and hide and give death a chance to finally find her.

Did spiders lay eggs in corpses?

Didn't matter. She'd be dead.

Slowly, clumsily, she twisted and began to drag herself toward the door. The rough, dirty plywood of the shed's floor rasped and tore at her bare skin.

Didn't matter.

She moved herself incrementally forward, eyes fastened on the gap between the door and the wall, falling into a slow rhythm—arms reaching and pulling, legs feebly pushing. Time settled around her like a thick, syrupy haze. Reach. Pull. Push. Dragging herself forward like a slug, leaving an erratic, blood-smeared trail.

She stopped halfway, breathing hard, sweat tickling her skin, to rest her forehead on the plywood. How many miles was it to the door? Her elbows were scraped raw, and her knees burned, and she thought she'd felt a fat splinter work its slow way into the skin of her left hip. Didn't matter. She'd be dead. Was it worth it? All this effort just to be allowed to die? A small eddy swirled the still air, making the dust motes dance through the slashes of gray sunlight, and she thought she caught the ghost of his musky scent. It made her empty stomach clench, and she gritted her teeth against the nausea. Yes, it was worth it. To die without his hands on her body, it was more than worth it. She raised her head again, fixed her eyes on the door, braced her bleeding elbows, gathered her strength, and heaved—

His boot caught her between the shoulder blades, stomping down to smash her against the filthy floor like a bug.

He must have come in through the wall behind her. Black despair pounded through her veins, saturated her tissues, settled into her bones, and dragged her down with it into a sucking stygian pit, pursued by the sound of his mocking laughter.

Hanna thrashed awake, banging her elbow sharply against the back wall of the closet. Pain shot down her arm, and she welcomed it because it meant she was really awake now. She felt Mr. Bickles's reassuring lumpy presence under her ribs and hugged him to her face for a few minutes, breathing in his familiar smell, and let herself remember.

He hadn't kept her long after her failed attempt to escape. Perhaps he could tell, even when she was safely paralyzed again, that all the fight had gone out of her. That she had given up. That he had won.

He *had* won.

And Hanna had woken up one morning in her own bed, clean, un-injured, and unscarred. Her parents said she'd been sick. For a while, Hanna thought maybe she had been. Maybe she was just crazy. She hoped she was crazy

But the memories seemed so *real*. She couldn't sleep because every time she closed her eyes she felt his hands, his blade, his body against her skin. She couldn't go out because every time she did, something triggered a panic attack—the sound of a man's chuckle, the smell of gas-oline, dust motes dancing through a long ray of sunlight, the brush of someone's cold fingers against her arm. Worse yet, those things some-times triggered full-blown flashbacks, making her think she was in the shed again, that it was all happening again. Sometimes she fought back against her phantom attacker, only to discover that she'd injured some-one in real life. The memories were so real to her. But there was no proof. Nothing she could look at and know for sure that she hadn't just made it all up.

It was a week before the splinter embedded beneath the smooth, unscarred skin of her hip had begun to fester. Three days after that, Hanna had sliced it out of herself with a craft knife. It was real. It was *all* real. No one believed her, but it was all real.

She'd lost track of how many days had gone by, then, before she swallowed all those pills and woke up in the hospital for the first time. She had wanted to die.

But she had lived. Night after night, year after year, she went on living.

She sighed and flipped back the deadbolt on the closet door. She checked all the locks and put a mug of water in the microwave to heat before padding into the bathroom. Her face was pale in the mirror over the sink, and her eyes looked haunted. Her hair clung to her sweat-damp cheeks. She turned on the tap and held her fingers in the flow of the water for a few minutes, letting the cold, wet reality of it reassure her. She cupped her hands and bent to splash a double handful of the cool-ness over the hot skin of her face, washing the last tendrils of the dream down the drain.

When she straightened again, her eye caught a movement in the mirror. Something in the shadows behind her shifted. A red eye gleamed out at her, and she heard the echo of a whisper of a deep chuckle. She whirled around, heart in her throat, trembling hands flying up in front of her face as she flinched back against the sink.

But of course, nothing was there.

Chapter
26

THE NEXT TIME HANNA AWAKENED, someone was knocking loudly on her front door. She tumbled out of the closet into her sunlit bedroom. Her head ached. What time was it? She yanked on a pair of crumpled sweatpants, dragged a t-shirt over her head, and combed her fingers quickly through her hair. It had been a long night; her visitor would just have to take her as she came.

She flicked back the curtain to peer out the window; Kamm stood on her porch looking grim, and behind him, Narista scowled at her feet. What could they possibly want? Hanna arranged a smile on her face before she undid the locks and opened the door.

Kamm bowed solemnly. "I hope we aren't intruding. My sister has something to say to you."

Narista stepped forward, drawing a small, jeweled knife from a scabbard that hung around her neck like a pendant. She knelt and laid the knife on the chipped concrete of Hanna's front porch. Clasping her hands behind her back, she bowed her head. "Hanna Bradley," she said, her voice solemn and formal, "I have brought you pain. I come to know if I can take it away again with me." She waited, silent, obviously expecting some kind of response from Hanna. Caught off guard, Hanna didn't have any idea what to say, and her sleep-deprived brain was too sluggish to improvise quickly.

Before Hanna could think what to do, Narista glared over her shoulder at her brother. "You see?" she said.

"Just wait," Kamm instructed firmly. "This is for you as much as it is for her." Narista heaved a sigh and resumed her penitent pose.

Hanna glanced at Kamm, hoping for some kind of clue, but he just smiled encouragingly at her.

"Look," Hanna said, rubbing her forehead. "This is obviously some kind of Talessanin thing I don't know about yet. I have no idea what I'm supposed to do. I'm tired, and I have a headache. Why don't you just come into the kitchen, and have a muffin, and say whatever it is you have to say, and we'll save this part for another time when someone can explain it to me."

Kamm patted Narista on the shoulder and said, "You see?"

Narista spoke through gritted teeth. "I thank you for consenting to hear me, Miss Bradley."

It wasn't until Hanna started leading the way into the kitchen that she remembered the state in which she'd left that room in the gray hours of morning. Dirty dishes were piled in the sink, sticky pans sat on top of the stove, drips of several kinds of batter had dried onto the countertops, and there was chocolate spattered across one wall where Hanna had flung a stirring spoon. Several containers of fresh baked goods cluttered the table.

The clock on the stove read 11:48. Nearly noon, and she hadn't even showered yet. What must they think of her? "I hope you'll overlook my chaos," she said as Narista followed her through the kitchen doorway. "I had a lot of thinking to do last night, and baking helps me think." She popped the lid off a muffin tin on the table and added, "Please, sit down and have a muffin."

Narista hesitated, fingering the hilt of her knife, which she had replaced in its pendant scabbard, then lowered herself into the chair Hanna indicated. She glared at Kamm, who gazed sternly back at her. Hanna sent Kamm into the studio for another chair, and the three of them sat at the table, picking at blueberry muffins.

"Right," Hanna said into the awkward silence. "What was it you wanted to tell me, Narista?"

Narista swallowed and began, "It was I who left the note on your back door with the dead mouse. I wish to apologize for any distress I might have caused and to assure you that—"

"Stop," Hanna interrupted. "I'm not interested in a fake apology. Just say what you really want to say to me, and we can talk about it."

Narista stared at her for a minute. She glanced at Kamm and back again to Hanna.

Hanna's head hurt. She had no patience for this. "I'll start you off," she said. "I would guess you want to begin with something like, 'Stay away from my brother, you human hussy, you're not nearly good enough for him.' Is that about right?"

Kamm frowned, and Narista's eyes narrowed speculatively.

"It's your turn," Hanna prompted.

Narista hesitated. "You know nothing about Jon," she said, then stopped, looking defiantly at Kamm.

"That's a good start," Hanna said. "Go on."

Narista shifted her gaze to Hanna. "You know nothing about his life. You know nothing about his family. You know nothing about his culture or customs. You simper, and smile, and flirt, and make believe you're civilized, but you're not. You have nothing to offer him."

"Very true," Hanna said. "Jon has told me very little about himself, and I have nothing worth having to offer anyone. Keep going."

"You see my brother as just a man from the stars who happened to make his home across the street from your little cottage," Narista said, leaning forward, her face growing intense. "But among his own people Jonantathinel of House Kanestelan Ehr is a legend. He is the firstborn of the Empress Among the Stars, and he would have been our next emperor had he not abdicated. He bears the blood of the ancient priest kings. He became the youngest Commander of the Nine Winds in the history of our people and held that office longer than any other Commander. He led the forces that put down the Rebellion of Five Worlds. Under his command, the Nine Winds infiltrated the Anathala Pirates and brought them to their knees. He went alone into the wilds of the Jenantat and captured Arenthalenat Al-Khenat. My brother walked into the Imperial High Council while it was in session, an act punishable by death; he demanded a voice and a vote on the Council for the Commander of the Nine, and they gave it to him. No one else has ever done that. Ever.

His deeds of heroism are without number. His name is loved and feared by more people than you can even imagine here on your dumpy little backwater planet."

Narista's voice was forceful, her face passionate. "By his own choice, Jon is no longer Ehrat of House Kanestelan. But he is still an Ehr. His blood is the oldest and highest in the Empire, and yours—yours is nothing. Who are you to aspire to attach yourself to Jonantathinel of House Kanestelan Ehr, greatest Commander of the Nine Winds, the Viper in the Night, Subduer of Worlds, legend of the Talessanin people? It's obscene! I will not watch it happen and do nothing! You're not of a noble House, let alone one of the Great Houses. You're not a citizen of the Empire. You're not even Talessanin. Your children wouldn't be Talessanin. You would pollute our truest bloodlines. You're nothing more than a filthy—"

"Narista!" Kamm interrupted sternly. "You forget yourself."

Narista looked at Kamm, chin high, eyes sharp with defiance. "I'm finished."

The two glared at each other until Hanna said quietly, "Thank you, Narista. I appreciate your honesty." Her voice sounded much calmer than she felt. Her head throbbed, and she wasn't sure she'd followed everything in Narista's recitation, but it certainly seemed as if Jon had left out a few important facts when he told her about himself.

Both of her guests turned to look at Hanna.

"If I may," Hanna continued, "I have a few questions for you, Narista, now that you're finished."

Narista looked wary. "Of course."

"Do I understand correctly that you just said Jon's parents—and yours—are the emperor and empress of the Talessanin Empire?"

Narista looked scornful. "Kanestelan is the Imperial House. Who else would our parents be?"

Hanna shrugged. "If it makes you feel any better, I don't know the family name of the British monarchs either. To be honest, royals have never interested me much. As you said, I tend to think of Jon as some guy who moved in across the street."

Narista looked outraged. She opened her mouth to say something, but Kamm interrupted. "It would be more accurate to say that Jon is the son of the empress and her first husband, who died when Jon was very young. My father, and Narista's, is the current emperor, who is our mother's second husband."

"I see," Hanna said. "And . . . Jon was next in line for the throne, but he abdicated?" Her head throbbed.

"Yes," Kamm said. "On his sixteenth birthday, as soon as he was legally of an age to do so. In Earth years, that would be about . . ." He frowned, thinking, ". . . twenty years old."

"Why?" Hanna asked.

"He said he believed I would be a better emperor, when the time came," Kamm explained. "When we were children, I had a great interest in the history of our people and the many different forms of government employed by the component peoples of the Empire. I spent many hours in the archives and with tutors discussing matters of state and diplomacy. Jon was a restless student when it came to such things, and the tutors were forever scolding him. He has a keen mind and possesses much wisdom regarding many matters, but he wasn't a good student of governance.

"Jon's gifts were more military in nature. In fact, when it came to battle training, Jon was somewhat precocious. He was a quick student of tactics and strategies on both small and large scales. And he exceeded all expectations in the arms training we received. He is a consummate marksman with any weapon you may choose, and by the time he was sixteen, only the arms master could defeat him hand to hand in the ring.

"Our mother took great pride in Jon's skills and used to say that with him at its head, the empire would be a power like no other in the history of the universe. But despite his gifts, Jon likes the idea of the empire being viewed as a benevolent guardian, a diplomatic entity more than a military one. He worried that taking his place as emperor would damage that image, so he chose to step down."

"And now *you're* next in line for the throne?" Hanna asked, just to be sure. Kamm smiled and inclined his head, and Hanna continued. "So I've just sent the second most powerful man in the empire, which might as well be the entire universe as far as Earth is concerned, down the hall to fetch a chair so he'd have a place to sit in the wreckage that is my kitchen and eat one of my blueberry muffins."

Kamm laughed. "Probably the third, though it is difficult to say at present. But Jon introduced you as my equal, and I'm happy to take his word for it, so you may send me down the hall for any number of chairs you like." Narista shifted angrily in her seat and began to say something, but Kamm cut her off. "Yes, Narista, you have made it very clear that you do not share my confidence in Jon's judgment on this matter. There is no need to repeat yourself. My decision stands."

"Wait," Hanna said. "The third?"

"Yes," Kamm explained, "though I should first emphasize that my mother, the empress, outranks all of us, since it is her line through which we come to the throne. But you were speaking of men. I would say that certainly my father is more powerful than I am at present. It is more difficult to judge when it comes to Jon."

"But I thought you said he abdicated." Hanna wondered if all this would make more sense to her once her head stopped hurting.

"He did. However, he then proceeded to make himself into a legend, as my sister has just explained. The acclaim of the people carries great power. He also holds the respect of the top leaders of all branches of our military and has the unquestioned loyalty of the Nine Winds, which is not a thing to make light of. The Imperial High Council honors him for his depth of understanding and level-headed wisdom, and the Chancellor of the Assembly is Jon's personal friend. Jon currently claims no title other than Ehr of House Kanestelan, but there are many kinds of power that do not come with titles. I strongly suspect that at present Jon could demand the Throne, and it would be his. In fact, some factions among our nobility have begun dropping small hints that they'd support such a move, and Jon certainly has the bloodlines to legitimize his claim. I suspect this is one reason Jon has suddenly taken it into his head to retire quietly on the outskirts of the empire, in a small town he remembers fondly from a previous visit to our newest planetary protectorate."

Hanna stared at him. "Jon came here before? Why don't I remember that?"

Kamm looked down at the remnants of his muffin. "It wasn't publicized."

"Oh . . ." Hanna felt entirely at sea. And her headache was getting worse, not better. She suddenly just wanted them to go away. "Well," she said, "this has been very enlightening. I think I understand your objections, Narista, and I will certainly take your concerns into consideration."

Hanna went to the cupboard under the sink to retrieve the dagger, still wrapped in the brown paper bag. She set it on the table in front of Narista. "I believe this is yours. Next time, if there ever is a next time, I hope you'll just come knock on my door and tell me what's on your mind instead of sacrificing an innocent rodent in order to make your point."

Narista's face flushed, and she looked down at the half-eaten muffin in her hands. "It was already dead," she said. "From Jon's security system." She looked up at Hanna. "Thank you for hearing me out. I'm sorry about the mouse. I was angry, and perhaps I went too far. I hope you'll forgive me." She actually sounded sincere.

"You're forgiven," Hanna said.

Kamm studied Hanna's face. "I must ask, Hanna, for the sake of legal clarity, whether you are satisfied with this as a resolution to this matter, or if you'd prefer to seek further action."

Hanna shrugged. "I'm satisfied. And if there's nothing else you need from me, I hope you'll excuse me; I have a lot of cleaning up to do." She stood, and the Talessanins rose as well, turning to go.

Then Hanna remembered. "Oh!" she exclaimed. "If it's not too much trouble, would you take this back with you for Tala?" She held up her covered cake dish. "It's the chocolate bundt cake I keep promising her."

Kamm gave her a broad grin, a fatherly twinkle in his eyes. "She will be most pleasantly surprised," he said. "Thank you, Hanna, you are very kind to my impertinent daughter." His expression grew thoughtful. After a moment, he handed the cake plate to Narista. "Please deliver this cake with Miss Bradley's compliments. There is one more thing I wish to mention to Hanna before I go."

Narista scowled sourly, glancing back and forth between Hanna and Kamm. She sighed and gave Hanna a slight bow. "Thank you for your hospitality," she muttered sullenly.

Kamm waited until they heard the front door close behind Narista before saying, "I've taken too much of your time already, Hanna, so I'll be direct. What I'm about to say trespasses inexcusably on your privacy. If I overstep too far, you may freely tell me this is none of my concern, and I will say no more."

He paused, as if waiting for a response. Hanna walked across the kitchen and fished around in the spice cupboard until she found the bottle of Tylenol. "Go on," she said. She took out a glass and went to the sink for water.

Kamm cleared his throat, "When we returned home from New York last night, Jon was sitting on the roof, looking at the stars. That's what he always does when he's particularly troubled about something. When I asked what had disturbed him, he said you asked why Narista referred to him as the Viper in her note, and that when he explained, you had the very good sense to wish not to continue an association with someone who has tortured and killed people. He didn't share the details of your conversation, but I know my brother well enough to guess he didn't present himself in a very positive light; Jon can be hard on himself. And just now, Narista told you Jon is a legendary hero who's out of your reach anyway. Perhaps you've already drawn your conclusions about my brother and have no desire to hear any more about him, but I wonder if a third perspective might be of any use or interest to you?" Again he paused, waiting for Hanna to say something.

Hanna swallowed the pills and motioned for Kamm to sit down again, then slid into her own seat. "Jon will be my neighbor whether we're friends or not," she said. "You know him much better than I do, and I'd like to hear what you have to say."

"You're very kind." Kamm's face grew intense, solemn. "Hanna, Jon is neither the demon he sometimes believes, nor the angel Narista likes to think him. He is only a man. I grew up with Jon, and for the past decade or so I have also served on the Imperial High Council, where I've observed Jon's conduct as Commander of the Nine in great detail. He has done many difficult things and faced many impossible choices. He is one of the most honorable men I have ever known, but he's still just a man. And he feels things as a man. I'm not certain what he has felt for you, but I know he was up on the roof last night, and that losing your friendship grieves him deeply.

"I won't pretend to know all of your reasons for ending your . . . association . . . with Jon, but perhaps I can speak on his behalf with regard to the two objections he mentioned—that he has tortured and killed people."

Kamm's tone became more deliberate, reminding Hanna of the courtroom lawyers on TV, laying out their cases before the jury. "Hanna, Jon is a soldier. More than that, he is a gifted warrior. Our empire needs warriors. In every intelligent species we have encountered, there are a few individuals who harm and manipulate others for their own gain with no apparent sense of remorse. We could debate the reasons for this until all the suns die out, but the fact remains that they exist.

"These individuals nearly always consider themselves intellectually and morally superior to everyone else, and when they cause problems, whether at a local or interplanetary level, persuasion and diplomacy are rarely effective in achieving workable solutions. Sometimes the only way to stop an act of aggression or violence is with an act of force. Sometimes the warriors among us are all that stand between evil and the rest of us. Sometimes killing is necessary to prevent greater harm.

"But one of the reasons Jon demanded a voice on the Council was that he felt the Council recommended killing too quickly and without giving sufficient consideration to other alternatives. He believed that those who had to do the killing should have a say in whether or not it was truly needed. Indeed, Jon is well-respected among the Council for his ability to find inventive ways to solve problems without violence. But there are times when even Jon cannot find a better solution. And when death needs to be dealt, Jon is very good at that too. He does not do it lightly or because he enjoys it, Hanna, he does it because it needs to be done, and he possesses the skill to do it well, with minimal unintended complications."

Hanna sighed. "I understand the need for police and soldiers. And I've known since the beginning that Jon was a soldier. I can respect that. But last night he told me he has killed children. On purpose. In their sleep."

Kamm frowned. "Jon told you that?" He looked down at his hands. "Yes. I suppose Jon would." He looked back up at Hanna, studying her face carefully. "There may have been other times before I served on the Council, but I know of two instances when Jon was required to take the lives of children, though there was more than one child in each case. He argued vehemently against it both times. One time he was outvoted on the Council, and the deaths of the children were part of the official recommendation to the Throne. On the other occasion, the Council voted to allow the children to live, but the emperor decided against the Council's recommendation, which is his right. In both cases there were extenuating circumstances in which the children's parents had placed them, and which we could find no way around.

"Disobeying the direct order of the Emperor would constitute treason. And because of who Jon is, even a small treason on his part could have far reaching consequences in the empire." Kamm hesitated a moment, looking appraisingly at Hanna, as if judging how much to say. "He did disobey orders once." He hesitated again.

"Eight million people," Hanna said softly.

"Give or take. He told you, then?"

Hanna nodded, feeling a little sick at the confirmation.

Kamm sighed. "It wasn't entirely his doing, you know," he said. "There were many factors involved. But Jon feels responsible. He was certainly guilty of insubordination, as far as that goes, and was charged with treason. If he had been anybody else, they might have just killed him—there were certainly enough cries for blood over the mess. But Jon's father was *ehrat* of the old imperial bloodline, and his mother is the empress of the new. Executing Jon for treason against his stepfather would have been seen as a political maneuver calculated to remove the competing bloodline. It would have divided the empire and resulted in a lot more than eight million deaths. So the Council ruled that Jon was not guilty of treason by virtue of the fact that he had received the order via the Commander of the Nine, and not directly from the emperor himself, and he was only flogged for insubordination against his Commander." Kamm shifted in his seat. "The Commander was quite thorough with his discipline. When I saw Jon afterward, I thought for a moment that they *had* killed him." Kamm rubbed at his face, as if trying to erase the memory. "After Jon became Commander himself, of course, he received all his orders directly from the emperor. And at that point, any open disobedience at all would have been disastrous. For all of us."

"It would have been treason," Hanna said softly. "They would have killed him."

"Possibly." Kamm kept his eyes fixed on her face. "Though that would have started a war."

Hanna frowned. "But not killing him would undermine the emperor's authority."

"Yes." Kamm's eyes held Hanna's, and he seemed to be waiting for her to say something else.

"And that might have started a war too?" she guessed.

Kamm nodded solemnly. "Very likely. Jon's loyalty reinforces the power of the Throne and helps assure stability and peace within the empire. But as Commander of the Nine, Jon was sometimes faced with a choice between loyalty to the Throne and fidelity to his own conscience."

Hanna felt her gut clench. "Follow orders and kill a child, or disobey and trigger a war."

"Jon faced a number of such impossible choices. In the end, all of us—Jon, the emperor, the other members of the Council—we are just men and women. We do the best we can, and we live with the consequences. Some are harder to live with than others."

Hanna shifted in her seat and said quietly, "I understand what you're saying, but how can I be . . . friends . . . with Jon if I can't get that picture out of my head, of Jon standing over a child's bed and . . ." she trailed off, unable to finish.

Kamm's voice was gentle. "Like us, you must do as you think best."

After a moment, Hanna asked miserably, "And what about the torture?"

"Ah." Kamm said. "As to that, torture is strictly forbidden in the empire. It's a barbaric practice, and there are nearly always better ways of accomplishing the same ends. However, the Throne recognizes that very occasionally circumstances might arise when even barbaric cruelty may be justifiable. The law makes no allowance for this, but the Throne can pardon the perpetrator."

He watched her face as he continued. "A little over two years ago, Jon confessed to torturing some prisoners. He was his own accuser. When one of the Winds is accused of a crime, the usual procedure is to present the evidence to the Throne—the empress and emperor—for judgment. However, because of Jon's relationship to the Throne, his case was referred to the Imperial High Council. I was required to abstain from voting, for obvious reasons, but I was allowed to observe the proceedings and ask questions.

"Put briefly, the case was this: several thousand students and employees of an educational institution in orbit around a highly populated planet were taken hostage by a group of subversives who had placed explosives in strategic locations and jettisoned all the life pods. The subversives' demands would have been impossible to meet—particularly before the deadline given, after which they claimed they'd detonate the explosives, killing everyone in the institution and sending debris raining down on the people of the planet below.

"The local authorities appealed to the Throne for assistance, and the Nine were sent. The Winds quickly apprehended all the subversives, but not before one of them triggered the countdown to detonate the explosives. Jon had no time to call in a team of explosives specialists as he'd intended, and he had no way to evacuate the hostages in time. Jon's solution was to interrogate several of the subversives separately until their explanations of how to defuse the explosives matched up sufficiently to act upon. Time was short, and some of his interrogation techniques crossed the line, but he succeeded in defusing the detonator.

"The Council voted unanimously that the circumstances justified his methods and gave him a full pardon and a commendation. But I think Jon has had a difficult time forgiving himself."

"Hanna," Kamm leaned forward in his seat and waited until Hanna met his gaze before he went on, "Jon is a good and honorable man. He has a generous heart and a brave spirit. But his work has been demanding and disheartening. He carries burdens no man should ever have to bear, and so often he chooses to carry them so others will not have to. He is weary and heartsick, and it has been far too long since I saw my brother smile and laugh as he did with you." Kamm reached out as if to take Hanna's hand but thought better of it and only laid his hand on the tabletop, fingers close together, hiding the webbing. "Hanna, you've shown patience with my daughter and forbearance with my sister. I wonder if your generous heart might also find compassion for my brother."

The two of them sat for a while, a heavy silence hanging low in the air between them. Finally, Hanna sighed and rubbed at her forehead. "You're a good brother, Kamm. And I can see why Jon thought you'd make a good diplomat. I'll think about what you've said."

Kamm stood and inclined his head solemnly. "Thank you for hearing me, Hanna. I'm sorry to take so much of your time when you're feeling unwell. I'll let myself out."

Chapter 27

HANNA HAD FINISHED EXCAVATING HER kitchen and was trying to decide what to do about the chocolate stain she couldn't seem to get off the wall, when there was another knock at her door. This time, Tomin stood on her front porch.

When she opened the door, he held up the flip-flops Hanna had left by Jon's hot tub. "I told Jon he should bring them to you himself," Tomin grumbled, "but he said you wouldn't want to see him. I don't know what happened between the two of you, Hanna, but I don't suppose you could just forgive him, could you? He's been in a mood all day, and some of us have to live with him."

"It's not as easy as that, Tomin," Hanna said, taking the shoes. "And it serves you right anyway. You might at least have told me they were the imperial family."

Tomin looked surprised. "Is that what all this is about? Hanna, it doesn't matter. Jon doesn't care about any of that."

Hanna glared at him. "No, that's not what this is about, but I don't suppose it ever occurred to you that *I* might care?"

Tomin opened his mouth to say something, then closed it again. His brows drew together, and he looked down. "No, I don't suppose it did. Jon is trying to keep a low profile in the neighborhood at present. And

I guess I just thought every woman wanted to go to the ball and dance with the prince."

"Well, I'm not every woman, Tomin, and *I* want to know what I'm getting myself into."

"I'm sorry, Hanna. How can I make it up to you?"

His look of contrition was so sincere that Hanna couldn't stay angry with him. She stood back and motioned for him to come inside. "You can start by teaching me the proper greeting between someone like me and someone like them—inferior to superior, or whatever you call it, so I don't go around offending everyone by pretending I'm their equal when I so clearly am not." She sighed. "And then you can eat some of the extra cookies. I got a little carried away last night."

Tomin grinned. "Oh, that greeting isn't hard. It's just like the one between equals, but sideways. Here, I'll show you." He held out his webbed hand as if to shake hers, and she did the wrist-clasping handshake he'd taught her for the greeting between equals. But as her fingers closed around his wrist, he rotated their hands so his was underneath, facing palm up, and hers was on top, palm down. "There you go," he said. "You are now my superior, and I'm your subordinate. Offer your hand flat, palm up, if you want to show submission. If you want to claim superiority, offer your hand palm down."

"That's easy enough," Hanna said. "Why didn't you just teach me that in the first place?"

"It wasn't the right one for the occasion." Tomin sighed. "And you already had enough things to try to remember."

Hanna frowned. "And what should I call them? I'm betting someone like me wouldn't generally be on a first name basis with people like them."

Tomin shrugged. "If they said you could use their short form names, you can do so until they tell you otherwise. But if you really want to be all formal about it, you'd address Kamm as 'my lord' for the simplified English construction, or 'Honored Ehrat' if you want to be more correct. Narista would be 'my lady' or 'Honored Ahn.' At this point, addressing Jon as 'my lord' or 'Honored Ehr' would have more or less the same effect as slapping him. Maybe you want to do that to him, I don't know, but if not, it would be kinder to address him as Jonantathinel Ehr and just leave it at that."

Hanna sent Tomin home with two big plastic bags filled with assorted cookies and had just closed the door behind him when the phone rang. It was Mr. Purcell, the buyer from the gallery.

"Hanna, are you familiar with the State Arts Council's Future Vision 20/20 event?" he asked her.

"Sure," Hanna said. "It's a charity event to raise money for arts education. The Council invites twenty galleries from around the state to provide twenty works of art each, and then charges rich people to come to the capitol to eat an overpriced dinner and bid on the art."

"Exactly," said Mr. Purcell. "And half of the art is created by established artists, and the other half by emerging artists, but the signatures are covered so the patrons don't know whether they're getting a bargain price on work by a famous artist or making an unusually large investment in work by a complete unknown. It's all sorts of fun. Have you ever been?"

"Well," Hanna admitted, "I knew someone who knew someone who let me pick up an extra shift as a waitress at the event a few years back, but not officially, no."

"Would you like to?" Mr. Purcell asked, then plunged on without waiting for an answer. "My predecessor had already selected the four artists to represent our gallery, but one of them has backed out, so we need an alternate. Would you be interested?"

"Of course I'd be interested!" This was exactly what she needed. On so many levels. "Thank you for thinking of me, Mr. Purcell. What do you need from me?"

"Well, we've sold a few of your things, so we're down to only two paintings of yours in the current inventory, and one of them is too small for the entry guidelines for the event," Mr. Purcell said. "So we would need four new paintings. And I'm sorry for the short notice, but since the event is a week from Friday, we'd need them by next Wednesday. Could I stop by then to choose canvases? The one you showed me before with the covered bridge might work. What else do you have?"

Hanna thought. "Well, I've been doing some work on commission recently," she said, "so as of today I don't have much in the way of new things, but I have some earlier pieces I could show you. And I already planned to spend the next week or so painting in the field, so I should have several new landscapes by next Wednesday. If I use acrylics instead of oils, the paint would have time to cure sufficiently. I'm sure we can come up with enough for the event."

"That would be wonderful, Hanna. I knew I could count on you."

The next several days blurred together. Hanna left her house in the dark hours of morning to be in place with her easel and paints when the sun began to cast its warm, slanting, early light. She moved to different locations as the day progressed, relying on the notes she'd jotted in her sketchbook during her exploratory excursions to match locations with the angle of the sun for the time of day, going back the next day to work more when the light was at the right angle again. She returned home, sunburned, mosquito-bitten, and exhausted, after the sun had gone down each evening. After the first couple of days, she was tired enough that the nightmares woke her only once or twice each night.

The hard work and intense focus also kept her from thinking much about her neighbors across the street, and Hanna was grateful. Every time her thoughts drifted in Jon's direction she felt lacerated inside. What was he? The kind, gentle man she thought she'd come to know? An unapproachable legendary hero? A cold-blooded killer? The bogeyman in every child's dark closet, she'd said—and she'd seen a terrible, almost tangible pain come into his eyes.

And what was he to her? What did she *want* him to be to her? She struggled to separate the icy knot of horror that clamped down inside her at the thought of his work from the blistering terror that threatened to drown her during the nightmares. Jon was not the sadistic beast who had done that to her. She knew he wasn't. But he had tortured people; he'd said so himself. He'd hurt children—had killed them. More than once. What was he, if not some kind of monstrous villain? Part of her felt crippled by a numb sense of dread at the thought of ever seeing him again. But another part ached to have his strong arms around her, to breathe in that spicy Jon scent, and to hear his velvet voice murmur, "You are safe, Little Mouse."

What kind of person longed for the embrace of a killer?

When she painted, all of that drifted away, and she settled into a quiet non-space where nothing existed but light and color, line and texture, and the race to get the paint laid right before the acrylic skinned over and refused to move.

She saw Jon only once during those hectic days. She woke in the pre-dawn hours to find that a heavy mist had risen from the lake, blanketing the woods and fields. She knew it would be a mistake to try to drive in it, but it would make for a lovely sunrise, especially down by the water. So she scraped her hair into a ponytail, tucked a canvas into the carry case, slung her daypack over her shoulder, and set off down the footpath that curved around the edge of the lake. After all, Jon had said she could visit his grounds whenever she liked.

She knew the perfect spot from which to catch the sunrise and had her easel set up before the gray dimness began to give way to the coming light. Hanna lost herself in the cool blues and violets of the shadows and let her soul soar into rose and gold with the rising sun, fingers flying, eyes flicking back and forth from the lake to the canvas, the canvas to the lake. The mist slowly cleared as the air warmed, and when a light breeze began to stir away the last remnants, Hanna drew a deep breath and stood, stretching. The painting would need a few touch-ups back in the studio, but for the most part she was happy with it.

She looked out over the lake, as her mind shifted back to the solid here and now of material reality, watching the breeze tickle ripples across the surface of the water. A bird fluttered up from the trees, arcing black across the pale sky. Wondering what had disturbed it, Hanna peered toward that part of the shoreline. It was where they'd gone for the picnic not so long ago—the place where the two rocky outcroppings reached like longing arms out into the water, cradling the secluded swimming hole. A figure stood at the far end of the longest outcropping, dark against the sky, stretching, tall and lithe, to greet the morning sun. Jon was dressed for swimming, in just his loincloth, and the sun gleamed golden on his bare skin. As Hanna watched, he lowered his arms, danced the few steps to the edge, and flung himself into the air, arms out, fins extended, echoing, for a moment, the flight of the bird. Then he fell, twisting elegantly and effortlessly, and knifed cleanly into the water below. Hanna caught her breath, pulse pounding suddenly in her throat. So beautiful. How could someone so beautiful be—whatever he was. He surfaced farther out into the lake than Hanna expected and rolled onto his back, floating like a languid otter, looking back toward the cliff.

As Hanna watched, another figure swayed out onto the diving ledge—a woman's graceful form this time, slender and supple. As she soared from the high perch, the golden sunlight glinted from the woman's coppery hair. Salenia. What was Salenia doing at Jon's house before dawn? She must have stayed the night. Jealousy scorched through Hanna, and for a long, cold heartbeat she forgot how to breathe. Then she clenched her teeth against the tears that stung at the backs of her eyes and berated herself. It was none of her business who was spending the night with Jon. She couldn't be with him, even if she wanted to. Not really. She was too broken. But that didn't even matter, because she didn't want to. Did she? He killed children. He tortured people. *"Impossible choices . . ."* Kamm's words came back to her. *"A generous heart and a brave spirit."* What *was* Jon?

It didn't matter. Whatever he was, he belonged to Salenia. Anyone could see that.

Hanna snatched the water bottle and brush soap from her pack and began cleaning her brushes, forcing herself to concentrate on the things that belonged to her own life. Her real life. The life in which she didn't have time for romantic nonsense because she had an opportunity to really launch her art career—if she could finish enough good paintings in time for the exhibition. She didn't need Jon. She had a good life.

A shout and a shrieking laugh echoed faintly across the water, and Hanna looked reflexively out to where the dark figures played against the bright glitter of the sun on the lake. There were three of them now—no, four—splashing each other and laughing as they skimmed through the water, and Hanna's heart fluttered as she recognized Narista. Maybe it hadn't been a romantic tryst, then, after all. Maybe Salenia had just come with Jon's sister for a visit.

It didn't matter, Hanna reminded herself.

But it did matter, and she found herself watching Jon and his friends taking turns diving from the ledge while she worked the soap into the bristles of her brushes. As she tucked the last brush into the case, a squealing giggle pealed exultantly out from the diving ledge, and a tiny figure flew from the cliff, spinning wildly before curling into a tight ball just as it hit the water. Tala. A smile tugged at Hanna's lips. The little girl was so full of life. Hanna remembered being like that as a child, herself. She hoped Tala would be sheltered from the dark things.

A tall figure remained behind, silhouetted on the ledge, standing long enough to wave back at Tala when she surfaced, then folding into a brooding crouch. For a long while, Jon remained there, motionless, like a gargoyle keeping watch from a cathedral spire, with the morning sun gleaming through the membranes of his extended fins. Hanna couldn't make herself look away.

Eventually, the others began to move back toward the shore, disappearing behind the rocky escarpment into the little sandy cove, and Jon stood, and stretched, and stepped off the high ledge, falling feet first, arms and fins tucked tight against his body as he pierced the water. Hanna waited a little longer, packing and repacking her supplies, giving the Talessanins plenty of time to gather their own things and head back to the house. She didn't want to have to talk to any of them.

The sun was well into the clear sky before she started for home.

Chapter
28

J ON KNELT IN THE SAND near the water's edge, face turned sky-
ward, arms held out to his sides, palms up. Drops of lake water
trickled from his braids down his naked back. White smoke drifted
from the *taless* seed where it smoldered on the grate of his pocket brazier, balanced on the rounded surface of the stone in front of him—the
stone where Hanna had sat to sketch before the picnic.

Her absence was a constant pain in the pit of his stomach. The fear
and horror he'd seen on her face before she fled haunted him. He had
done that to her. The knowledge ate through his gut. He had soothed her
fears and made her feel safe, knowing—*knowing*—what he was, and how
it must terrify her when she found out. He should never have done that
to her. He should have let her keep her distance, shouldn't have pushed
her for more. But it had been so delightful to think that she liked him
just for himself. To imagine that she, perhaps, if anyone could, might see
past the Viper to the man underneath and, perhaps, truly care for him.
And now Hanna was the one paying the price for his foolish hope.

He remembered the first time he had seen her, there on his front
porch with her brave smile and her chocolate cake. He thought of that
first night when she had allowed him to stay and watch the movie with
her, and of the way his heart had surged when she took his arm at
the picnic. He remembered the rush of hope he had felt when Tomin

announced her name at the dinner party, and there she stood, hesitating in his doorway, and felt again the breathless joy of being kissed by Hanna in the treehouse as if it were the most natural thing in the world for her to do. He had thought maybe . . .

But he should have known. He *had* known, beneath it all. And he should not have let it hurt her. Tiffany had told him of Hanna's pain, had asked him not to hurt her more. But he had done it anyway. He should have protected her from himself. The best thing he could do now was to stay away from her, to try not to make it any worse—she had been hurt more than enough before she ever met him. The smoke from his tribute drifted up into the morning sky, toward the vast reaches of the galactic ocean beyond it, carrying his prayer with it. *Let her find peace.*

Something crackled in the woods behind him, and Jon spun to his feet, fingers flying to the dagger strapped to his thigh beneath his *lanat*.

She stood frozen on the footpath in the shadow of the trees, face pale, eyes wide and startled.

"Hanna," he breathed. Her hair was coming loose from its tie at the nape of her neck, and a few stray brown curls fell darkly over the pale, delicate curve of her collarbone. A streak of dark blue paint stained her cheek. *She was so beautiful.*

She cleared her throat. "I'm s-sorry," she said softly. "I thought everyone had left." There were shadows under her frightened eyes, and she looked tired. Nightmares, she'd said. Flashbacks. Well, he'd done that to her too. The knot in his stomach tightened. Her eyes flicked from his face to his hand, and she swallowed hard.

The dagger weighed suddenly heavy in Jon's grip, and he felt the hot blood surge through his body. Fool! Half naked, fins on full display, and pointing a weapon at her—this would not make things better between them. "Forgive me." He made his voice as gentle as possible as he shifted out of his fighter's ready stance. "It is a reflex." He half turned and slowly bent to lay the dagger on the stone beside the small brazier, then held out his hands toward her, showing his empty palms. "The others have gone back to the house. I . . . stayed behind."

She didn't relax, exactly, but a little color returned to her cheeks, and she drew a deep breath. "I . . . um . . . didn't mean to interrupt your"—she made a vague gesture with her free hand—"whatever you were doing."

She shifted her big bag higher on her shoulder and adjusted her grip on the handle of the rectangular case that swung against the side of her leg.

Jon looked down at the brazier. "A prayer," he said. "But you are a welcome interruption." He looked back at her again. She hadn't run from him—yet. That was something. He cast about for something to say that might keep her here a little longer. It was selfish, perhaps, but he ached to have her close. He looked down again, unable to meet her eyes. The seed was mostly ash now, and he tipped the lid of the brazier closed.

"I suppose I should build a proper haven," he said, trying to make his voice cheerfully conversational. "But I am not accustomed to living in one place very long and coming out here makes me feel closer to the Sower."

Hanna cleared her throat again. "You . . . you worship the Sower?"

Jon's eyes flicked back to her face. Could she be trying to keep the conversation going too? He studied her face as he said carefully, "I *follow* the Sower." As if that clarification would mean anything to her. "I worship the Maker. I reverence life in all its abundant forms."

A small, bitter sound escaped from Hanna, and she blushed furiously.

Jon tilted his head inquiringly.

Hanna shrugged and met his gaze; her eyes held a challenge. "You kill people, Jon."

His heart sank. He was a monster. "Yes," he said softly. "Such are the gifts the Maker has given me. I try to use them in service of the Sower. Sometimes in the dance I stumble so close to the Destroyer that it is difficult to tell the difference. But I do try, Hanna."

She said nothing, but her chocolate eyes studied him. Measuring. Weighing. Asking.

He wanted to have the right answers. He knew he didn't, but he wanted to. Wanted to put his arms around her as he had in the treehouse and hold her; to feel the soft solidity of her against his body and just listen to her breathe. Wanted that to be enough. "I hurt you," he said softly. "I did not intend to, but I did. I am sorry, Little Mouse . . ." Without thinking, he took a step toward her.

Hanna stumbled back, color draining from her face. "I have to go," she whispered hoarsely.

And she disappeared down the footpath into the trees.

Chapter 29

WHEN SHE GOT HOME, HANNA stuffed the sunrise painting behind a cupboard in the studio. It wasn't going to be in the exhibition. She couldn't look at it anymore. He reverenced life by *killing* people? That didn't make any sense. But then, why did her heart still race when he looked at her that way? Why did it soar when he called her Little Mouse?

She showered and changed and threw herself back into her work. Life went on—day gave way to night, dark made room for light, and time shifted through the greyness of dawn or dusk, blurring like paint on a muddied canvas. During the days, Hanna lost herself in the lines and shadows, the richness of the colors, the textures, and the light, and she completed five paintings she was happy with. And at night . . . at night, in the darkness, *he* came to her with his hands, and his knife, and his mouth, and his groping, heaving body. Sometimes he wore Jon's face.

But sometimes there were other dreams, in which she danced with Jon in the treehouse, and she was safe.

Mr. Purcell came on Wednesday and went away with the old covered bridge painting as well as one of an aspen grove that the previous buyer had rejected. He also took three of the new paintings and asked her to bring the other two to the gallery after the show.

Hanna took Rachel and Tiffany out for dinner to celebrate. She worried at first that her friends would grill her about Jon again, but Tiffany had developed a tremendous crush on the new UPS man who delivered packages at the salon where she worked, and the three of them verbally dissected him instead.

It wasn't until Thursday, when Hanna was trying to catch up on the house and yard work she'd let slide in the rush to meet the deadline, that she saw Jon again. But it was only from a distance as he played a chasing game with Tala, who kept running in and out of the gate from the back yard to the front, squealing with laughter. He looked over once, and Hanna thought he stumbled when he saw her out pulling weeds. She almost raised a hand to wave at him, but a hot rush of uncertainty swept over her. How would he interpret a wave? For that matter, what would she mean by waving? She kept her head down, pretending she hadn't noticed him, and a moment later he was gone. They must have moved on to another game after that, because she didn't see him again.

And then it was Friday and time for the biggest exhibit of her entire life. She set out early to drive the five hours to the state capital so she could check in to her hotel and dress for the gala without rushing. She was glad she'd splurged on the new gown. Who knew she'd need formal attire twice in the same month? At least this time there would be real forks. And no dancing. And no Jon to confuse her. Only the anxious anticipation of wondering whether anyone would bid on her paintings.

Mr. Purcell met her at the annex entrance as he'd promised and introduced her to the three other artists who represented their little gallery at the event. He helped her pin on her official artist name tag, showed her to the exhibit hall, and left her to wander the nooks and corridors that had been constructed of temporary half-walls hung with art.

The work on display was incredible, and Hanna couldn't help but worry that her landscapes would stand out as inferior. But as she came to each of them, she found that the gallery had chosen frames that set off the colors nicely, and the bright, busy paintings they'd hung on either side made hers seem peaceful and idyllic. The minimum bid prices listed on the cards next to her paintings were higher than she'd ever sold a painting for in her life. But then, she supposed a lower price would be a sure tip-off that the work had been created by one of the "emerging" artists in the show, not one of the recognized professionals.

Servers offered trays of cocktails and hors d'oeuvres to the patrons as they viewed and bid on the art, and employees from each of the participating galleries hovered throughout the exhibit hall, wielding electronic tablets and managing the bids. After bidding closed, the gallery employees would rapidly pack the art for safe transport while the patrons ate a leisurely dinner in the banquet room next door.

As the time for bidding neared its end, Hanna rounded a corner to find Mr. Purcell standing in front of her painting of the aspen grove with one of the tablet-bearing assistants. Their heads were bent over the screen, and they spoke together in low, excited murmurs. Mr. Purcell glanced up and saw Hanna; a grin broke across his face, and he motioned her over.

"You might find this interesting," he said. "We can't discuss the identity of the artist where anyone might overhear, of course, but this lovely painting of the aspen grove is apparently making quite a stir with some of the bidders."

"This one?" Hanna's surprise showed in her voice.

"Come see." Mr. Purcell caught her elbow and drew her in closer. The screen of the tablet showed a photograph of the painting, its title, dimensions, and medium, as well as identification numbers for the artist and gallery. Underneath, a long column of bids began at the minimum bidding price and rapidly escalated, running off the bottom of the screen. The salesman scrolled down until the amount of the most recent bid showed.

"You can't be serious," Hanna said.

"Oh, but I can," said Mr. Purcell. "Sometimes it's just a matter of finding the right buyers and giving them the right motivation. Right now, this piece is the highest priced item in the show, though some of the same artist's other paintings are also doing very well. Once a piece begins to rise to the top, people start buying works with the matching artist identification number."

"But," Hanna stammered, "I don't understand. That can't be a real bid."

"It's real, all right." Mr. Purcell laughed. "Here's the thing, Hanna. We have some unusual guests tonight. Some Talessanin lord or duke or something is here on vacation." Hanna's heart seized up. *Surely not. Not here!* Mr. Purcell went on, apparently not noticing her reaction, "And he's looking for Earth landscape art to take home with him. There aren't many landscapes in the exhibit tonight, and his lordship took a shine to this piece."

"Say that again?" the salesman asked suddenly. Hanna was confused for a moment until he said, "Thanks," and she realized he was talking to someone over an electronic earpiece. "Mr. Purcell," he said, "they're coming. He wants to look at it again in person before he decides about increasing his bid."

Mr. Purcell nodded at the salesman, then turned back to Hanna, speaking rapidly. "Also among our guests is one of our senators who has repeatedly spoken out against allowing the off-world export of Earth cultural items, such as original art. He is rather well-to-do himself and seems determined to outbid the extraterrestrial contingent. And because of this little rivalry, the artist and the gallery that represents him or her are going to make out like bandits no matter which of them comes out on top, even taking into consideration the cut that goes to the Arts Council."

"And who is coming to see it again?" Hanna asked, heart beginning to pound. *It wasn't Jon. It could not be Jon. Not tonight.*

"The Talessanins," the salesman said. "Don't worry, they're civilized enough. You might want to step back so his lordship can get a good view, though." He grinned at Hanna. Then he looked at something behind her, over her head, and said softly, "Here we go."

Hanna's heart climbed up into her throat and started strangling her. *Please let it not be Jon!* Numbly, she turned to see who was coming up behind her.

"My lord," the salesman stepped forward and offered a small bow, "it's a pleasure to see you again."

The man he spoke to was definitely Talessanin—and to Hanna's great relief, definitely not Jon. This man was older, sturdily built, with thinning, iron gray hair and a slightly sallow complexion. He wore a dark gray longcoat with elaborate silver and blue embroidery. An elegant, white-haired lady glided along with him, one hand tucked into the crook of the man's elbow, and the other balancing a champagne flute. Hanna started breathing again. The two newcomers inclined their heads in response to the salesman's bow.

"A pleasure," the man echoed sourly. He eyed Hanna and Mr. Purcell. "And are these our very persistent adversaries in the bidding?"

The salesman answered smoothly, "No my lord, just interested observers. Mr. Purcell represents one of the participating galleries, and Miss Bradley is one of our artists. They came to see the painting that was drawing so much attention."

"Checking out the artistic competition, Hanna?" The familiar voice was cheerfully teasing and came from behind Hanna. She turned, heart pounding once again.

Kamm looked very dignified and very nearly human in his black tuxedo. Narista was on her brother's arm, dressed in an exquisitely sophisticated black and white gown that would've been at home on a red carpet in Hollywood. She eyed Hanna critically up and down, and Hanna was struck abruptly with an acute awareness that she possessed only the one formal gown. "Miss Bradley," Narista murmured, raising a disapproving eyebrow. She extended her hand toward Hanna, palm turned downward.

Well, she was the daughter of the empress, after all. Hanna forced a smile onto her face and clasped Narista's wrist with her hand turned palm up beneath Narista's. "It's nice to see you again, Honored Ahn." Hanna was glad her voice managed to stay even.

"We didn't expect to see you this evening, Hanna," Kamm said, glancing from Hanna to Narista and back with a vaguely troubled expression. "Your name wasn't listed among the artists in the preview catalog."

Mr. Purcell spoke up. "I'm afraid those catalogs were already printed when one of our artists withdrew from the event, my lord. Miss Bradley was kind enough to allow us to use her work instead. Her name does appear in the artist list in the back of the event catalogs being distributed this evening."

The older Talessanin woman frowned. "Are these . . . friends . . . of yours, Narista?"

Narista took half a step forward so she stood slightly between Hanna and the older couple and turned a glowing smile on the woman, "We know Miss Bradley slightly. She's Jon's new little human neighbor. Lord and Lady Trakanaleth, may I present Miss Hanna Bradley." She turned to Hanna. "Miss Bradley, please meet Lord and Lady Trakanaleth. You have been introduced to their daughter, Saleniastanelen Ahnat."

Hanna swallowed. Salenia's parents. Salenia's parents were buying her painting? First, Lady Trakanaleth, then her husband, offered their hands to Hanna, haughtily, palm down as Narista had done, and Hanna clasped each in greeting, subordinate to superior.

As Lord Trakanaleth released Hanna's wrist, he looked over her head and smiled. "Ah. There you are at last," he said. "We were beginning to wonder if you had changed your mind."

Hanna turned. For a gasping moment, her pulse beat loud in her ears as all her blood rushed to her face at once, and then drained out the back of her skull leaving her a little light-headed. Jon wore an immaculately tailored black tuxedo. A lock of his loose, dark hair had fallen across his face. Salenia clung to his arm, barely contained in a jade-green gown that beautifully complemented her upswept coppery tresses. Again, Hanna was struck by how perfectly the two of them fit each other. They even wore matching startled frowns.

"Look who we've found," Narista enthused as Hanna blinked away her consternation and collected herself. *She could do this.* "It happens Miss Bradley is one of the artists with work in the exhibit," Narista went on. "And this is her good friend . . . oh dear, I didn't catch his name." She looked pointedly at Mr. Purcell.

"Harold Purcell," Hanna supplied, twisting her mouth into a smile. The buyer inclined his head looking a bit confused.

"Miss Bradley." Salenia glided forward, hand outstretched, palm down. "How very unexpected." Her voice dripped with contempt and condescension. Hanna clasped the woman's wrist, noticing how pale and stubby her own fingers looked next to Salenia's elegant manicure.

For a long heartbeat, Jon hesitated, his frown deepening as the awkwardness of the moment percolated through the group. Finally, Hanna drew a slow, steadying breath and offered her hand to him, palm up, subordinate to superior as she'd greeted the others. "Jonantathinel Ehr," she said quietly into the stillness, "it's nice to see you again."

Jon shifted uneasily. Then something twitched in his jaw, and he stepped forward to receive the greeting. As their hands closed on each other's wrists, however, he gently, but firmly, rotated his arm, turning both of their hands over, putting hers in the superior position. Hanna's heart stopped beating as Jon looked directly, almost defiantly, into her eyes. "Miss Bradley," he murmured. "It is always a pleasure to see you." He bowed over their clasped hands, his forehead brushing the back of her wrist. A variation. *Why hadn't she asked Tomin about variations?* Jon's breath, warm against her fingers, sent a shiver up her spine. He straightened—so tall—and looked down into her face again. Into her eyes. Almost directly into her soul.

Part of her wanted to fling her arms around him, bury her face in his chest, and never let go again. Fortunately, that part was quickly wrestled into submission by the part of her that was still afraid of him, the part that knew he really belonged with Salenia, and the part that had a deep and abiding desire to avoid making scenes in public. There was a loud crash behind Hanna, and she whirled, her hand sliding away from Jon's gentle grasp. Lady Trakanaleth's empty champagne flute lay smashed on the hard tile of the floor.

The salesman spoke rapidly into his earpiece, and a moment later a man swooped in with a broom and dustpan to clear away the broken glass. "My lord," the salesman said to Jon, "three minutes remain to place bids." Hanna's heart tripped over itself. Jon? *Jon* was buying her painting?

Jon blinked at the salesman as if only just realizing he was there. "Thank you," he said. "A moment, if you will." He looked around at the group and asked, "What do you think? Should I purchase it or allow the honorable senator the pleasure of paying the bill?" They all turned to contemplate Hanna's aspen grove. It was one of her larger pieces, painted on a bright afternoon last fall when the leaves were changing. The sky was very blue, and the sunlight filtered through the golden leaves as they danced in a soft breeze. She had always liked that painting.

Salenia tucked her hand possessively into the crook of Jon's elbow. "The colors would go well with the leather sofas in your living room," she said, "but it does seem very yellow. I've never much cared for such a bright yellow."

Her mother spoke next, "I still don't understand why you would wish to have paintings of Earth trees on your walls when you have so many Earth trees outside your windows." She sniffed. "But you must do as you think best."

"I like it," Narista said. "It's cheerful. Something about the way the artist captured the light coming through the leaves."

Jon regarded the painting thoughtfully. "Hanna," he said, "you are an artist, what do you think of this painting?" He turned to look at her. "Or perhaps you would like to show me one you painted, and I will buy that one instead?"

Hanna's cheeks warmed again. "I can't tell you which ones are mine," she said, trying to sound gently reproachful, but settling for not allowing her voice to crack. "It's supposed to be a secret. If I tell, they won't invite me back again next year." She shrugged. "As for this painting, I think if you're the one who has to live with it, you're the one who should decide. It doesn't really matter if an artist likes it, or if your friends like it, it only matters if you do."

Jon gave her a long look, nodded, and turned his gaze back to the painting.

"One minute left, my lord," the salesman said.

"Ah," Jon said. "Yes." He frowned at the painting. "Please raise my bid another two thousand dollars."

Hanna nearly choked.

The salesman tapped rapidly on the tablet. "Done, my lord," he said. He paused. "And the bidding is now closed. Congratulations, my lord."

Jon grinned, and Kamm clapped him soundly on the back. Narista looked appraisingly at Hanna, while Salenia glared daggers, and her parents looked disapproving.

Kamm turned to Hanna. "We're about to go in to dine," he said with a friendly smile. "Would you like to join us at our table, Hanna? I'm sure we could arrange for another place."

Jon looked sharply at his brother. Everyone else looked at Hanna.

"That's very kind," she said slowly, "But I think I'd better sit with the other artists where I was assigned. I think we're meant to be . . . um . . . on display."

Mr. Purcell stepped in, "You're exactly right, Hanna, though I'm not sure I'd put it quite that way. May I show you to your seat?"

"Yes," Hanna said. "Thank you." She took his arm, and he led her off through the maze.

As soon as they were out of earshot from the Talessanin party, Mr. Purcell laughed softly. "Well, Hanna Bradley, you are full of surprises, aren't you."

"I think I need to sit down," Hanna said. There didn't seem to be quite enough oxygen in the air.

Chapter 30

APPARENTLY, AN UNIDENTIFIED EXTRATERRESTRIAL NO-BLEMAN paying a record-breaking price at Future Vision 20/20 for a work by an unknown, first-time participant made a good human-interest story. Over the next week or so, Hanna was interviewed by several newspapers and two different morning television shows. She told them all that no, of course she never expected anything like this to happen; that yes, the Talessanins had been very nice when she met them; and that of course she found it exciting that there was a chance her painting would travel the stars. Then she gave out the contact information for the gallery through which her work could be purchased and thanked everyone for their interest. To her great relief, she managed to pull it all off without any embarrassing panic attacks—at least, not public ones. It was good publicity, but she was still glad when the reporters found a new headline, the whirl of excitement died down, and life took on its usual shape again, more or less.

Several more days passed before Mr. Purcell knocked on Hanna's door. She invited him into the kitchen, and he laid a check on her table.

"Congratulations, Hanna," he said, holding out his hand. "There's another one coming for work sold directly through the gallery, and you'll need to come by the gallery for some more paperwork, but this covers your share for all of the paintings sold through the Future Vision exhibit. Thank you for taking me along for the ride."

Hanna shook his hand firmly. "I appreciate you giving me the opportunity, Mr. Purcell."

"Please, call me Harold." he said. "I haven't had so much fun in a long time." He grinned. "I peeked out from the back room when the associate came in to get the paperwork for the aspen painting. The tall guy who paid for it dropped the sale contract like a hot rock when he saw your name on it."

A hollow knot formed in Hanna's belly. "He did?"

"He did. And then he picked it up and looked at it again, and his face lit up like Christmas morning. For a minute there, I thought he might kiss Maria—that's the associate. When he showed the others, the brother started laughing like it was some great joke, and I thought the redhead might faint. The older guy looked like his blood was about to boil. It was like a bad episode of reality TV. Have you seen them since? Did they say anything?"

Hanna hoped her laugh adequately hid her discomfort with the subject. "I haven't seen any of them since we ran into them at the show. I'm sorry, Harold, you'll just have to wait for the next episode like everybody else." She actually *had* seen her neighbors a few times, coming and going, but she'd kept her distance, and none of them had bothered her. The nightmares had receded somewhat, and she had only imagined seeing *him* in the woods twice over the previous week.

Hanna helped Harold carefully pack the last two landscapes in his car so he could take them back to the gallery for framing. He wanted to know when there would be more because there was now a waiting list for her work. She explained that she was out of canvases but showed him the partially constructed stretcher frames she'd already begun building in her garage and said she'd move as quickly as she could stretching the canvas and applying and smoothing the layers of gesso priming so she could get back to painting as quickly as possible. She understood that they didn't want anyone on the list to wait so long that the excitement wore off, and they changed their minds.

Harold gave Hanna a quick hug and a peck on the cheek as they stood in the gravel driveway and told her it was a pleasure to work with someone who understood about the business side of art. As she turned to go back inside, a movement caught at the corner of her eye from across the street. It took her a moment to realize that Jon was sitting on the roof of his house with his back against a chimney and that what she'd seen was him shifting positions.

Without thinking, she waved. After half a heartbeat, he gave her a small, seated bow in return. Hanna didn't want to think about what that little exchange might mean, so she went inside to put the check away and call Rachel to schedule a meeting at her office about investing the windfall.

A couple of hours later, Hanna was in her garage meditatively sweeping up the sawdust around her chop saw when a hand gripped her elbow. She flinched back, gasping in fright and surprise, and whirled to see Tomin standing there looking abashed.

"I'm sorry for startling you," he said, "but I couldn't seem to get your attention from the doorway."

Hanna drew a deep breath to slow her pounding heart and smiled sheepishly as she pulled the rubbery plugs from her ears. "Sorry," she said. "I usually wear earplugs when I work out here because some of my equipment can be pretty loud. I hope I didn't disturb you with my noise; I'm still not used to having neighbors."

"Not at all." He made a dismissive gesture. "I just had something to ask you."

She straightened and set the broom aside. "Actually, I've been wanting to ask you something too."

"Have you?" Tomin looked intrigued. "Then you go first."

Hanna laughed. "It's nothing really, I just wondered about variations for that greeting you showed me the other day—you know, the subordinate to superior thing."

Tomin's brow furrowed. "Variations? I don't think there are any variations for that one. Just up or down."

"But . . ." Hanna frowned, "I saw one."

"Are you sure?" Tomin scowled thoughtfully. He held out his hand. "Show me."

Hanna clasped his wrist turning their hands so hers was underneath. "It started out the same," she said, "so I thought it must be a variation, but maybe I was wrong. It was like this." She bowed over his hand, touching her forehead to his wrist.

Tomin snatched his hand away. "Don't do that!" He looked horrified. "Hanna, don't ever do that. Wherever did you see such a thing?"

Hanna was confused. "Why? What does it mean?"

"It means . . . it means servitude. No, stronger than that. Bondage. Assent to the other person's ownership. It's a very vulnerable position for a Talessanin, as it leaves all the upper *enan* exposed and in striking range." Tomin's hand rose to absently finger the smooth protrusion at the end of his first dorsal fin spine beneath his collar. "Historically, it was a slave's greeting to his master, but these days it's only ever used as a gesture of surrender when an enemy who has suffered utter, abject, humiliating defeat wishes to beg for mercy. You shouldn't ever do that. It's debasing. You're nobody's slave."

"But . . . then . . . why would he do that?" Hanna asked.

"Who? Where did you see this done?"

"At the art show. Jon . . ." She gestured helplessly.

Tomin frowned. "Someone surrendered to Jon at the art show? That doesn't make any sense."

"No, Jon greeted me that way. I didn't know what it meant."

Tomin stared at her. "Jon?" He waved a hand vaguely in the direction of the house across the street. "*Our* Jon?"

Hanna nodded. "Why would he do that?"

"I don't . . ." Tomin stopped and stared at her again. "What did you do? After he did that, I mean."

Hanna pursed her lips, trying to remember. "I don't think I did anything. Lady Trakanaleth dropped her glass, and it broke, and everyone turned to look, and he sort of . . . let go."

"He did that in front of other people?" Tomin sounded even more shocked.

Hanna shrugged. "Yes. And then the salesman said time was almost up, and Jon put in his last bid, and we all went in to dinner."

"I would've dropped my glass too." Tomin shook his head. "What did the others do?"

"I . . . I guess I didn't really notice."

"Did you walk in to dinner with him?"

"No. Kamm invited me to sit with them, but I was supposed to sit with the other artists, so I went with Harold Purcell. I think Jon walked in with Salenia. Should I have gone in with Jon?"

"It might have restored a modicum of his dignity if you did, but if he's going to behave like that, he deserves what he gets, even if he is . . . well . . . Jon."

"What if he does it again?" Hanna asked. "What should I do?"

"If he has any sense, he *won't* do it again."

"I'm serious, Tomin, what should I do?"

"I don't know. It's not as if there's a protocol for that. It isn't something people do. Except Jon, apparently."

"Right." Hanna stared at Tomin a moment longer, then shook her head to clear it. "You had something to ask me?"

"Yes," Tomin said, sounding relieved at the change of subject. "The thing is, Kamm is needed at the embassy tomorrow and will be taking Jon with him. Chance and I will be here, but it would be highly improper for Tala to be home alone with two adult males who are not related to her. All of Tala's tutors are on leave while Kamm and Tala are vacationing here, and Narista has her own plans for tomorrow. Kamm is wondering if you might be willing to come over and stay with Tala for a few hours. But he emphasizes that he can make other plans if you're not available. Tala asked me to be sure to explain that the two of you could finish your tea party if you come and to say that you may wear her pearl hair comb."

Hanna laughed, and Tomin grinned at her as he continued. "It would be from about three in the afternoon until five or six in the evening, and Kamm will see that she gets her supper after he gets back, so you wouldn't have to worry about meals or anything. Chance and I would be there as security, but we'd stay out of your way unless you wanted us for something."

Hanna considered. She was definitely going to need a break from building canvases by then. Tala was sweet. And Jon wouldn't be home. "Sounds fun," she said, "I'll be there at three."

Chapter
31

HANNA RANG JON'S DOORBELL A little before three o'clock
the next day, shoulder bag well stocked with sidewalk chalk, a
jump rope, a plastic bottle of bubble fluid, crayons, and a large
batch of homemade play dough. Tomin welcomed her into the living
room and went to fetch Kamm and Tala.

The aspen grove painting hung in a prominent place on the living
room wall. Salenia had been right about it going well with Jon's furniture, and the wall color set off the bright yellow of the aspen leaves as if
it had been chosen for that purpose.

The soft scuff of a careless footstep came from the hall to the bedrooms, and Hanna turned with a smile to greet Kamm, but it was Jon
who strode into the room. He didn't see her at first, focused as he was
on adjusting a sleeve fastener while he walked. The black leather jacket,
fitted trousers, and high, flexible black boots he wore reminded her of
the dress uniform he'd worn at the dinner party, but this was sleeker,
less ornate, more businesslike. This must be his real uniform. His working uniform. The one he wore when he killed people. Hanna caught her
breath.

Jon looked up at the sound and froze, startled.

"Hanna," he said. "You are early."

Hanna swallowed hard. "I didn't want to make Kamm wait for me." A tense silence stretched between them, neither moving until Hanna waved vaguely at the painting and said, "That looks nice in here. I think it likes its new home."

Jon's mouth formed a wary smile. "I was most pleased when I learned the name of the artist." His smile turned wry, and he looked down at his feet. "I must apologize for my behavior at the exhibit. I fear I embarrassed you. That was not my intent."

Hanna shrugged one shoulder. "I wasn't embarrassed. Seeing all of you surprised me, but I had no idea what your greeting was until I asked Tomin about it yesterday. I think you embarrassed Salenia, though. I imagine it must be rather uncomfortable for a woman to see her date offering surrender or servitude or whatever it was you meant by it, to some other woman."

Jon's eyes flicked back to her face, intense, almost fierce. "I was not her date. I did not even know she would be there. Narista and Salenia planned for our families to meet at the exhibit without informing Kamm or me. The Trakanaleths have been friends with my family for many years, and this is their first visit to Earth. It would have been dishonorable not to escort her when I was unattached. But I was not her date."

He took a cautious step closer. "When I stepped around that corner and saw you, I remembered what you said at the dinner party—that you were afraid I would walk in with Salenia on my arm and not remember you. And there I was, with Salenia on my arm, watching them greet you as an inferior." His head tilted, and his gaze intensified. Hanna's heart climbed into her throat as he said, "I wished to make it very clear to . . . to everyone that I am not courting Salenia, that I have not forgotten you, and that you are not inferior to *anyone*." Abruptly, he looked at the floor again. "But my . . . greeting . . . was very impulsive, and I did not consider how it might make you feel for me to be so forward when you were with another man. Human customs are so different. I am very sorry if I caused trouble for you."

For several heartbeats, Hanna couldn't respond. What could she say? But it hurt her to see him looking so miserable. Finally she said softly, "Harold Purcell is the art buyer for the gallery that sells my work. Since it was my first time participating as an artist in the Future Vision exhibition, he helped make sure I got where I needed to be, when

I needed to be there. He was just doing his job. He wasn't my date. And he had even less idea what you were doing than I did." She shrugged and attempted a small smile. "He found you quite entertaining, though, and I'm sure he'd love to sell you more paintings. You overpaid for this one by rather a lot."

Jon looked quickly up at her, then at the painting. "No," he said, tilting his head thoughtfully, "I do not think I did. Perhaps I will speak with this Harold Purcell about acquiring additional works by the same artist." He shifted his gaze back to Hanna and asked hesitantly, "So when he visited you at your home yesterday, he was not . . ." He looked away and didn't finish.

"He was dropping off a check and picking up two paintings," Hanna said. "And making sure I understood that I need to hurry and make more while I'm still somewhat of a temporary celebrity because one of my paintings was bought by a space alien, and some reporters said so on TV."

Jon coughed out a bitter laugh and shook his head. "I saw him kiss you, Hanna. When he was leaving."

Abruptly, he drew a ragged breath and straightened, looking away, his expression both ashamed and desolate. "I am very sorry, Miss Bradley. You do not owe me any explanations. Please excuse me." He bowed stiffly and moved to step around her toward a door on the far side of the room.

As he passed, Hanna's hand flashed out, startling them both as it pressed against his bicep, stopping him. "Jon," she began—and was suddenly intensely, breathlessly aware of his closeness, of his scent, of the heat of his body beneath the warm leather under her fingers. She drew a slow breath and didn't look at his face. "He did kiss me. On the cheek, like you might kiss Narista. It didn't mean anything."

Jon stood very still for a heartbeat. Two. Three. Then he murmured hoarsely, "Thank you, Hanna. It was difficult to tell from the roof. And I am sorry, I did not mean to spy."

Hanna didn't know what to say, so she just stood there, inhaling the spicy, leathery scent that was Jon and feeling her heart pound in her throat. What she really wanted, she discovered, was for him to put his strong arms around her, and hold her, and call her Little Mouse. But she couldn't forget what he was, what he had done. And she couldn't look at him.

Neither of them moved. The moment elongated, slow, and taut, and searing, until Jon leaned down to whisper, tentatively, "Hanna . . . when you kissed me in the treehouse . . . did that . . . mean anything?"

Childish laughter echoed down the hall, followed by a patter of footsteps, and the two of them shifted away from each other as Tala burst into the room. "Miss Bradley!" she squealed. "You came!"

Hanna laughed around the lump in her throat. "Of course I did, Tala. I said I would. And I brought some things for us to play with." She heard the door open quietly behind her, as Jon moved into the next room. Tala grabbed Hanna's hand and tugged her over to one of the couches so the two of them could look through Hanna's bag together.

From that vantage point, Hanna could see through the door Jon had left ajar. He stood just on the other side, turned sideways to her, looking into an open cupboard. She could see that, though this one was much subtler than the one on his dress uniform, this uniform, too, had a striking viper worked into the back of the jacket. Apparently, hidden sheaths and pockets had also been worked into it because Jon was methodically taking things out of the cupboard and stowing them in various places about his person. Several slender-bladed knives and daggers, some straight, others with sinuous curves and wicked-looking barbs, slid into channels on his back, forearms, and calves, their protruding hilts blending with the embellishments on his uniform. He tucked away several tools Hanna didn't recognize, then strapped a black holster to each thigh and stowed what she presumed to be more weapons in them.

He looked up from tucking something in the top of one boot, saw her watching him, and stilled, gazing back at her. One of his hands slowly rose to his forehead, dropped to his lips, then to his heart, where it turned outward and tipped toward Hanna, as if nudging something through the air in her direction. She didn't know what the gesture meant, but there was an intensity in his expression when he did it that stopped Hanna's breath. He held her gaze a moment longer, then turned back to his task.

"Miss Bradley," Tala chirped, "what is in this jar? May I open it?" Hanna looked down to see the treasure trove from her bag arranged neatly on the seat of the couch on the other side of Tala. The little girl was turning the bottle of bubble fluid over and over in her small hands, trying to guess from the picture on the label what wonders the bottle might contain.

"Let's go outside to open it," Hanna said. "Sometimes it makes a mess."

As the two of them stood, Chance stepped out of the room Jon had entered, pushing the door farther open. Behind him, Hanna could see banks of odd-looking electronic equipment and more large cupboards. "Honored Ehrat," Chance said, "the flutter pilot just called in. He will be here momentarily."

"Thank you. We'll be ready." Kamm's uncharacteristically solemn voice came from behind Hanna, and she turned to see him leaning against the frame of the broad arch that led to the dining room. He saw her looking and added, "Thank you for coming, Hanna. Do you need anything before we go?" His expression was thoughtful and intense. How much of her interaction with Jon had he seen?

Hanna was sitting on the top step of the porch blowing bubbles for a giggling Tala to chase around the yard when the pulsing beat of a flutter drive vibrated through the air, and the craft flickered into being out over the street, then lowered to the ground. Kamm emerged from the house, with Jon stalking beside him looking thoroughly lethal.

Tala skipped across the lawn and flung herself around her father's waist. "Goodbye, Baba!"

Kamm looked fondly down at her and ruffled her hair with his hand. "Goodbye, my Tala. Be good for Miss Bradley. Remember the rules." He smiled at Hanna over Tala's head. "Thank you again, Hanna, for staying with her."

Tala unwound her arms from Kamm and spun over to tug on Jon's hand. He dropped to one knee, and she wrapped her arms around his neck. "Goodbye, Bahta Jon," she said, and kissed his cheek. She looked him in the eyes and asked, "You will keep my Baba safe?"

Jon looked solemnly back at the little girl and said, "My life before his, little Tala." He smiled at her. "But today there will be nothing dangerous to protect him from. He only wants me to stand behind him and look frightening."

She giggled. "You do look frightening, Bahta Jon." She kissed him again on the cheek.

Hanna was struck by the loving trust the little girl had for her deadly uncle. She didn't see him as a menacing force of darkness or a bringer of death; to her, he was a protector and preserver of life, a force who shielded her and her father from all the darkness out there between the stars. She remembered Kamm saying it was the warriors who stood between evil and everyone else. This was what he'd been trying to tell her. Jon wasn't a weapon, he was a shield. Perhaps he'd been wielded as a weapon sometimes, but that wasn't his nature. He was a protector. This was why she'd always felt so safe with Jon's arms around her.

He had taken those children's lives at the order of his emperor, but he did not flaunt their deaths like medallions on his uniform. No, those deaths were carved into his soul like the scars he wore carved into his skin. There were reasons, he'd said, but there was no justification. No justification. No healing. Perhaps they weren't scars, but open wounds. What had he said that night in the treehouse? *Some wounds are too tender to uncover overmuch.* They'd been talking about her wounds then, and he'd offered comfort and acceptance. She'd felt so safe with him. But when he showed her his own wounds, what had she offered him? Fear. Contempt. Rejection.

Jon reverenced life enough to take life to protect it. It must be a terrible paradox to try to reconcile. He danced close to the Destroyer, he had said. And Kamm had said Jon carried burdens so others wouldn't have to.

Who made Jon feel safe?

He was standing, now, to go, and Hanna felt frozen to the porch step. He looked back at her, and the pain behind his eyes stung as he offered a small bow and turned away.

"Jon?" Her voice was cracked and sounded hollow. He turned toward her again, and she searched for something to offer him. Something that wouldn't wound him even more. "Yes, Jon."

His brow furrowed slightly; it wasn't enough. She cleared her throat. "What you asked me before," she said. "Yes, it meant something." Understanding dawned in his eyes, and a slow smile lit up his face. She couldn't help smiling back. He took a small step toward her, then looked over his shoulder to where Kamm waited. "You should go," Hanna said. "We can talk when you get home."

"Thank you, Hanna." His voice was a rough whisper. He held her gaze with his for one more long, compelling heartbeat. Then he turned again and left.

Chapter 32

J ON DIDN'T RETURN HOME UNTIL well after midnight. For the most part, Kamm's mediation had gone well, though it had not gone as planned. But it had taken far too long for Jon's liking.

Almost as soon as the meeting began, one of the Genatu ambassador's bodyguards attempted to plant a pulse tab on the Hikanu First Minister. The Hikanu bodyguards intervened, then retaliated, and a brief, small-scale battle ensued right there in the embassy conference room.

Kamm, seated at the head of the table, raised one hand, and Jon, who was anxious to get this over with so he could go home and speak with Hanna, solved the problem by turning off the oscillation dampener on his transpod and teleporting onto the center of the conference table. The mind-numbing *whomp* produced by the unregulated release of the tiny flutter fold broke the glass in three of the observation windows and left everyone who had been standing sprawled on the floor.

Kamm, the Ambassador, and the First Minister remained seated at the table, though the Honorable Ambassador and His Dignity, the First Minister looked rather shaken.

The Viper slunk silently down the remaining length of the polished wood tabletop, directing a stern glare at each person in the room. When he reached the foot of the table and turned, one of the Genatu bodyguards pulled a weapon. Jon flicked a throwing knife into the man's wrist almost without looking and continued his slow, deliberate prowl back up the table. When he neared the head of the table, he paused at the place where the stunned Ambassador and First Minister sat across from one another. He locked eyes with each for a moment, until each gave under the weight of his gaze. "Settle this," he said firmly.

Kamm arched an eyebrow at his brother, and Jon responded with a small, slightly defiant tilt of his chin. Maybe Jon's methods were unconventional sometimes, but they were effective. And he was in a hurry.

The Viper bowed respectfully to the Kanestelan Ehrat before re-engaging the oscillation dampener on his transpod and, with the flutter fold now properly regulated, teleporting silently back to his position behind Kamm's chair. Kamm continued what he had been saying as if there had been no interruption, and the negotiations went smoothly after that.

In fact, in Jon's opinion the negotiations went a little *too* smoothly. At the end of the scheduled time, the adversaries were on the verge of settling a boundary dispute that had festered for generations, and Kamm consented to continue mediating their negotiations after a brief break for a meal. Jon chafed at the delay.

During the break, Kamm phoned Hanna to ask if she could stay later than originally agreed upon or if he needed to make other arrangements for Tala. Jon grew increasingly and unreasonably jealous of his brother's easy smile and laughter while he spoke with Hanna about his daughter.

Jon desperately wished he could think of a good reason to call Hanna himself, just to hear her voice again. *Yes, it meant something.* What did it mean? Something different from the "nothing" that the kiss of a friend or a brother meant to her. But what, exactly, did that mean? And did it *still* mean something, or had its meaning been obliterated when he told her about himself?

He longed to ask her. To feel the press of her hand against his arm again. To hear her laugh. But he had to settle for a quick security report from Chance instead, and the absurd rush of exhilaration he felt when Chance told him Hanna was playing with Tala in the treehouse. Jon told himself he was twelve kinds of a fool, but the thought of Hanna's hands touching the boards he had nailed into place made him smile anyway. He tried to imagine Hanna's expression when Tala showed her the framing for the small house, which he'd built since she last visited. And his mind filled with the bewitching memory of her sitting on the platform in the moonlight with her gown disarrayed from her imaginary tea party . . .

And she had stayed. What would it be like to go home to his own house and find Hanna waiting there for him?

Of course, when the diplomats finally stopped talking, and Kamm was at last willing to actually go home, it wasn't Hanna who came out to meet them on the front lawn, but Chance. Jon realized the plunge of disappointment he felt was irrational, but that didn't make it go away.

"Report?" Kamm asked Chance while Jon collected himself.

"A good time was had by all," Chance replied solemnly. "Hanna taught us a new game called hopscotch, and she and Tala made all the letters of the English alphabet with some kind of modeling compound and then made little statues of all of us doing nonsensical things. We had pizza with pepperonis delivered to our very own doorstep, and Hanna taught Tala how to make chocolate bundt cake. But we're not allowed to eat it until you get home because Tala wishes you to see that she made it all by herself. Also, because Hanna insisted that Tala must go to bed at a somewhat reasonable hour, I have been charged upon pain of death to deliver this to you immediately upon your arrival."

He handed Kamm a folded piece of paper, which Kamm opened to find a childish drawing of Tala standing in front of a waterfall with a rainbow arching overhead.

"Pain of death?" Kamm asked.

"That's an exaggeration," Chance admitted, "but she was very insistent." He handed another folded page to Jon. "Hanna didn't want you to feel left out." Jon unfolded the paper and discovered a clever, stylized drawing of a little brown mouse smiling mischievously out at him. Over the mouse's head arched another rainbow, an addition clearly made by a different artist's enthusiastic hand. Chance continued, scrutinizing Jon's face. "She's asleep on the couch in the family room and asked me to have you wake her when you got home."

Jon tried to keep his expression neutral but felt one corner of his mouth quirk upward momentarily.

Chance nodded. "That's what I thought. Beyond the shallows and into the deeps. Are you sure you know what you're doing, my friend?"

This time, Jon offered him a wry smile. "I am sure I do *not* know what I am doing. But I am equally certain that I wish to continue doing it anyway."

Chance regarded him thoughtfully. "You do know people will . . . talk."

Jon met his eyes. "I am the Viper. People talk about me." He tilted his head inquiringly. "What about you, Chance?"

Chance heaved a dramatic sigh. "After all we've been through together, you have to ask?" Jon glared at him, and Chance put a hand on his big friend's shoulder. "I stand with you, Jon. My life before hers if you ask it of me. And you could definitely do worse than Hanna, even if she is a human."

Jon grinned at him. "Ah, well, as long as you are with me, I always have a Chance."

Chance rolled his eyes. "Funny how that works in English, isn't it?"

Jon's face went solemn, and he shrugged disconsolately. "It may not matter very much where you stand on such a thing. Hanna is difficult to read, but I think she is merely strolling idly along the shore, trying the feel of the waves on her toes. In all likelihood, she will decide she does not like to get her feet wet and will go home where it is dry to have her lunch. With a nice human man who has no fins and does not go around killing people."

Chance grinned wickedly. "And who could blame her, really. And then you would be forced to settle for your choice of a hundred beautiful, wealthy *ahnats*. But if Hanna is what you want, I wish you fair skies and good hunting."

"And," Kamm interjected, "if Hanna is what you want, maybe you should go wake her up."

"Yes." Jon hesitated. "And then what?"

The other two laughed, and Chance said, "That's always the question when it comes to women, isn't it?"

Kamm added, "We'll give you a count of twenty before we come in, but I'm not going to stand out here all night."

Jon glared at both of them, squared his shoulders, and headed for the house.

Hanna was indeed curled up on the sectional sofa in the family room. Her hair tangled across a pillow Jon recognized as one from his bed, and the soft throw from the chair in his bedroom was draped over her sleeping form. Had she gone into his room to get them herself, or had Chance or Tomin fetched them for her? Best not to imagine Hanna in his bedroom, he decided. But his pillow would smell like her tonight.

He knelt on the floor beside the couch and studied her face—her delicate, *human* face. Humans were so like Talessanins. Her features were a little more rounded, perhaps, than a Talessanin woman's would be but only enough to make her seem elegantly exotic. With her hands and arms covered by the blanket, it was difficult to see much difference. Relaxed in sleep, her face lost the slight, wary tightness it habitually wore like armor. Her mouth was full and soft. The gentle curve of her neck just below her ear called out for him to trail his fingertips along it. He wanted to push the blanket back and trace the clean lines of her finless forearm. But it would be unforgivable to touch her without her consent.

For a few long moments he just knelt there, drinking in the sight of her face like a draught of cold spring water after a long, hot day at sea. He drew a deep breath and whispered her name. "Hanna." She shifted slightly in her sleep but did not wake, so he tried again a little louder. "Hanna?" Her eyelids fluttered and opened, and he smiled as her sleepy gaze focused on his face.

Hanna's eyes sprang wide, and she sucked in a sharp breath, flinched back against the couch, and froze. Blood drained from her face, and her breathing became quick and shallow. He had triggered another panic attack.

"Hanna," Jon said soothingly, "it is—" Hanna's quick backhand caught him by surprise, connecting solidly on his cheekbone right under his eye and knocking him off balance. The sudden shock of unexpected pain triggered an auto-response in his armor's defensive systems, and his transpod flicked him instantly to the other side of the room.

Hanna rolled off the couch and tried to stand up, but her feet tangled in the blanket; she scuttled backward until her back fetched up against a wall, where she sat gasping and shuddering.

And, of course, that was when Kamm walked into the room and saw her, disheveled and white-faced, cringing against the wall.

"Hanna?" he said, sounding confused. Then his voice became alarmed. "Hanna, what's wrong?" He hurried toward her, following her wide-eyed gaze to where Jon knelt on the other side of the room, his hand pressed to his cheek.

"S-sorry," Hanna gasped. "Need a minute." She closed her eyes, and her breathing became slow, deliberate.

Kamm knelt protectively beside her, directing a horrified glare at his brother. "Jon," he demanded, his voice a low growl, "what did you do?"

"I startled her," Jon said. "Hanna, I am very sorry."

Kamm looked back and forth between Jon and Hanna. "She doesn't look startled to me, Jon, she looks terrified."

Hanna opened her eyes again and placed a placating hand on Kamm's arm, clenching her teeth and battling to get her breathing under control.

Kamm took her trembling hand in his and asked earnestly, "Hanna, what did he do? Should I have him taken out back and flogged or just make him scrub all the bathrooms every day for a week?"

Hanna's voice, when it came, was a whisper that sounded close to a sob. "Just please tell him to take that thing off his face."

Jon's hand drifted to the other side of his face, and he realized that he still wore his *enkalan*. No wonder he had startled her so badly; she'd never seen him wear it before. He slid his fingers under the edge and pressed the disengagement node. The display darkened as the red electronic eye turned off and the neural links retracted, then the dermal bond released, and the black half-mask came away in his hand.

"I am sorry, Hanna," he murmured again. "I did not realize. I suppose I have become so accustomed to the display that I do not always think about it. I forgot I was still wearing it. I am sorry I frightened you, Hanna."

Hanna nodded. Her breathing was still shaky and very deliberate, and her jaw kept clenching and unclenching, but a little color was returning to her face. "May I s-see it, Jon?"

He stood carefully, not wanting to startle her again, and walked slowly across the room. Crouching down next to his scowling brother, he handed his *enkalan* to Hanna.

Hanna avoided Jon's eyes as she took it from him, holding it cautiously by the edges with shaking fingers, as if it might sting or burn her at any moment. She studied the darkened red reptilian eye and the snake scale patterning on the front side of the *enkalan* and ran a thumb down one of the two long fangs that curved from the bottom edge. She turned it over and ran a fingertip lightly over the smooth inner surface, feeling the slight static charge that lingered there. "What is it?" she asked softly. Her breathing was beginning to even out.

"It is called an *enkalan*." Jon kept his voice low and gentle. "It is the neural interface that allows me to operate various technological systems in my armor without using my hands. It also extends my sight into several non-visible spectra and shows a visual display of useful information."

"Technological systems," Hanna said, turning the *enkalan* again in her hands. "That's how you got over there." She waved a hand toward the other side of the room.

"Yes. One of the systems works a lot like a flutter drive. At least, it folds and pierces relative space in much the same way, but the distance it can move things is comparatively limited."

"You can walk through walls." Hanna made it a statement, not a question. "And you can be invisible."

"I . . . can." Jon said. "Among other things. It is one of the reasons we are called the Nine Winds. This technology allows us to move unseen, like the wind, and gives us greater mobility in battle. The secrets of constructing these armor systems are carefully guarded, and the use of some is restricted to a few specialized military units."

Hanna drew a deep breath and avoided looking at Jon as she held out the *enkalan*. When he reached to take it, Jon's fingertips brushed hers, and she flinched away.

"Your hands are cold," she whispered.

Jon tucked the *enkalan* into its storage pocket in his armor. "That happens when we teleport," he explained. "Something about rapid moisture evaporation in the Void. The armor has a heating system, but still, too many 'ports in a short time can cause hypothermia."

Hanna absently wiped her hands on her knees. Was it the feel of the *enkalan* she was trying to rub away or the touch of his hand?

"Hanna . . ." Kamm's quiet voice held an intense undercurrent. "How do you know about the invisibility and phase shifting? They're not common knowledge among humans."

She flicked a glance up at Kamm but looked down again at her knees and drew a deep breath before she spoke. "A long time ago . . ." She paused, as if considering what to say. When she continued, her words were careful and measured. "A long time ago, I woke up in the middle of the night, and there was a man in my room. He wore one of those masks. He . . . did something to me so I couldn't move, and he took me . . . away."

Jon felt suddenly sick. "No!" He lurched to his feet. "Kamm, they were not supposed to remember! We were promised they would not remember!"

Kamm shook his head. "There were a statistically insignificant number of subjects for whom the memory patch didn't work properly. It was thought they'd all been found and the problem fixed." He sighed and made a helpless gesture with one hand. "Too much time has passed to patch it now. The memory chain would be far too long."

"What are you talking about?" Hanna's voice was tense, pinched. "You *know* about this?"

"It was before my time on the council," Kamm said grimly. "But I have seen the reports." He sighed and settled back on his heels. "Earth was first discovered by smugglers. We don't know how long ago for sure; they kept a low profile. But eventually their activities here drew the attention of intergalactic law enforcement, and an official exploratory expedition was dispatched. The discovery of alien beings that so closely resembled Talessanins caused quite a stir among the researchers, and they sought and received permission to collect a number of sample specimens from various locations around the planet for the purpose of biological research."

"Biological research?" Hanna said, her voice small, like a frightened child. Tentatively, she added, "It did seem like a laboratory. They . . . had needles. And things. I couldn't move." Her breathing became ragged again. "They cut me. But then they fixed it, and nobody believed me because there were no marks."

Kamm frowned. "It was usually noninvasive, but sometimes they fixed things, if they found a problem."

Hanna blinked at him, brows furrowed. "Fixed?"

Jon's stomach felt like he'd swallowed a stone. "Oh Hanna . . ." His voice had gone hoarse. "It . . . it might have been me. I am so very sorry."

Hanna looked up at him and blinked. "Wh-what?"

Kamm explained. "Specimen collection on Earth was one of Jon's duties after he joined the Winds. Their special abilities are useful for such tasks. That was when Jon first came to Freebridge. It was one of the collection nodes."

"Not publicized." Hanna turned her frightened eyes to Jon. "That was four years before the embassy ships."

"Yes." He nodded miserably. "In the autumn. I . . . liked it here." He looked down. "I am sorry, Hanna."

"It wasn't you," Hanna whispered hoarsely.

"It might have been. There were so many. It was so long ago. I don't remember their faces." Perhaps he should. "It might have been me."

"No. He was shorter than you. His . . . *enkalan* . . . had a fur texture, and more teeth, and he had a scar on the other side of his face." Her finger traced a line down her face from forehead to chin."

A wave of relief passed through Jon. She was right; it had not been him. "Dalathek," he said. "That would have been Dalathek."

"You know him?" Hanna laughed. At least, Jon thought it was a laugh—there was more than an edge of hysteria to the sound. She scrubbed her hands over her face. "Of course you know him." Her voice was so brittle.

Again, it was Kamm who explained. "Dalathekenial of House Kanestelan commanded the Nine at the time, Hanna."

"Kanestelan . . . you're *related* to him?" Hanna's voice skewed higher in pitch, and she pressed back against the wall, drawing her legs more tightly up into her chest.

Kamm frowned. "Not by blood. Senior members of the household staff also carry the family name. Dalathek came into House Kanestalen as arms master when my father married my mother. Before Dalathek went into the Winds, he taught Jon to fight. But he was ejected from our House and banished from the empire when Jon took his place as Commander. He is now known as Dalathek Al-Khenat because he belongs to no House."

"Arms master." Hanna looked back and forth between Jon and Kamm before finally settling on Jon. "He . . . Dalathek . . ." her tongue tangled in the unfamiliar name, and she drew a shuddering breath to begin again. "Dalathek was your commander?" The words rasped against each other. "He was your . . . your friend?" She rubbed at her forehead with shaking fingers. "Your . . . m-mentor?"

"Yes." Jon kept his voice gentle. "What is it, Hanna?"

For a long moment she stared at him, her eyes wide and haunted, barely breathing. Jon backed a little away from her, giving her space. She drew several slow, gasping breaths, fighting back her panic. Then, hesitantly, she choked out words. "After the . . . the laboratory, he took me to a sh-shed. He kept me there, and . . . and he . . ."

Realization hit Jon like a tsunami and rage flooded through him. "Dalathek was the one who raped you?" he demanded.

Hanna cringed. "Yes." Her whisper cut through Jon, dagger sharp, and he choked on his own breath.

"Raped . . .?" Kamm rasped.

Hanna's gaze remained focused on Jon's face. "He taught you to kill. He taught you to . . . to torture people. To . . ." Her voice trailed off, but her eyes searched his face.

Jon's blood turned to ice. What did she see when she looked at him now? He was her tormentor's apprentice. An implement of anguish that had been smelted, shaped, tempered, and polished at the forge of the demon who inhabited her nightmares. Jon was the spawn of death and darkness. How could she ever care for him now?

He swallowed hard. His voice was barely more than a fierce whisper, but he held her gaze steadily as he said, "I am not Dalathek, Hanna. I make my own choices."

She stared back at him, weighing what she saw. What she knew. "No," she breathed at last. "You're not him."

"Oh, Hanna," Kamm said softly, "I am so very sorry. We didn't know he'd done it before."

"Before?" Hanna gasped, and her eyes flickered to Kamm.

Kamm sighed. "After the Winds completed sample collection on the North American continent, they moved on to Europe and Asia and then to the more southerly land masses. They were nearly finished with the task when Jon noticed his commander engaging in secretive behavior and disappearing for long periods of time without explanation. On one such occasion, Jon followed Dalathek and observed him entering a small cave. Jon waited for him to come out, and when he didn't, after a while, Jon followed him in. Dalathek was standing over a girl who was lying, drugged, on a grass mat in one corner. She'd been . . . raped."

"And . . . c-cut?" Hanna choked.

Jon remembered the bloody, crisscrossing patterns carved into the other girl's skin. Had Dalathek done that to Hanna too?

"Yes." Kamm looked at her, his brows drawing together. "And cut. Dalathek was repairing her injuries. He claimed he'd just found the girl like that and had been helping her."

"The damage was too fresh." Jon rubbed at the back of his neck, remembering. "It happened while I sat outside doing nothing." He closed his eyes. *No one had helped Hanna either.*

Kamm cleared his throat. "Jon took her to the researchers, who repaired her injuries and patched her memories. Then she was returned to her family. Based on later observations, she didn't remember the experience."

"She said it was him," Jon muttered. "Before they patched her memories, she said it was him."

"Jon brought an accusation against the Commander before the Throne," Kamm went on. "It was referred to the High Council for judgment. The Council's finding was that the medical evidence was inconclusive, the timing was impossible to establish with sufficient certainty, and the girl's mental condition might have made her mistake a rescuer for an attacker. Furthermore, they concluded that because humans are not citizens of the Empire, they are not entitled to the same protection under imperial law. They decided to drop the charges. Perhaps they would have decided differently if they knew he'd done it before."

Jon pushed himself to his feet and paced to the other side of the room, scrubbing a hand through his hair.

Kamm continued. "Jon was angry and challenged Dalathek before the Throne for command of the Nine Winds, knowing the challenge was to the death. Jon soundly defeated Dalathek, but my father could not bear to see his friend killed by his stepson, so he intervened. Dalathek was cut off from House Kanestelan and banished from the empire."

"I should have killed him." Jon almost didn't recognize his own voice when it pushed out of him, bitter and harsh. "I should have killed that contagion when I had the—"

A terrible gagging, sobbing sound wrenched from Hanna's throat, and Jon spun to look at her. Her arms curved around her belly, and she seemed to deflate, folding down over her knees, burying her face in the blanket that still tangled around her legs. Her breath began to shudder in and out in ragged gulps, and her shoulders shook silently. It took Jon a heartbeat to realize that she had begun to sob uncontrollably.

He found himself on his knees beside her almost before he knew he had moved in her direction. He wasn't sure what to do. He wanted to hold her, stroke her hair, wipe away her tears. But what if touching her made it worse? He looked helplessly at Kamm, but his brother only frowned and shook his head. Jon leaned toward Hanna, careful not to touch her. "Hanna," he said softly, "how can I help you?"

Hanna leaned slowly into him, resting the side of her head against his chest. He placed one hand carefully on her shoulder, not wanting to frighten her. At his touch, she unwound her arms from her knees, and wrapped them around his chest, twisting to press her face into the leather of his body armor. Her shoulders shook even harder. Jon slid down next to her with his back against the wall and gathered her into his lap like a little child, rocking her and whispering gentle nothings. He barely noticed when Kamm left the room.

After a while, the wrenching sobs subsided, and Hanna's body relaxed into Jon's embrace. The two of them just sat there a little longer in the dim silence with their arms around each other. It felt good. Right. Healing.

Without moving, Hanna drew a shaky breath and whispered, "I'm sorry." Her voice was small and shaky. "I didn't mean to come apart like that."

"Do not be sorry. You had good reason."

"It's just . . . nobody ever believed me before. I told my parents what happened to me, but they remembered me staying home from school for several days with a stomach bug. They didn't even know I was gone."

"He probably used a memory patch on them," Jon murmured.

Hanna nodded mechanically. "My father said only a filthy-minded whore would make up a story like that. He left us about a year later." She sighed and settled closer against him before continuing, "The psychiatrist at the hospital told my mother it had probably been an isolated psychotic episode or a hallucination brought on by a high fever, because I seemed to believe it actually happened, even though it obviously could not have. They put me in a residential treatment facility for a while.

"After the embassy ships landed I tried telling another therapist about it, but she said my brain was just trying to make sense of my previous hallucinatory experiences by mapping them onto something from real life.

"One therapist told me it was okay to treat it like a real experience because my brain thought it was real, and it had traumatized me the same as if it had been real, and the nightmares and panic attacks were certainly real. But nobody ever actually *believed* me before." She shrugged, her body moving tantalizingly against Jon's. "It caught me off guard."

Jon freed a corner of the blanket from the tangle and used it to dab carefully at the tears that were drying onto her cheeks. "It should never have happened to you, Hanna. I am so very sorry."

Finally, she pushed a little away from him and sat up enough to look up into his face. Her eyes were red from crying.

"It feels good to have some answers after all these—" She stopped, and her mouth twisted into a vague frown. "Jon," she said softly, "you're bleeding." She gently touched his right cheekbone, then brushed her fingers near his eyebrow. "Did I do that? I'm so sorry."

Jon chuckled softly. "No, you did not do that, Little Mouse. You did this." He smiled and pointed at his left cheekbone, which he could feel beginning to swell. "The blood is from my *enkalan*. The neural link connects through my skin directly into two facial nerves that run near the surface there, and it bleeds a little when I take it off. But Talessanins heal quickly, and it is nothing to worry over. It has probably already stopped bleeding."

Hanna used another corner of the blanket to wipe at his face, still frowning slightly. "You're right," she said. Her face softened. "Still, I'm sorry I hit you. For a moment I thought you were him."

Jon grinned. "Then I am glad you hit me. He certainly deserved to be hit."

Hanna choked on a startled giggle. Then she leaned forward to place a kiss on the arch of his eyebrow, one on his right cheek, and a gentle whisper of a kiss on his swelling left cheekbone.

For a stunned moment, Jon hardly dared to breathe; it was such a sweet torment that he didn't want to break the spell of it. But *what did she mean by it?* She was human; it was a puzzle.

Slowly, he took her hand in his and placed a kiss in her palm, folding her webless fingers around it. "Hanna," he asked softly, hesitantly, "did those kisses . . . mean anything?"

Her lips made a soft, enticing smile. "Yes, Jon." She leaned forward and placed another kiss on the tip of his nose. "They meant I'm glad you're home. And they meant I made a mistake, and I'm sorry, and I hope I haven't ruined everything, and I hope we can be friends again." Her brows drew together ever so slightly, and her lips drew into a pensive pout as she studied his face, waiting for his response.

Jon swallowed. "Friends?" He tried to keep the disappointment from his voice.

She heard it, though, because her smile widened again, and her eyes sparkled as she added teasingly, "Very good friends. Maybe with a romantic claim of the sort that lets you kiss me whenever you like. But I might need to know more details about what that would entail before I commit that far."

Jon's heart rolled over. She *did* care for him! In spite of everything, she could still care for him.

But what did she mean? Was that an invitation to kiss her? What if he tried, and it hadn't been, and it made her hate him again? What if it had been, and he didn't do anything, and she thought he didn't *want* to kiss her?

Gently, cautiously, he raised one of his hands to cradle the side of her delicate face. "Could I kiss you now?" he whispered, hardly daring to hope.

Hanna laughed. "I wasn't sure you'd want to," she said. "But I'm really hoping you will."

So he did. His kiss was tentative at first, a sort of question without words. She answered him tenderly in the same language, and his other arm slid around her waist, pulling her closer. She snuggled against him, and her hands slid up his chest to his shoulders and tangled in his warrior's braids. When her fingers found his first *enan*, he pulled back again, just to look at her.

And when his lips met hers again, his kisses stopped asking questions and began answering them instead, thoroughly, hungrily, and with great conviction.

Chapter
33

HANNA'S FEET CRUNCHED ACROSS THE gravel. Jon's soft boots made almost no sound as he glided beside her, and his black uniform blended into the night. He might almost have been a phantom, a figment of her overactive imagination. Except, the big hand that enveloped hers, with the finger webbing that gave gently to make room for her own fingers between his, that was solid, and strong, and substantial. And when she stepped into the pool of light at the bottom of her porch steps and drew him along behind her, the rest of him solidified too, undeniably real. And that look on his face—soft, unguarded, and content, perhaps even a little bit smug—that was not a look that could be faked. Her cheeks warmed under his gaze, and she gave him a small, self-conscious smile.

He tipped his head inquiringly, and she laughed as she let go of his hand. "You look like the cat who stole the cream," she teased, fishing in her pocket for her front door key.

Jon lounged back against the porch post, grinning impudently back at her. "I think I am much more pleased than that," he said, "and what I took was freely given." His grin slipped and turned into a slightly troubled frown. "It was, was it not?"

Hanna laughed. "Yes, Jon. Very freely given."

Jon's frown only deepened.

"What's wrong?" Hanna stepped closer to him. "What are you thinking about? "

Jon shrugged and looked at his feet. "I was wondering . . ." He shook his head. "It does not matter."

Hanna put her hands on her hips. "If it's going to make you scowl like that, it matters to me," she said. "Out with it."

Jon shifted uncomfortably against the post and studied Hanna's face. Then he looked at his feet again. "It is not important."

"Did I do something wrong?" Hanna asked. "I don't know half enough of your Talessanin customs yet. If I do something wrong, you should tell me so I can fix it."

Jon's eyes flicked up to Hanna's face. "You did nothing wrong, Little Mouse. It is only . . ." He drew a deep breath and straightened, his expression earnest and almost shy. "I do not understand why you changed your mind about me. I am a little afraid that you might change it back." He stepped toward her and laid a big hand gently against her cheek. "But I am also afraid that if I press you to answer such questions I will push you away again, and it is more important to have you with me than to know your reasons for being here."

Hanna smiled teasingly. "I didn't know the Viper could be afraid of anything."

"You might be surprised." He looked down, and his webbed fingers dropped away from her cheek.

She caught them on their way down with her free hand. "Please ask me anything you want." She was very serious now. "Whenever you like. I might not always have a good answer, but I will always try."

Jon's gaze rose again to meet hers. He shrugged one shoulder. "Why, then? I am the same man from whom you fled so quickly that you forgot your shoes. You know so many things about me that you do not like. None of that has changed. None of it will ever change. What is done, is done. I am . . . how did you put it? I am . . . the bogeyman in every child's dark closet. Why would you allow me near you? Why would you allow me to touch you? To . . . to kiss you? In the morning, in the light of day, will you come to your senses and regret . . . this?" There was a plaintive note threading through his voice, and he looked away again as he finished speaking.

Hanna shifted closer to Jon and squeezed his hand, waiting until he looked at her before she answered. "You're the same man who watched chick flicks with me too," she said, "and the one from the dinner party. And the art show. You're not the bogeyman, Jon. You're the thing lurking in the bogeyman's dark closet. You're what the monsters are afraid of. I'm sorry it took me so long to figure that out. I think I was simplifying things too much, trying to make it all black and white when it's more complicated than that.

"The things I know about you that I don't like are things I'm pretty sure you don't like either. And that says a great deal about the kind of man you are. Those things aren't demonstrations of who you really are, they're more like . . . like violations against your true self. Otherwise, they wouldn't hurt you so much. I'm glad I know those things about you. They help me understand you better. I'm not saying I'm happy about them; I'll never be happy about them. But I think they have helped shape you, in some ways, into the man I like so much. The one who can be both strong and gentle. Who knows how to just sit quietly together, but also talks to me like I matter and knows how to listen. The one who is loyal to his family and his empire. Who values life enough to dance with the Destroyer to protect it. You're the bravest man I know, Jon. And you make me laugh. Taken all together, looking at all of you as a whole, I think you're the kind of man I want to be with." She looked down, scuffing at the porch with the toe of one shoe. "I don't know if I can. I've never been any good at relationships, and the truth is, this one scares me in a lot of ways. But I want to try anyway. At least . . . if you still do too."

In answer, Jon gathered her into his arms and drew her against him. She snuggled her cheek into the solidity of his armored chest, and he propped his chin on the top of her head. After a moment he cleared his throat and released her from the embrace. Gentle fingers under her chin tilted her face up until her eyes met his. Jon's gaze was intense, and she thought for a moment that she saw a tear on his cheek, but he leaned in abruptly to kiss her again, long and lingering, and she wasn't sure. When he straightened again, he murmured gruffly, "Good night, Little Mouse." And then he just turned and left.

Hanna watched him until his black-clad form was swallowed up in the darkness of the night outside the circle illuminated by her porch light before she unlocked her door and went inside.

Chapter
34

J ON STOPPED AT THE EDGE of his lawn and turned to look back, heart pounding, hands clenched to keep them from trembling. He waited until Hanna went inside and closed the door before he continued across the grass and into his own house.

When he entered the armory, Chance was already executing the final check and nightly lock down of the security system. He watched Jon from the corner of his eye, a musing expression on his face.

"Yes?" Jon's voice was more abrupt than he intended. He pulled the door of his weapons locker open and began divesting himself of his equipment.

Chance grinned. "I've seen you abort missions on occasion, but I don't think I've ever seen you run away before."

Jon continued checking weapons and tools and carefully placing them where they belonged. He wished the thoughts whirling through his mind could be sorted and put in order as easily. "I have not engaged in this sort of skirmish before," he said after a while. "She caught me off guard."

Chance snorted. "I've watched women throw themselves at you from one end of the empire to the other, Jon—the ones that aren't terrified of you, anyway. If it's not the imperial bloodlines, it's the mystique of the Viper in the Night."

"Hanna is not throwing herself at me." Jon scowled at his friend. "But I suppose you watched the whole thing on the feed."

"You needed a chaperon. Kamm thought Hanna would be more comfortable without an obvious audience. Think of it as a compromise."

Jon's scowl deepened as he broke down his pulse pistol and laid the parts in their padded compartments. "I am living on Earth. Hanna is a human. I should be allowed to court her according to human customs."

Chance choked on a laugh and raised a suggestive eyebrow. "Human . . . *customs*?"

Jon slammed the pistol case closed and shoved it onto its shelf. "You know that is not what I meant."

Chance sighed. "Hanna may be human, Jon, but she's still a woman, like all the other women."

Jon fished the last knife from his boot and stowed it. "No. Hanna is different. And not only because she is a human. When Hanna looks at me she does not see the Kanestelan Ehr, and I do not think she sees the Viper anymore. She knows those things about me, but when she looks at me, she sees *me*. She sees the man I am underneath the bloodlines, and the stories, and the political positioning. She sees the things I am proud of, as a man, and the things that shame me, and still she wants me." He closed the locker. "It is . . . disconcerting."

Chance still looked skeptical. "And Hanna is the only woman who can give you that? What about Salenia? Your families have been friends since the two of you were children. She must know Jon, the man, even better than Hanna does."

"I do not want Salenia. I want Hanna."

"Salenia would be a more logical choice. She's beautiful, intelligent, accomplished, and when she inherits, you'd inherit with her. Everyone practically expects it already—your brother as the next emperor and you at the head of House Trakanaleth. All neat and tidy and without any of the fuss that would come out of the Viper courting a human. And she followed you here for a reason. It isn't as if Earth is her regular vacation spot. She might say she's visiting your sister, but she's here for you."

Jon rolled his eyes. "Salenia is certainly decorative. And she has all the proper political connections. But she does not want to be with me, Chance. She only wants to be *seen* to be with me. I think nothing would make Salenia happier than if I married her in the most lavish ceremony ever witnessed in the empire and then went off and died heroically so she did not have to actually live with me afterward. Unless I rescinded my abdication first. That might make her happier. She has known me for a long time, but when she looks at me, it is not a man she sees, it is wealth, and power, and position, and the triumph of fulfilling her parents' expectations. Hanna sees *me*."

Chance shook his head, frowning. "And what do you see when you look at her?"

Jon glanced over at the feed monitor, which still showed Hanna's little cottage. A light came on in what must be her bedroom, and his pulse quickened. He drew a deep breath. "I see . . ." How to put it into words? "Home. I see home, Chance."

Chance knew better than anyone else what that meant to Jon. He studied Jon's face more closely. "Beyond the deeps, then, and into the dark reaches of unexplored ocean abyss." He nodded, solemn. "And where is Hanna?"

Jon shook his head. "Off the shore, perhaps, and splashing in the breakers." He closed his weapons locker and leaned his forehead against the cool wood of the cabinet door. "Am I a complete fool, Chance?"

Chance chuckled and clapped a hand down on Jon's shoulder. "You know I've always said so, Commander," he said brightly.

Jon shot him a sideways glare. "Commander?"

Chance grinned wickedly and shrugged. "My lord?"

Jon rolled his eyes. "Why do I feed you?"

On his way down the hall, Jon slid out of his jacket and detached the electrical connections from the contact points on his conductive under-tunic. The things itched abominably. He hung the jacket in its case in the back of his bedroom closet and engaged the recharging unit.

As he began to close the case, his eye was drawn to something caught on the edge of one of the fasteners—a long strand of Hanna's hair. Carefully, Jon untangled the strand and coiled it around his finger. When had it caught there? When he held her while she wept, or later when she pressed her cheek into his chest before he kissed her goodbye? Thinking about holding Hanna made his heart beat faster again.

He crossed the room to his desk and took out two small boxes. One was his pocket brazier, which began to heat up when he tipped the lid open. The other was made of ivory and held a number of *taless* seeds.

He poked through these with his finger before selecting one. Carefully, he wound the strand of Hanna's hair around the seed. He touched it to his forehead, his lips, his heart, and placed it in the center of the small brazier, then knelt, head tipped back, palms raised, as the white smoke began curling up from the seed, filling his room with the rich aroma of his prayer for Hanna.

He remembered the way she'd laughed after she caught him staring at her painted toenails. Their first dance at the dinner party when he'd placed her hand over his heart, and she'd left it there. The cool smoothness of her skin the next evening when he trailed his fingers along the lines of her damp foot with its tiny, painted lemon slices, and the gentle touch of her fingers tracing the scars on his own skin. It had been so delightful, then, to think she liked him just for himself, not even knowing about his family or his work. But he realized now that the delight had held an undercurrent of fear and sadness because he knew she would not want him anymore once she found out more about him.

Except she did. She knew the worst, and she neither delighted in the dark things nor pretended they did not exist as other women had done. She knew, and she understood what he was, and she accepted all of him, even the parts she didn't like. The thought wound around some deep seed of his soul.

Chapter
35

HANNA TURNED ON THE LIGHTS and checked all the locks. She hummed softly as she turned the lights off again, undressed, and shrugged into an oversized T-shirt and soft leggings for bed. If there were nightmares tonight, they'd be a small price to pay for the way she felt when Jon kissed her. Just thinking about it sent shivers through her body again.

When she went to brush her teeth, she caught her reflection in the bathroom mirror smiling a soft, dreamy smile, and shook her head at herself. Silly. She glanced down for a moment to put toothpaste on her toothbrush, and when she looked up again her eye caught a movement behind her in the reflection, a glint of red in the black shadows of the hall.

It was starting already.

She sighed.

Then the black form stepped out of the shadows and through the bathroom doorway, filling the space behind her in the mirror.

She froze, gasping, and choked on a familiar sour, musky odor in the air as his scarred face leered over her shoulder. Dimly, as if they were far away and detached from her brain, her hands scrabbled on the bathroom counter for something—anything—to use as a weapon. His arm snaked inexorably around her shoulder, and his cold hand clamped over her mouth, solid, unyielding, and very, very real.

Dalathek!

Chapter
36

JON'S PRAYERS WERE INTERRUPTED BY the sharp, buzzing noise the security system made when a sensor was triggered. Probably another bird or one of those furry creatures that kept trying to get into the trash receptacles. Chance was still calibrating the system to account for the variety of local wildlife. And Chance would take care of it. The *taless* seed was burned nearly to ash, though it still held its shape, with only the thinnest trickle of smoke drifting upward. An insistent, piercing beep joined the buzz, and Tomin's footsteps padded down the hall toward the armory. Tala's sleepy voice called out, but Jon couldn't tell what she said. Nor could he make out Kamm's soothing response. Chance's booted footsteps beat rapidly down the hall, and the door to Jon's bedroom flew open, slamming against the wall. The *taless* seed crumbled to dust in the bottom of the brazier. The heating element clicked off.

"Jon. Come now." Chance's voice was tight, his dark face tighter. "They have Hanna."

For half a choking heartbeat, Jon just stared. Then he was on his feet and striding toward the front of the house. "Who?" he demanded. "Who has her?" *He would kill them.*

"I already called for backup and a medic flutter," Chance reported. "We just need to stall until they get here."

"How do we know she's even still alive?" Tomin's voice, calling out from the front porch.

Jon's blood froze. He stumbled.

Chance caught his elbow. "Slow, Jon. And calm."

He was right. Going out there in a panic would only escalate the situation, whatever it was. Jon took a deep breath and exhaled slowly before stepping out onto the porch next to Tomin. A faint burnt smell hung in the night air, and a warm shivering sensation trickled over his skin and made his hair try to stand on end; the particle shield had been activated.

Jon's gaze rapidly assessed his surroundings before focusing on the dark, armor-clad figures who occupied the street outside the shield, illuminated by a security lantern that cast one side of the figures in stark whites and the other in inky blackness, like actors in a shadow play.

Two pairs of flank guards made four. In the center, four more stood guard around a fifth man, who crouched next to something on the ground.

Hanna.

She lay crumpled on the cracked pavement, and the man was doing something to her neck. She wasn't moving. Jon reflexively gave the mental commands that should have triggered night vision and bio data, but of course he had taken off his *enkalan*, so there would be no night vision, no heart rate, no weapons recognition, no teleporting. He wasn't even wearing his jacket, so the best he could hope for from his armor was a limited level of impact reduction if something hit him in the leg.

The man straightened and shoved Hanna hard with his boot. "Wake up, you filthy sow!" he bellowed. "Prince Honorable's idiot lapdog wants to see you breathe." Nothing happened, so the man kicked Hanna hard in the ribs. This time she stirred and moaned softly.

"You see?" the man called out. "It's still alive. For now." He looked back toward Tomin, and the surreal lighting showed Jon the triumphant leer on the scarred face.

Dalathek. Dalathek had Hanna.

"Ah, there you are, Lord Commander." Sneering mockery twisted Dalathek's voice. "I was beginning to wonder if a mouse was the wrong bait for the Viper after all."

Jon took half a step forward, but Chance tightened his grip on Jon's elbow. "*Think* Jon!" he whispered urgently. "You are unarmed and unarmored. You can't help her if you're dead." Jon managed a slight nod, and Chance's fingers relaxed again.

"Very well," Tomin called back, his voice steady and calm, "she is alive. What do you want in exchange for her?"

"What do I want?" Dalathek called back. "I told you! I want that plague-ridden serpent who stole my life!" He thrust an accusing finger at Jon. "I want justice!"

"If you got justice, you'd be dead! You raped that girl!" Jon spat the words without thinking, then desperately wanted to call them back. The last thing Hanna needed was for him to antagonize her captor.

Dalathek barked an incredulous laugh. "It was a *human*, Jon! Legally they aren't even people. The worst I was guilty of was a little animal cruelty." He kicked Hanna again, and this time she struggled to push herself up to her hands and knees, but one hand slipped in the loose gravel and she collapsed again. Dalathek laughed and leaned down to grab a handful of her hair, wrenching her up onto her knees. "You are such a hypocrite, Jon! I saw you pawing at this one not half a span ago."

"Keep him talking," Chance murmured. "Embassy security reports backup in two minutes. The medics are ready, but they can't shift until it's safe."

Jon couldn't think what to say. His mind whirled, and his eyes were riveted to Hanna's wide-eyed, bewildered face. What had they done to her?

"Of course humans are people," he called. "Genetically, they're almost indistinguishable from us. It's only a matter of time before the laws recognize it."

"Indistinguishable? You think so?" Dalathek sneered. "Shall we cut this one open and see?" He slid a slender dagger from a sheath on his thigh and trailed the tip of it down one side of Hanna's face, down her neck, across the base of her throat. As it came to rest just above her collarbone, a dark trickle oozed from under the dagger's tip.

Dalathek yanked Hanna's hair again and spat in her upturned face. "Or maybe you'll come with us, and I'll let it live." The dagger moved slightly, and the trickle grew bigger, unmistakable even in the uncertain lighting.

Jon shifted forward, and Chance tightened his grip on Jon's elbow again. "Find your roots, Jon," he hissed.

He was right. Jon slid into his pre-battle breathing exercises, calming his mind, slowing his heart, bringing everything into focus.

"I'm not going to wait all night, Jon!" Dalathek called out. "I know you've got company coming. If you don't want this malignancy back, I'll just take it with me and try it out myself." He shifted his grip to Hanna's waist and hauled her to her feet, pressing the length of her body against his.

Jon twisted his arm away from Chance and strode across the lawn. Dalathek's guards shifted into shielding positions, and the flankers drew in closer.

"Jon!" the voice behind him was Kamm's. He must have joined the others on the porch. Jon hoped Tala was still safely in her room; whatever happened here, Tala should not see it. But Jon was *not* going to let Dalathek have Hanna. Not again.

Jon's mind slid into the clear, still space from which a warrior fought just before he stepped through the stinging tingle of the particle shield. No going back now—things could pass through the shield in only one direction.

"Stop!" Dalathek ordered. Jon stopped.

"I'm unarmed." Jon held his hands out in front of him, empty palms displayed.

Two of the flanking men pointed pulse pistols at him while their companions checked Jon quickly, but thoroughly, for weapons and lashed his wrists together.

"You have me. Now let her go."

Dalathek laughed. "I said I'd let it *live*, boy, not that I'd let it go." Dalathek took several steps closer to Jon, dragging Hanna with him. "I'm still going to have my fun with it. But if you're very good, I'll let you watch." The tip of his dagger drifted from Hanna's collarbone and skittered down the front of her baggy shirt, leaving a tattered line of rips in the fabric, coming to rest just below her waist. "I've been watching you," he added conversationally. "For days. It has not been easy trying to find a way through your security system." He shook his head reproachfully. "Your protocol encryption is particularly devious."

"Let her go," Jon said again, more forcefully. "She has no part in this."

"Oh, but I think she does." Dalathek laughed mockingly. "It wasn't until I saw you with her that I realized I didn't have to go to you, I could get you to come to me." Hanna swayed as Dalathek wound his fingers into her hair again. This time her legs bore her weight, if unsteadily, but her face was still a mask of disoriented terror. Dalathek twisted his hand, pulling Hanna's head back and around until she looked up into his scarred face. "We'll have lots of fun together won't we, Little Mouse," he crooned. He leaned down and kissed Hanna full on her mouth. Hanna's body went rigid, and Dalathek turned a triumphant leer on Jon. "It *is* a tasty morsel, isn't it?" he taunted.

Everything that happened next came to Jon with perfect, slow-motion clarity, but he couldn't move fast enough to stop it.

Hanna's body convulsed, and she vomited down the front of Dalathek's body armor.

Dalathek flinched. His face transformed into a mask of rage and disgust, and he released his hold on Hanna. Unsupported, she staggered, falling forward into the dagger, plunging the blade deep into her belly. As she collapsed, the dagger tore upward through her body, and Jon heard metal grate against bone.

His reflexes flung him into action even before Hanna hit the ground. Bound hands moving together, he smashed one guard's throat with the back of his elbow, throwing him back into the guard behind, who was taking aim with a pulse pistol.

The man on Jon's other side went down under his return swing, blood spattering from his shattered nose. Jon fell with him, twisting sideways and back; the beam from the fourth guard's pulse pistol grazed the top of Jon's shoulder before hitting the particle shield. Feedback from the shield shot back up the pulse beam, spewing sparks, and the pistol exploded. The stink of burned meat permeated the air.

Jon rolled. The ground where he'd lain spat dirt as a round from a projectile gun thudded into it. He rolled again and used the momentum to regain his feet. Dodged sideways.

Chance shouted.

No time to listen. Jon grasped a charging guard's wrist with both bound hands. Spun outside and down. Peeled the dagger from the guard's fingers and yanked down, breaking the arm over his shoulder. Pain skipped across Jon's ribs—knife in the guard's other hand. Jon whirled and plunged the dagger he held through the guard's eye into his brain. The guard's collapse yanked the dagger from Jon's grip.

Keep moving.

Dalathek roared at his men.

Three loud pops from the projectile gun. One round crackled as it ricocheted off the shield. Another hammered into Jon's armor over his left hip.

Move.

Which guard was shooting bullets? Found him. Lunged closer. A spinning kick to the wrist sent the gun flying. Next kick caught the guard in the throat.

A blade thudded into Jon's shoulder, and he whirled, feet skittering on loose gravel. A pulse pistol beam sang through the air where he'd just stood. Jon danced aside as another throwing knife grazed his arm. Rolled beneath a pulse beam. Came up just in time to see the gunman's head explode.

Chance was there, his own pulse pistol drawn. "You insane?" he bellowed.

The distraction gave the knife-thrower time to close on Jon, dagger drawn. Jon flung his hands up. Caught the blade on his right forearm. Fin spines shattered and black sparks swam in Jon's vision. He kicked in the man's knee, felt the joint break, and danced away, shaking his head to clear it. Chance's pulse pistol sang again, this time toward the tree line, picking off another dark figure.

A vibrating purr thrummed through the air. Another. Then a third. Embassy security forces began dropping to the ground even before their flutter craft landed.

Where was Hanna?

She still lay where she'd fallen. A pool of blood spread slowly across the asphalt under her, puddling in the cracks. *Too much blood.*

Jon's knees hit the pavement beside her. "Hanna?" His voice was hoarse. He cleared his throat and tried again. "Hanna?" This time his voice was plaintive, like a child's. He wanted her eyes to open like they had when she was only sleeping on his couch. He wouldn't even mind if she backhanded him across the face again. "Hanna, please!"

She didn't respond, but her chest rose and fell in slow, shallow breaths. *She was alive!* Carefully, he pulled back the edge of the gaping rip in her shirt and examined the wound. Dalathek's dagger was still wedged in the bottom edge of one of her ribs, but the point extended down into her abdominal cavity, not up through her diaphragm and into her heart or lungs as he'd feared it might. Blood trickled from the gash in her belly in the kind of steady stream that indicated organ damage, and there was a smell he knew meant nothing good, but there was no arterial spurt, and that gave him hope.

Chance knelt beside his friend. "I'm so sorry, Jon. The medics will be here as soon as the perimeter is secured."

Jon moved his still bound hands up to Hanna's face, stroking her cheek with the backs of his fingers, leaving bloody trails across her ashen skin. Pain stabbed through his broken fin bones every time he moved his right hand, but he didn't care. Chance reached over and cut Jon's bindings. "Hanna," Jon whispered. "Please wake up. His left hand kept stroking her cheek, while his right drifted down to where her hand lay flung out on the pavement.

Tenderly, he bent to place a kiss in her cold palm, closing her limp fingers around it. "Please wake up, Little Mouse."

Chance patted Jon's shoulder and stood to survey the scene.

Hanna's fingers twitched in Jon's hand. Her eyes opened ever so slightly, watching him from under her lashes. Her lips pressed together, then parted slightly with the exhale of her shallow breath. "Jon?"

"I am here, Hanna. Stay with me," he begged.

"Hurts," she breathed.

"I know it hurts, Little Mouse. Help is coming. Stay with me."

She just watched him for a few breaths. Then, "Cold." Tears began to trickle from beneath her lashes and she closed her eyes.

"Stay with me, Hanna." He had nothing to warm her with but his bloodstained undertunic. He stripped it off and draped it over her. "Hanna, open your eyes, you need to stay awake." He stroked her cheeks, kissed her hand.

Her eyes stayed closed.

Then Chance was pulling at him. "Jon, you need to move, the medics are here."

Jon looked up blankly.

"You need to get out of the way," Chance repeated.

Two men in the red tunics of medical professionals shouldered in next to Jon, and a third dropped to the ground on the other side of Hanna's body. Their hands moved efficiently over Hanna, examining her wound, checking for a pulse, for a breath. Please, Gentle Gardeners, let her breathe.

Jon let Chance pull him away from her but not very far.

Two more medics hurried over and began connecting tubes and wires from some kind of medical machine to Hanna's body. One of them swore and skittered around to the back of the machine, punching buttons furiously. One of the other medics shouted a long stream of technical medical jargon at the button-pusher. Jon didn't understand very much of it. Something about blood. A third medic stood and stepped over to where Jon stood with Chance still gripping his arm to keep him out of the way.

"What's happening?" Jon demanded.

"Some of the equipment isn't calibrated for humans," the woman explained, "but we're fixing that. We need to know what medications she was given."

"Medications?" Jon was completely at a loss.

"There are two very fresh transjection burns on her neck. Do you know what medications she was given?"

Jon had never felt so helpless.

Chance said, "We don't know. Probably something to knock her out and something to wake her up again, but we don't know what or how much."

The medic's mouth tightened into a thin line. "We'll figure it out."

Jon's hand clutched the woman's arm as she turned to go. "Do not let her die." It sounded too much like an order. A threat. "Please," he added, "she cannot die." Now he sounded like he was begging.

Perhaps he was.

The woman's face went grim. "Honored Ehr," she said, "we are doing our best for her." She inclined her head and pulled away to go back to Hanna.

Jon let her go.

Chapter 37

JON PACED THE LENGTH OF the corridor and back. Again. He was sure the soft lighting and the vining plants that grew from niches in the stone walls were meant to sooth, but after so many hours of waiting, they only seemed to mock him, to sneer at his complete impotence. He was a reaper of life. Not a sower. Not a cultivator. There was nothing he could do to help Hanna.

He stopped again to look out the open, stone-framed window at the corridor's far end. Somewhere on the other side of the complex, the sun was going down, cooling the fresh air that came in through the window and casting the snow-capped peaks in a soft, rose-colored light. Too soft. Too calm. As if her world knew she was dying and was smoothing her way to the Beyond.

No, he reminded himself. She wasn't going to die. They said the repairs had been successful, and she would recover; she just needed time to heal. She would be well again. He knew that. In time.

But that kind of knowing was not enough. He needed to see her. To hold her. To look into her chocolate eyes and feel the warm softness of her skin against his. And for that kind of knowing he had to wait.

He paced back to the other end of the corridor. Kamm didn't look up from his seat on the bench carved into the stone wall just outside the doors to the surgical chamber. The hum and whir of medical equipment seeped out from behind the doors, mingled with the solemn murmur of unintelligible voices.

When would they let him see her?

Would she even *want* to see him? Would she let him touch her? Or would she flinch away from him again as she had when he'd told her he was the Viper? Had she seen him kill Dalathek's men, or had she already been unconscious? If she had seen, would it change the way she felt about him?

He paced back to the window and stared out at the darkening horizon.

Behind him, Kamm shifted restlessly. Cleared his throat. "I need to see about Tala," he muttered. He sounded as weary as Jon felt.

Jon didn't turn around as his brother's footsteps thumped across the floor. The small door halfway up the corridor hissed open, letting in an irritating tinkle of soothing music, which cut off as the door slid closed, then intruded once more when it hissed open again. New footsteps entered, stopped just inside the door, and then shuffled aside as a second person entered the corridor and the door closed. Tomin and Chance.

"How is she?" Tomin asked.

"Recovering. As far as I know. They haven't let me see her yet." Even Jon could hear the wretchedness in his voice.

Tomin sighed. "At least come wait in the visitors' lounge. It's cold out here in the corridor."

Jon set his jaw. "I'm not going anywhere."

Footsteps approached, and a hand landed on his shoulder—the one without the pulse pistol burn. "She's going to be all right." Chance leaned both elbows on the window ledge and looked solemnly out at the mountains before adding, "And she'll be safe here. I've checked all of Kamm's security measures—the ones for the orbital port, the ones for the embassy, all of them. The medical facility is under tight watch, the high security guest suite they've prepared for her could withstand a plasma canon barrage, and all the key access points in the entire complex have doorknobs fitted with high quality scanning systems, so no one is getting in without the proper authorization."

Jon nodded numbly. Chance was probably right. She would be well. She would be safe. But he still needed to see her open her eyes.

He sighed and changed the subject. "You have a report, Tomin?"

"Nothing new. The trackers are still closing in on him. It's just a matter of time."

Time again. Time seemed to be piling up on top of Jon, mocking him with its refusal to be hurried.

He sighed and scrubbed one hand back through his braids. He was such a fool. "I should have . . . maybe if I hadn't—"

"Jon." Chance nudged him with his elbow. "You can't play that game. You know better."

That was true enough. Done was done. Second-guessing after the fact did no one any good. Commanding the Winds had taught Jon that, if nothing else. Still, this was different. This was Hanna.

"Her heart stopped twice in the flutter shuttle on the way back to the medical facility." Jon had never felt so powerless in his life. "What if—"

"How's your arm?" Tomin interrupted gently, leaning against the wall by the window.

They were right. It did no good to chase the tail of what could never be undone.

Jon sighed and turned toward Tomin, folding his arms across his chest. "I'm to have another crooked fin spine; broken one too many times to fix without regrowing it. But they say it'll hold. The rest are patched together well enough."

Tomin prodded gently at the tight bandaging that swathed Jon's forearm, inspecting the hair-thin filaments that protruded from between the layers. "Looks like you held still long enough for them to get the bone stim nodes inserted." He nodded approval. "A couple more days, and they'll be good as new. No hard swimming for a while, though I imagine."

"It doesn't matter." Jon's voice was gruffer than he intended, but he didn't want to fuss about his arm when Hanna's injuries were so much worse. He stalked down the corridor and slumped onto the bench Kamm had vacated, groaning softly when the move reminded him of his other injuries.

Chance sat beside him, studying Jon's face. "You need to get some rest. We'll wait here while you shower, and get something to eat, and sleep for a couple of hours. One of us will fetch you if anything changes."

Jon shook his head and stopped prodding at his bruised hip. "I'm fine."

Tomin snorted. "You're not fine. You haven't eaten since they brought her in yesterday. And sponging off behind a screen doesn't even come close to counting as proper hygiene. You won't help her by making yourself sick."

"I can't leave her."

"Kamm said they're keeping her sedated until morning. She won't even know you left."

"I'll know."

Chance made an exasperated chuffing sound and paced down the corridor. "I know she's important to you, but—"

"She let me kiss her, Chance. Without asking. You saw." Jon didn't even try to hide the desperation in his voice. "How can I leave her now?"

"She *kissed* you?" Tomin stared. "Are you serious? A week ago, she could hardly stand to look at you."

"They worked it out," Chance said wryly. "Be happy for him."

"I am happy for him. It's just . . ." He sighed. "Jon, are you certain you really want to do this?"

Jon leaned his elbows on his knees and scrubbed both hands through his braids. "I am certain of very little, Tomin. Courting a woman is not the same as planning a battle. And courting a human is . . . confusing. I am not even certain she will still want me when she wakes. I am only sure that I want this. I want *her*. And I am not leaving."

Tomin cleared his throat again. "You need to think this through carefully, Jon. What will your mother—"

Jon leapt to his feet. "I am not a child. My mother has no say in this."

"Your mother is the empress; she has a say in everything. And your stepfather—"

"I resigned. I no longer dance at the emperor's command."

"But if the Assembly doesn't—"

"I thought you were with me on this, Tomin."

"I *am* with you." Tomin raised a placating hand. "But sometimes being with you means reminding you of reality instead of just cheering from the sidelines while your theatrical fancies run away with you."

"This is not a whim."

"I know that. I do. You've retired. No more going off to battle. You've decided to settle down somewhere on the edge of nowhere and play house instead, and to do that properly, you're going to need a wife. Fine. I get that."

Jon started to speak, but Tomin cut him off, deepening his voice into a sardonic imitation of a master storyteller's solemn intonation. "And since you are the only product of that fateful union between the Imperial Kanestelan bloodline and that of the Holy Mithekarian priest kings of the Old Empire," he dropped the solemnity, but not the sarcasm, "it's probably high time you started producing lots of little *ahns* and *ehrs* to follow in your illustrious footsteps and all that. Which also requires a wife."

Jon glowered at him. "That is not—"

"I just want to make sure you're thinking this through. I like Hanna. I consider her a friend. I want to see her well and happy. But Jon, *think*. Is she the best match for you? I'll grant you she's convenient—a tempting little human tidbit right across the street from your new little human house in your new little human town. And she's pretty enough. I can imagine she must be soft, and sweet, and fun to play a little kiss and cuddle with when nobody's looking. And she's certainly a quick learner. But you're the Viper, Jon."

"Not anymore," Jon growled.

Tomin set his jaw. "You are Jonantathinel of House Kanestelan Ehr, eldest son of the Empress Among the Stars, greatest Commander of the Nine Winds, Subduer of Worlds, legend of the Talessanin people. There is still talk that you could be our next emper—"

"No." Jon snapped. "My abdication stands. It will always stand. Kamm is the diplomat, not me. He is still the one the empire needs at its head. None of that has changed just because I retired from the Winds."

"Maybe not. But with the factions gaining strength in the Assembly and the Council, you are—"

"I am a man, Tomin. And I am tired. I do not want to be a legend. I do not want to be an emperor. I want to be just a man. I want to eat cookies and have picnics and build treehouses and watch silly, two-dimensional movies with my feet on the furniture while I eat popcorn and drink strawberry slushies. I want to go to art shows and try to guess which paintings are Hanna's. I want to sit for hours and watch her face while she sketches down by the lake." Something in her eyes went . . . distant . . . when she sketched, as if she must be seeing everything, all at once, all the way through. It was not a thing he could describe adequately, but he had seen it that night at the lake, and he wanted to see it again.

He sighed. "When Hanna kisses me, I can tell that it is *me* she is kissing. Not my reputation, not my bloodlines, not my inheritance from my father. Me. Jon. The man."

"Jon, you could have your pick of a hundred beautiful, wealthy, Talessanin *ahnats*. If you picked one from a minor House, that would make it all the easier to fade out of the public eye if that's what you're after. Getting involved that deeply with a human will only call more attention to you. And you've only known Hanna for a couple of months. Earth months. Half of which she wasn't even speaking to you."

"Tomin." Jon glared at his friend. "I want Hanna."

"And you're sure about that? Even if it makes a mess?"

"Yes, Tomin. I am sure."

Tomin studied Jon's face one last time, judging his resolve. Then he straightened, folding his arms across his chest, a broad grin spreading across his freckled face. "Good," he said brightly. "Because this is a mess I've been looking forward to making ever since I saw the look on your face when she brought that cake over the first day."

"I swear to you, Tomin," Jon growled, "If whatever you are scheming in that head of yours does anything to damage this for me, I will—"

"I know." Tomin stood. "Viper and all that." He grinned. "Don't worry, I like playing in messes. Especially other people's messes."

Chance chuckled darkly. "Why else would anybody join the diplomatic corps?" He shivered. "You're right about one thing, though, Tomin. It is cold out here."

With a resigned shake of his head, Tomin muttered, "Fine. Chance, you stay with him. I'll get someone to bring over a tray from the kitchen. And a clean shirt. And a coat. And an update on Dalathek."

Chapter 38

LIGHT BLED, JACK O' LANTERN orange, through Hanna's eyelids and left a taste at the back of her throat like watermelon taffy mixed with furniture polish. Her heart thumped a slow rhythm in her ears, throbbing hard against her temples. Nearby, voices called nonsense to each other. The high one. The low one. The high one again. Her eyes drifted open, blinked blearily into the hot whiteness of the blinding light suspended above her.

The low voice. The high one. The breathy drone of a machine. Thin tubes hung down from the dark void above the light, shifting in the air like seaweed in a lazy ocean current. Near her elbow, a floating glass tray supported what looked like a collection of surgical instruments. Or dissection tools. The dimness beyond was exaggerated by the dark afterimage the light left on her retinas.

Hanna knew this dream. The lab came between the moonlight in her bedroom and the horrors of the shed.

And if she knew it was a dream, she could wake up. She *had* to wake up before *he* came to take her to the shed.

Except . . .

Sluggish, drug-fuddled memories oozed up from the dull ache below her ribcage. A black shadow in the hall. A webbed hand over her mouth in the bathroom mirror. A stinging flash of silver at her neck.

Not a dream.

His hand in her hair. *His* mouth on her mouth. *His* arm pinning her body against his.

Not a dream!

Panic welled up, hot and blinding. *He* had already come for her! And now she was back in the lab. It was all happening again.

"N-no!" Her defiant scream burbled from her lips as a barely coherent mumble.

Her mind and body strained against the anesthetic torpor, and she flailed clumsily, trying to sit up. Her efforts succeeded only in making her rotate slowly, tilting at an awkward angle, until the light was behind her, casting her shadow on the glossy floor a few feet below.

There was nothing holding her up! She hung suspended in the air between the floor and the light like a dead animal floating in a jar of nonexistent formaldehyde, tangled in the seaweed tubing and the clinging fabric of a thin, white chemise. She thrashed again, trying to angle her feet toward the floor.

One drifting arm caught in the tubing—warm against her skin, pulsing as if it were alive. When she jerked reflexively away, her elbow snagged another tube. Pain flared sharp in her gut, and the end of that tube slithered out through a hole near the waist of her chemise, trailing drops of blood that wobbled in the air as if they'd forgotten how to fall. Another thrash, and a second tube ripped free of her abdomen, sending wobbly drops of pale diamond to dance with the ruby blood droplets.

An alarm shrilled. Voices jabbered.

He would hear them! He would come! She had to get out!

She flailed, and her foot caught the edge of the glass tray, sending it careening. Metal implements scattered, some gyrating lazily through the air near her hand, while others spun off to one side and clattered to the floor.

If they could fall, she could fall. She just needed to find the edge of . . . of whatever was holding her up. She wriggled, groping numbly for the way out.

A hand clamped down on her outflung wrist, and she yanked back hard. Instead of pulling her free, though, the motion flung her whole body sideways, slamming her into the hand's owner. Gravity engulfed her, flinging her onto the floor. Pain stabbed through her belly when she hit, then dissolved and trickled off into the muddled drug haze. She rolled and shoved against the floor with both hands. She had to get up. Had to get away.

A wave of sick dizziness made everything slide sideways, and the floor tilted up to smack her in the shoulder. Something glinted on the floor beside her hand. One of the metal instruments she'd knocked over. She snatched at it—better than nothing, whatever it was—and heaved herself backward until she collided with the wall, where she scraped herself into an unsteady crouch and raised her weapon. The thing had a blade, scalpel-small and sharp, curved like a scythe. Like a claw.

Red-robed figures converged on her, sliding and lurching in her uncertain vision, reaching toward her.

"NO!"

This time the scream tore free of her throat, a raw, animal shriek that echoed off the walls.

Across the room, a door burst open. Footsteps. A booming shout as a new figure loomed into the chaos, face obscured behind the burning white of the hanging light.

He had come for her! *Dalathek* had come for her!

Again!

The red figures backed off as he stepped in front of the light, a shadow now, haloed from behind.

He would take her. She couldn't stop him. But she refused to cower at his feet. She levered herself against the wall and pushed, swaying, to her feet. She raised her claw blade.

He stopped. Hesitated. Took half a step closer, holding his palms out to show they were empty. "Hanna? Hanna, it is all right. You are safe." It was Jon's rasping voice.

Her blade wavered.

"J-Jon?" She squinted up at him, trying to see his face through the dizziness and backlit shadow.

But sometimes, in the dream, he wore Jon's face. *Was this a dream?*

Slowly, he lowered himself to his knees on the floor in front of her, and the change in the angle of the light showed her the dark braids, the high cheekbones, the pleading hazel eyes—she could fall into those eyes forever and never find the bottom. He wore a black longcoat draped over his shoulders like a king's robe. Like a knight's cloak. Like a super-hero's cape.

"My honor, Hanna," he said solemnly. One hand touched his fore-head. His lips. His heart. "You are safe. You are in the medical facility at the Talessanin Empire's North American Continental Embassy on Earth. And you are safe."

The mental haze was slowly clearing, drawing in its wake a trem-bling weakness and a growing ache in her belly.

Another memory drifted to the surface. Pain. Stark shadows. The smells of blood and vomit and something burnt. Dalathek's harsh whisper: "*This is not finished!*" Jon whirling out of the darkness like an avenging angel, lit stark white on one side, black as death on the other, as his enemies fell before him—The Viper in the Night.

"You k-killed them," she gasped. She swayed on her feet.

His whole body went tense and still. "You saw? I was not certain." His voice had lost its urgency and taken on a careful wariness. "I am sorry, Hanna; I did not mean to frighten you."

"S-sorry?" A laugh—or maybe it was a sob—wrenched out of her, and the claw blade clattered to the floor. "You came for me!"

She staggered forward and collapsed into him, wrapping her arms around his neck and burying her face in his shoulder. He was real and solid and smelled of *taless* spice and leather.

Not a dream!

Relief bubbled up from somewhere inside and yanked itself out of her in choking gasps. Was she crying? She wasn't sure.

He settled backward to sit on the floor, gathering her into his lap with one arm while he shifted the other, wrapped in bandages, out of the way. "You are safe," he murmured again. "You are safe, Little Mouse."

She clung to him, savoring the warmth of his body and the sub-tle, flowing motion of his muscles beneath the fabric of his shirt as he rocked gently. *Not a dream!*

When the storm had passed and the fog in her mind had cleared a little more, she shifted so she could look up into his face and murmured, "Did you kill *him* too?"

"I . . ." He cleared his throat and drew a deep breath, as if steeling himself against her reaction. "I was too slow. Dalathek escaped. I am sorry. Kamm's best hunters are tracking him. It is only a matter of time. And you will be safe here at the embassy."

Hanna sighed and nodded. The movement was loose and uncoordinated like a bobble-head toy, but she could feel her body coming back to her as the anesthetic haze faded.

He let out a long breath and shook his head. Quietly, he said, "I am so very sorry, Hanna. It is my fault you were in danger in the first place. I should have known my interest in you might make you a target. I should have taken measures to protect you." His eyes closed, and a muscle twitched in his cheek, making the light shift along the planes of his face as he clenched and unclenched his teeth. "And when he came, I should have . . . I should . . ."

Carefully, she placed two fingers against his lips—the trembling was beginning to subside, and her aim was improving. "You came for me," she murmured. "You stopped the nightmare." She felt the smile crinkle the corners of her eyes before her lips realized it was coming. "And before that . . ." Other memories floated up from the dimness. "Before that, you walked me home."

"Yes."

"And . . . you kissed me." Her smile melted into a troubled frown. "Was that part real?"

"Yes." A whisper. A shy smile. Was he blushing?

Her own low whisper came out rough and throaty as her heartbeat quickened in her chest. "Would you kiss me again?"

He swallowed hard, and his gaze flickered to her lips before he met her eyes again. "Yes. If you still want me to when you are awake."

Hanna brought her hand up again and laid it gently against his cheek. It wasn't shaking anymore. "I'm awake enough to know what I want."

"You might change your mind." There was a tired bitterness in his tone.

"Why would I do that?"

"I am the Viper." He shrugged, as if that explained it. Maybe for some people it would.

"I knew you were the Viper when I kissed you before," she said. "And I knew what that meant."

He shook his head. "Being told someone has killed people is one thing. Seeing it happen is . . . different."

"I'm *glad* you killed those men. If you hadn't, they would have—" She bit her lip. She knew what they would have done, but she couldn't say the words. Instead, she whispered, "I'm not going to change my mind, Jon. I promise."

His head tilted slightly sideways, but he didn't say anything. For a long, breathless moment he just studied her with those deep hazel eyes, solemn and intense. Weighing. Then his lips slid into a slow, wondering half-smile. He shifted position, winding himself more tightly around her body, bending forward to give the tip of her nose a playful nuzzle with his own. She heard a catch in his breath as his lips brushed hers, feather soft at first, as if he still feared she might bolt. When she didn't, his kiss deepened, gained confidence, his lips moving tenderly against her own, sending warm tingles all the way down to her toes, lingering as if he were savoring something sweet and precious.

When he straightened, studying her face again to judge her reaction, she sighed contentedly.

"That was definitely worth waking up for," she murmured. "I think I could get used to that."

She felt the rumble of his low chuckle vibrate through his chest.

"I do not think I could," he murmured, "no matter how many times you let me do it. But I would be happy to try to find out."

Her laugh sent a stab of pain through her gut. He saw her wince and shifted his hold on her so he could see the bloodstained front of her white hospital chemise.

He frowned. "You woke up too soon, Little Mouse. Your injuries require more attention. You must let the medics help you." He gestured toward the red-clad figures with his bandaged arm. One was doing something to the dangling tubes, and the other, a woman, waited patiently nearby; the light glinted silver off something in her hands.

Hanna looked from the woman back to Jon.

"Please," he whispered. "I need you. Let them help you."

Jon trusted these people. Hanna trusted him. She looked back to the woman, held her gaze for a moment, then nodded consent.

The medic glided closer. Knelt beside Jon. Pressed cold metal against Hanna's neck.

Hanna stiffened, gagging on the phantom scents of old wood and gasoline as panic clutched at her throat and sent imaginary dust motes careening through the beam of the overhead lamp.

Jon snuggled her closer. "You are safe, Little Mouse," he whispered, and his spicy smell and the warmth of his breath against her neck drew her back from the terrors of the shed to the safety of his arms.

"Stay with m-me," she mumbled, as the blackness closed around her.

And he whispered, "Always."

THE END

An Invitation From the Author

If you enjoyed reading *Dancing with the Viper*, please tell a friend and consider leaving a short, honest review on Amazon or Goodreads. Reviews help books gain exposure and sales, and are critical to the success of any book, especially those published by independent authors and small publishers. Even just a line or two can make a big difference.

I also love hearing from my readers directly. Please visit my web site to find contact information or sign up for my Guild to receive periodic email updates. There's also a link to the Guildhall on Facebook, where you can chat with other fans. See you there!

www.amybeatty.com

Special Thanks

I like to think of Dancing with the Viper as my apprenticeship novel. When I began writing it, I had spent some time studying books about the craft of novel writing, but had made only a few exploratory excursions into the actual practice. I didn't yet have a good feel for how much story actually fit into a thousand words, and I wasn't sure I'd even be able to competently create enough story to fill an entire book. Still, study will only get you so far, and there comes a time when the only way to move forward is to put your bum in the chair and your fingers on the keyboard and just keep moving forward until you've succeeded—or until failure teaches you what aspects of the craft to study next. (And, I told myself, if it bombs, nobody ever has to see it but me.)

Since that first draft, the manuscript (which turned out too long for one book) has been split, unsplit, and re-split. It's been through more helpful hands than I had the sense to keep track of, and although I won't be able to list everyone who helped make this book what it is, I hope they all know how deeply they are appreciated.

With that said, there are a few people who have made special contributions to the project, whether of expertise or enthusiasm (which is just as important sometimes) and without whom I never would have come this far.

Special thanks go out to Jennifer Jenkins, my friend, my mentor, my first fan. I'm sorry you had strep throat, even if it did give you time to read the whole thing.

To Talei Lawson, my cheerleader and volunteer minion, who would've been my first fan if Jen hadn't gotten sick and finished reading first.

To Jo Schaffer, Lois Brown, and Nichole Van, for their guidance and patience in critique.

To my editor, Julie Frederick, who helped me find an ending for the first part at last—thank you for playing in my sandbox with me.

And last, but never least, to my dear family for putting up with my special brand of crazy, for telling me like it is, and for shoring me up when my courage wobbles. I could not do this without you.

ABOUT THE AUTHOR

Amy Beatty grew up in the wilds of Yellowstone National Park as part of an experiment in crossing the genes of a respected research biologist with those of a grammar aficionado. She spent her summers making forts under the sagebrush with her friends and catching garter snakes by the creek to populate elaborate sandbox villages-or holed up in her bunk bed exploring the exotic worlds hidden between the covers of books.

She currently resides in Utah with her husband and two delightfully unconventional children, under the benevolent dictatorship of a toy fox terrier who plans to take over the world as soon as she gets her minions whipped into shape.

www.ingramcontent.com/pod-product-compliance
Lightning Source LLC
Chambersburg PA
CBHW071147260626
47162CB00003B/955

* 9 780578 412740 *